GALAXYS EDGE

ORDER OF THE CENTURION

ORDER OF THE CENTURION

ANSPACH + COLE

Galaxy's Edge: ORDER OF THE CENTURION
by Jason Anspach
& Nick Cole

Edited by David Gatewood
Published by Galaxy's Edge Press

Cover Art: Fabian Saravia
Cover Design: Beaulistic Book Services
Interior Design: Kevin G. Summers

For more information:

Website: GalaxysEdge.info
Facebook: facebook.com/atgalaxysedge
Newsletter: InTheLegion.com

"The Order of the Centurion is the highest award that can be bestowed upon an individual serving in, or with, the Legion. When such an individual displays exceptional valor in action against an enemy force, and uncommon loyalty and devotion to the Legion and its legionnaires, refusing to abandon post, mission, or brothers, even unto death, the Legion dutifully recognizes such courage with this award."

98.4% of all citations are awarded posthumously.

01

The planet Psydon
27 years prior to the Battle of Kublar

Lieutenant Washam sat in a sweltering mobile hab several kilometers behind the front lines of the Battle of Psydon. Out of the action, out of the fight... his career over before it had the chance to begin. There was a war on, and Wash was one of the few legionnaires who would be denied the chance to see it up close.

Sweat stuck to his green uniform, making the collar cling to his neck. No matter how many times he peeled the fabric away to fan at his overheated flesh, the humid, swampy feeling never dissipated. Mobile office habs, like the one where Wash endlessly toiled through an unending supply of admin work, were supposed to have climate controls. That tech was hardly a miracle. Just about every house and speeder inward of galaxy's edge had them standard. Certainly every capital ship, starfighter, and freighter had the ability to control temperature. But not a Republic Army mobile office unit in the middle of a war-torn hellhole on a far-flung jungle planet.

It wouldn't be so bad if Wash could at least kit up in the climate-conditioned legionnaire armor. He could imagine the cooling relief that would come with putting on a Legion helmet and feeling the micro fans blow chilling air in his face.

But even though he was Legion, that gear wasn't meant for him. The House of Reason, in appointing him to the rank of first lieutenant, might have named him every bit a legionnaire as the next... but the House of Reason wasn't on Psydon. And General Umstead, who led the Legion's operation on Psydon, was having no part of this new appointee program. So Wash, as a newly pinned point, was stuck. Hot, bothered, and out of the fight. Regardless of whether he had any guts, there would be no glory.

"Point" was a pejorative shorthand for a legionnaire appointed to service by either the House of Reason or the Senate. The decision to directly commission officers from the Republic's galaxy-spanning government into the Legion—as had been done in the Army, Marines, and Navy for years—had not been a popular one. Not with the galaxy itself, and especially not with the Legion.

The Savage Wars were still fresh in the minds of the galactic collective, and it was the legionnaires, led by General Rex, who'd fought the hard fights, died the brutal deaths, and left behind the graves necessary to save the galaxy from domination and destruction at the hands of the Savage marines. Hard men trained to do hard things had ended the war scant years before, and their predecessors had been fighting for the same for centuries.

The galaxy was grateful for the Legion. And so anything viewed as detrimental to that famed warrior branch was, necessarily, unpopular.

But the House of Reason, encouraged by the relative stability of the galaxy—massive wars like the rebellion of Psydon excluded—felt it necessary to have a greater influence over the Legion. *Mutual growth for a beneficial relationship...* that was how they packaged it during the debates. But the Legion, and much of the galaxy, saw it for what it was.

A power grab.

The politicians in the House of Reason and the Senate resented, envied, and even feared the position that the Legion had staked out in the minds of the citizens of the Republic. It was, after all, only thanks to the Legion that the Galactic Republic—and thus its governing bodies—existed at all.

During the darkest times of the Savage Wars, when the collection of systems, planets, and colonies in the squabbling Unified Federation failed to muster a capable resistance against the relentless Savages—who had spread like a cancerous wildfire throughout the galaxy—it was the independent military force known as the Legion who fought back. It was the Legion's strength—not just its military prowess, but its strength of will—that made it possible to forge a government with the purpose of protecting life and liberty throughout the galaxy, for all species.

But it was also the Legion, knowing the conflicted hearts of men and the black hearts of career politicians, who insisted on including Article Nineteen in the

Republic's Constitution. This hard-reset clause gave the Legion the legal authority, if needed, to wipe the slate clean and start the government over again.

If things ever got too bad.

Just in case.

And Article Nineteen was a Sword of Damocles that the House of Reason and Senate desperately wanted taken down. *That* was the end game of the Appointment Program, and everyone knew it. The long con everyone saw and couldn't get out of.

Once known as the House of Liberty, the newly rechristened House of Reason had grown stronger than it was ever intended to be. Its influence had never been greater, and its agenda was shifting from protection and preservation to the shadowy, elusive, and ever-liquid concept of *improvement.*

Part of that improvement dealt with tempering the original concept of liberty.

Liberty is a thing that simply is. It's wild, natural, and frightening to stare in the face. It promises no comfort, no promises of safety, no easy answers. But it does provide unfettered opportunity. It's up to each individual to decide just how much liberty they can stomach.

The House of Reason was more than willing to explain why freedom and liberty were best tempered by their guiding hand. How freedom was suitable in small doses, but fatally unfair in its pure form. And so, in spite of promises that the House and Senate would never seek to impose their will on the Legion, their most radical members, the ones that the rest of the House could write off as extremists raving for their small base, called for change. The extremists became a movement, which became a platform, which demanded that the House of Reason must have some influence over the Legion. That it must be free to appoint officers in order to leaven the ranks to see things in a more balanced and fair way.

And so, yeah—the legionnaires hated guys like Wash. Not for who they were... so much as what they represented.

Wash was part of the first graduating class of points. He wanted nothing to do with the House of Reason's agenda. Because the Legion was made up of heroes. Men of such unyielding talent and resolve that they were able to stand against the very gates of hell and emerge victorious. He knew they would never accept him as one of their own, and he didn't hold that against them.

"Hey, Wash!"

Wash swung his chair around and saw the face of Major D'lay Berlin, a fellow appointed officer in the Legion. And Wash's closest friend.

"How's the major today?" Wash asked. "Another day in paradise?"

"Don't knock it, Wash. We're piling up time served in a combat zone when we could be stuck on cruisers."

Wash smiled. The two men didn't see eye to eye when it came to the appointment program. They had grown up on the same planet, in much the same circles, and were both appointed by the same House of Reason delegate, Mageen Stu't-grant. But they had wildly different views about what their purpose was in the Legion. Berlin was a dashing, gallant-looking man, who felt that he and

Washam had been chosen to serve as poster boys for the Republic. Handpicked officers meant to make the unpopular program not look so bad after all.

Wash, on the other hand, wanted to KTF.

Berlin leaned against the open doorway, a waiting repulsor sled still humming outside, its Republic Army driver looking miserable in his seat. As an appointed major, Berlin was allowed to wear the Legion armor. They still didn't give him a bucket, though.

Wash frowned. "You know you're not making it any cooler in here by keeping the door open."

Berlin seemed to consider whether he wanted to stay right where he was, then jauntily stepped inside. "Somehow I doubt it makes a difference. You're working in a sweatbox, Wash."

The closing door shut out the noise of the jungle, but the sweltering heat had already made its way inside. Wash could tell; he was an expert on the discomfort. "It makes a difference. I've got an overstuffed docket of supply requisitions to review, and now all that extra hot is going to make me just sit here and be miserable instead."

"You'd find a way to be miserable anywhere, buddy." Berlin leaned against Wash's desk, looking down at his friend. He seemed to be hiding something behind his back. "But me? I found a way to keep cool."

"I doubt that." Keeping cool was something that virtually no one on Psydon was able to do, unless they were stationed on an overhead cruiser or in one of the permanent buildings within the Psydonian cities. Wash had seen enough raging requests from the brass in all branches to know that the extreme Psydon humidity—it felt like breathing through a wet sock—had done a number on all the conditioning units. Parts and replacements were always the top request. There weren't enough spares, and they never lasted long.

"Doubt me no longer." Berlin tossed a legionnaire's bucket into his friend's lap.

Wash turned the helmet over in his hands. "How did you get this? Appointees are only allowed the open-face marine variant."

Berlin's only reply was a rakish smile.

Wash shook his head. "You didn't even undergo the full familiarity training at the Academy. You skipped that part, remember?"

"You should have, too. Not like they were giving us buckets."

"So... how?"

"Hilltop Defiance," Berlin said with a shrug. "Leejes were virtually wiped out there overnight. They took it back at sunrise, but you should've seen the place. Dead legionnaires everywhere. Spare buckets and gear all over the place."

"You stole a dead legionnaire's helmet?"

Berlin shrugged again. "He was done with it. I slipped the armorer twenty credits to get it refitted to fit my head. Did you know these aren't one-size-fits-all?"

Of course Wash knew. It was covered in the equipment familiarity courses that Berlin—along with every other point save Washam—had skipped. "Yeah. Amazingly enough, not every grunt has the exact same facial structure. Who'd-a thunk it?"

"Well, anyway, now I've got all the benefits of Republic tech to keep me cooled down."

Wash fought the urge to grind his teeth. Berlin meant well, but this wasn't something he'd earned—and therefore it wasn't something he should have. But it would be futile to argue that point with his friend. Or any other appointed officer, for that matter. Wash was the odd man out among his peers. And truth be told, he was probably just making everything harder on himself. Harder than it needed to be, because he was buying into the Legion's propaganda. "KTF" and "Forget Nothing" and all those other little phrases whose purpose, according to his appointed peers, was to make sure that young men went off and got themselves killed when asked.

But maybe, deep down, he felt that grinding frustration so strongly because his friend, who didn't even care about the Legion, now had something he, Wash, so desperately wanted.

Wash tossed the bucket back to its owner. "So tell me how you even managed to get close to Hilltop Defiance? I thought that was still hot?"

"Oh, believe me, it is." Berlin slapped his bucket as though playing a drum. "And the *Legion* wasn't going to let me near it. The last thing they want is for an appointed officer to do something worth noting. That would fly in the face of all their crying about how this program is a mistake."

Wash gave a *well-that's-one-perspective* raising of his eyebrows. The reality was that the Legion didn't want the heartburn that would come with a point getting dusted. That, and they were committed to total victory. They sought to win on every play. And the presence of a point reduced their odds.

"So, what? You crept in from the jungle?"

"Nah. The Legion might shut me down, but the rest of the branches, they see a major when they look at my armor. So when I tell a couple of privates to drive me someplace, they do it."

Wash shook his head and stood. He stretched his hands overhead. The air at the top of his hab, mingling with his fingertips, felt several degrees warmer. "I'm hot enough to tell a couple of privates to drive me someplace just to feel the wind against my skin. And I'm not too proud to strip down to my skivvies first."

"Wouldn't help," said Berlin, putting the helmet over his head. Its external speaker made his voice sound slightly mechanical. "It's like driving through a steam bath. But I'll see about getting you one of these." He rapped the side of the bucket with his knuckles. "The fighting has moved on from the hill, and there are still plenty of buckets around, just there for the taking. Though some Legion recon teams already gathered up all the weapons. So if you want something more than your pistol and that marine-issue blaster rifle, we'll have to sneak into the armory sometime."

Wash laughed at the thought. He wanted nothing more than to serve in the Legion, though he looked all wrong for the part. Berlin, on the other hand... he looked ready to

KTF. "No. I'm good with whatever the Legion sees fit. But just... watch out, Berlin. I just don't want you to get into any trouble over this."

"I'm not going to." Berlin modeled his fully jocked-up self. "Looks pretty slick though, right? I'm telling you, just say the word and I'll get you up to speed."

"I'll pass."

Berlin opened his mouth to speak, but Washam supplied his friend's words before he had the chance to utter them. "I knew you'd say that."

The two men laughed.

"I *did* know you'd say that!" Berlin sounded like he was smiling from behind his helmet.

"And I knew you knew it. We've spent practically our whole lives together. I don't know why we even bother talking anymore. We can just have the same conversations in our minds."

The comm light on Wash's datapad flashed, and he glanced down. He'd received several new messages in the few minutes he'd been talking to his friend, and an icon signaled fifty-two reports ready for processing. That number had been down to five before he'd gotten sidetracked by Berlin.

Wash let out a sigh despite his commitment to the Legion. It wasn't glamorous work, but it was the job the Legion had given him. The first Legion sergeant they'd ever been exposed to as cadets had told them, "Do everything as though your life depends on it." Then he'd made the corps of cadets pick up trash all along the training field. None of the other points had understood, nor cared about, the exercise in wisdom. But Wash had made it his own personal mantra. So much so that he didn't even think about it. It was just always there in his hard drive. Pushing him to do his best, regardless of how meaningless the task felt.

"Keepin' you busy, huh, pal?" Berlin said sympathetically.

"Not the way I'd like, but... yeah. Busy."

Berlin leaned in and spoke in a conspiratorial whisper. "Hey. I'm out of your hair in a few, but I'm working on an angle that I know you'll be interested in."

Wash slumped back into his chair feeling sweaty and miserable. "Somehow I doubt that."

"No, no. I'm serious. What would you say to going out on an armed recon patrol?"

Wash had no way of reading Berlin from behind his bucket, but he thought the major had to be joking. There was no way Legion command was going to let a couple of appointed officers go into the jungle probing for the dog-like doros. No matter how much Wash might want it to be so.

"Berlin, now you're wasting my time."

"That's only true if I'm lying." Berlin inclined his head. "And I'm not lying."

Wash knew he should just end the conversation and try to get caught up on his work before the end of his shift—not that anyone else was assigned to help with the flow of work that would come in overnight. This suck-fest was all Washam's. But the thought of actually getting out there and using the training he'd received at the Academy, of showing the legionnaires that he should rightly be called a brother and a fellow leej—the chance was too enticing to ignore.

"For the sake of argument, let's say you're not lying," he said.

"I'm not."

"Fine. How can you pull something like that off? And don't tell me the Legion is on board."

Berlin sat on Wash's desk, removing his helmet to reveal a Cheshire grin. "Like I said earlier, the other branches, they don't see an appointee. They only see a Legion major."

Wash nodded. He'd experienced the same among the Republic's soldiers.

Berlin continued. "I was talking to some marine pilots—the ones flying the SLICs. The guys are pretty much just flying legionnaires all over the place, dead and alive. Other than some gun runs, that's their life—taxi service to the Legion. And the thing of it is, they have no idea. A lot of 'em are on standby because everything in this fight is so fluid. A Legion officer tells them where to go, they go."

Wash could see where his friend was headed with this. "And so your plan is to order a couple of pilots to take you out on a nice hike into the jungle, rifles on our shoulders. No thanks."

"First, you're way off base."

"So that's not it?"

"Well... it *is*. But we'll have a marine recon team with us, too."

Wash rubbed his eyes and shook his head. "Berlin, this is stupid. And trust me, I get it. We go out, make the checkpoints, and the leejes give us some recognition, acknowledge we're willing to put in our share."

"No, that's what *you* want," Berlin said, the smile not fading from his face. "I want something a lot bigger. You know the score in this program: we serve, and then we use our time in the Legion to secure a seat on the planetary council. Maybe a governorship or a Senate seat. But I've got my eyes on a prize grander than local legislation. I'm going straight from Psydon to the House of Reason."

Wash clucked his tongue. The last place he wanted to be was the House of Reason, though he understood the drive. Becoming a delegate in the House of Reason was the be-all-end-all for those with political aspirations. A life achievement. But no one as young as him and Berlin— neither of them thirty standard years—had ever made it in. Even those few "young bucks" who had made it at not-quite forty had only done so by way of a hereditary hand-me-down. A delegate gets old, decides to retire, endorses a great-grandson or niece, and the adoring populace of their galactic sector votes in the chosen one out of gratitude. Just like they're told to. But what Berlin was talking about… that would require an honest-to-goodness power play. Going hard against an entrenched incumbent who was willing to do whatever it took to keep power.

"You're crazy."

"I know it sounds far-fetched. But think about this with me for a minute. What do we know about the delegates from our sector?"

"They're exceedingly rich and powerful, they're friends of both of our families, and they get whatever they want?"

Berlin smirked. "Okay. What else?"

Wash shrugged and raised his hands.

"They're positioning themselves more and more as anti-war. And I know it's all part of a broader plan of theirs—I do listen at those boring cocktail parties—but they're miscalculating, badly. The pain of the Savage Wars is still fresh in people's minds; the average citizen is not ready to turn up their noses at the military. So with *me* running as a former officer in the Legion who, unlike my opponent, actually *fought*, I know I can swing the delegate seat."

"Okay," Wash said, somewhat reluctantly. "That's actually a surprisingly good strategy."

"Thank you."

"But I don't think a quiet recon patrol is going to hold much water in the war hero department. And the Legion will never let you do anything bigger than that. It's not like you can order a company of legionnaires to get on the SLIC with you."

Berlin's smile faded, replaced by a gravity that, though not menacing, sent a chill up Wash's spine. "I know all that. And so here's the workaround: one, we're the only legionnaires on the mission. Everyone else is a marine. And two… it's not just a patrol. I looked at some theoretical Dark Ops intel, and we're going to take a stab at finding and destroying the doros' mobile artillery."

Wash felt the blood rush from his face.

"And so what I need from you, buddy," Berlin said, not unkindly, "is to tell me—are you coming with me, or have I got to go do this alone?"

02

The next morning brought Wash little more than nervous anxiety. Before leaving the hab the day before, Berlin had explained his plan two more times, and had then pressed his friend to give an answer.

"I'm not sure" was the best, most diplomatic answer Wash had been able to offer. "No way in the seven hells" would have more accurately captured his feelings on the matter.

And yet, when Berlin had sent him a text message in the wee hours, telling him to go to work prepared for a mission... Wash could still only give a noncommittal reply.

He felt like a deserter as he walked the short distance from his hooch to the steamy office hab that morning, and he couldn't make eye contact with any other being, humanoid or bot. Like he was preordained for some guilt and felt the heaviness of his sin weighing on his soul.

For that brief walk, he was going with Berlin.

But then, in the familiarity of his hab, he realized how massively stupid that was. He would stay.

As he scrolled through endless requisitions, audits, and angry messages about some supply problem or other, he began to feel normal again. He cruised through the first hour of work, and soon he was laughing at the idea that anyone would ever miss him, a point.

He looked up at a Legion recruiting poster hanging on the hab wall. He wasn't sure who put it there, but the honor and adventure promised in the poster seemed almost cruelly ironic for a point sitting in a sweatbox.

Wash was convinced that his plight was likely shared by every other appointed officer on Psydon. They were a bunch of guys assigned to junk projects that probably didn't matter. Things designed to make them *feel* like they were contributing. And for most of those points, that was probably good enough. They'd get their Legion crest for the rest of their lives, without ever having been asked to face the slightest bit of danger. None of his appointed peers had ever seemed interested in visiting the front lines. At least, not until the blaster fire stopped.

But for Wash, it was all he could think about.

What is combat like?

Would I feel different for killing a humanoid?

How bad would it really hurt to be shot?

He had no answers. Only orders to stay in a sweltering hot box of an office hab. Those answers were for other young men. Legionnaires allowed to be Legion.

They would see the elephant... and they would know.

Wash's datapad chimed, announcing another batch of messages. The sound was both mind-numbing and soul-crushing.

Do everything as though your life depends on it.

He reminded himself that he took pride in doing the job no one else wanted. In doing it well. He felt a sense of accomplishment in exceeding expectations and meeting all his obligations. No matter how mundane, the fulfillment of duty built character. Even if that meant sacrificing your own desires.

Wash made a decision. He would stay. He would tell Berlin to leave him out of his schemes and self-aggrandizing adventures.

At least this time. Maybe next...

Wash got up and walked across his mobile office hab to the kaff machine. He had to push the temperamental machine's brew button four times before it shot a jet stream of rich, deep-brown liquid into his old college mug.

Wash rolled his shoulders in an attempt to unstick his sweaty collar from his neck. Though the midday sun was still hours away, it was already hot enough in the hab to make him question why he would want another serving of the heated drink. A month in country, and a tech hadn't even so much as come by to look at the hab's busted climate control unit.

Wash picked up the drink and blew across its surface. The hot liquid gave no hint of steam in the ever-more-oppressive heat of the office. His hands began to sweat.

I wonder if there will be kaff in the field? he thought to himself. *The standard leej kits had instant tabs, but...*

It didn't matter.

You're staying, remember?

As Wash returned to his desk, he saw his N-16 blaster rifle leaning against it. If he was staying, why had he bothered bringing the weapon to his office this morning? It would be of little use against relentless waves of paperwork. Although a few blaster shots into his datapad *would* give him some cathartic release.

And then there was his ruck, which was filled with field macros, charge packs, rations, water...

Just how long did you plan on staying in the office to fend off the assault of incoming notifications?

"There's a war going on," Wash told himself. "Remember?"

Wash spoke often to himself. If he didn't, he could go entire workdays without ever having to use his voice at all. Which was probably exactly what the Legion wanted out of points like him. Out of the way, set aside, kept busy with some task so menial that they couldn't possibly cause any damage to ongoing combat operations.

For the first time, Wash felt disgruntled—if not actually angry. He didn't deserve this. He was the only appointed officer who hadn't taken a shortcut. He had gone through the Legion's combat training school. And he had prepared himself for months beforehand—dieting, exercising, undergoing feats of endurance, putting on mile after mile in hikes and runs—all in the hopes of making the grade. For real. Not just as a point.

He'd promised himself that if he didn't pass on his own merits, he wouldn't join the Legion at all. So while the rest of the appointees skipped the full Legion training or took the "appointed officer candidate course"—which was designed for men who had no business serving in the Legion—Wash endured the real deal. He suffered the indignity that came from being every Legion drill instructor's pet object of derision. He bore the scorn of those legionnaires who felt that he was being provided special privileges, even though they saw him on every run and march, joining them each night in the mess hall, shoving as much food into his mouth as he possibly could before an instructor came in and flipped over the tables and ordered everyone to clean up.

All of that Wash had done, and in doing so he had found an inner strength he hadn't known existed. The House's pilot appointee program consisted of five hundred men, and of those five hundred, he was the *only* one—at least that he knew of—who had become a legionnaire the right way.

The hard way.

The *only* way. As far as that old NCO who had given him his first lesson had been concerned.

And what was his reward for not taking the easy way out?

A broken-down mobile office hab. Sweltering Psydon heat without even the opportunity to see a shot fired in anger.

No, he wasn't going with Berlin. He wasn't crazy. But that didn't mean he had to be happy about where he was sitting.

He walked to the sink and dumped his new mug of kaff down the drain. He wasn't in the mood.

He pulled up the next item in his queue—a requisition form—and groaned. Whoever had written it had provided no clue to tell Wash why this form was even in front of him. Nothing about why it was in his system or why it was sent to him on an authorization channel. Every necessary field was either left blank or offered only some vague note like "New Order: One unit."

"One unit of what, kelhorn?" Wash growled.

He knew what would come next. He could file the report as inadequate, which, in theory, meant it would go back to the sender to be corrected so it could be processed properly. But what would *actually* happen was that it would be ignored—and then, two weeks from now, Wash would receive an angry message from someone higher up in the chain of command wanting to know why the cargo container of mortar bots—or whatever the hell was being requested, only it never actually *was* requested—wasn't where it needed to be.

And the answer would be because some sket-shoveling space rat, ordering supplies back in the air-conditioned safety of the cities the Legion had stabilized at the start of the war, didn't feel like typing those few extra characters to actually let Wash do his job. But that wouldn't be good enough. Because those mortar bots would be part of an imminent operation, and Wash would have to bust his butt finding something *right now* by staying up until the long hours of the night calling supply depots and begging for favors.

Well, not this time.

Wash scanned the email, looking for the electronic signature bearing a unique alphanumeric identifier. He logged into the quartermaster's personnel file and looked up the number. It belonged to a corporal. Probably some kid bored out of his mind just waiting for his tour to end, daydreaming about getting back home. Or some degenerate daydreaming about kicking out on a freighter to spend some time at an R&R port. The kid probably expected the requisition to be reviewed by another corporal. But Wash was the odd case of a first lieutenant assigned to this task. And while his rank didn't mean anything to the Legion, it still carried weight among the Republic Army basics.

Yeah, he called them basics. Just like the rest of the leejes did. And for the first time, he didn't feel sorry about doing so.

Stupid basic.

Without taking a moment to cool off, Wash sent his fingers dancing across his projected keyboard, eviscerating the hapless supply clerk one keystroke at a time. He sent the message without pausing to reflect whether he really should, because he knew that if he did, he would yield to his better judgment and let the issue drop.

"Take that, kelhorn!"

Wash leaned back in his chair, mumbling curses in vulgar Standard that would make his parents flush with shame. He didn't care. In fact, he almost *wished* someone would challenge him and test his mettle.

His datapad chimed, heralding a new request. It would likely be more of the same. Perhaps not quite as egregious as this last one, but no less frustrating. That's what his workday consisted of: skipped procedures and bureaucratic hassles that surely weren't in place during the Savage Wars. As the Army and Navy grew, the endless paperwork grew with it. In triplicate. And Wash was the only legionnaire on hand to KTF the stack.

He let out a sigh and felt his anger-fueled momentum fade away. These slackers deserved what they got. But with the number of notifications he had waiting on his datapad... He didn't have the energy to chew that many butts before noon.

Why not head back to your hooch and take a nap? It's not like anyone would even notice you were gone.

Wash shook his head, but internally he was thinking the option over.

Through the thin walls of the hab came the sound of a single SLIC approaching. Wash stood up, his interest piqued. It couldn't be the camp's platoon of legionnaires— the ones who wouldn't give Wash the time of day. They had all flown out on SLICs three days ago, but they were supposed to march back in—and even if that plan changed, it would take more than one SLIC to deliver them.

Part of Wash wanted to go out and see who was touching down, but the larger part of him was in too foul of a mood to bother. He reached for his mug, then felt a pang of annoyed regret at finding it empty. He remembered how he'd dumped the kaff down the drain, a willful abuse of taxpayer money. It would've been just cool enough to enjoy by now, too.

As he pondered whether to brew another mug, the door to the hab swung open, and the SLIC's intense repulsor noise blasted in as though it was literally right outside his door. It was close at any rate, and had to be kicking up a hell of a lot of dust in the camp.

"Really?" said Berlin, standing in the doorway, his newly acquired legionnaire bucket tucked under one arm as he held the door open with the other. There was a wolf-ish grin on his face. "You mean to tell me we're about to go on a recon patrol and you couldn't even be bothered to put on your armor? I know the Legion at least gave you that much gear. It's the buckets we have to find on our own."

Wash, who wore his usual gray fatigues, darkened by sweat, didn't feel in the mood for Berlin's levity. The truth of it was, he was surprised that his friend was actually following through on his plan, and he said as much. "You're not actually doing this, are you? This is stupid, Berlin. A bad idea all around. If you don't get yourself killed, you'll *definitely* get yourself court-martialed. Call me crazy, but that's not how I want to end my career in the Legion."

Berlin studied Wash a moment before saying, "Soooo... You're not going?"

"*No*, I'm not going!"

The major looked down. "I really thought you'd come, Wash. You're sure?"

Wash nodded.

Berlin turned, letting the door half close behind him. "Well, wish me luck, huh?"

Wash nodded again as the door closed behind his friend. He felt sorrow clutching at him, threatening to drag him into a malaise. But... he was *right* not to go along with this. It was idiotic, and he would not be a part of it.

He got up to make a new cup of kaff.

He would stay.

As the machine hissed out its brew, Wash crossed the room to grab his ruck. He threw it over his shoulder.

This is stupid. You're being stupid right now, Washam. Stay.

He picked up his rifle and slung it over his shoulder, feeling that he'd reached a moment of decision. The SLIC outside cycled up its repulsors.

You can still stay...

Wash left his malfunctioning, oppressive office hab. He shouted for Berlin, who was walking toward the SLIC, but he couldn't make himself heard above the noise. So he ran toward the aircraft. It was filled with Republic marines, their legs dangling over the sides.

Berlin climbed on board, turned, smiled, and held out his hand. "Knew you'd come!"

Wash was going.

03

Wash didn't know what the max capacity of the SLIC was, but he felt they must be close to it. Still, he was able to find a jump seat and wedged himself between two of the jungle-camoed hullbusters.

The marines wore greasepaint on their faces, some in stripes, others practically wearing black masks. Their durable green fatigues were paired with black combat boots and heavy flak jackets, some sealed up and others hanging open to reveal bare, muscular chests and tattoos of the Republic Marines insignia: a sea serpent tearing apart the hull of a capital ship.

Wash felt the man next to him looking him up and down. He wasn't intimidated—his Legion training had equipped him with suitable self-defense skills—but he did feel out of place. Though he had his ruck and weapon, which rested between his knees, he knew he didn't exactly look like a leej fighter.

Wash locked eyes with his black-haired observer and nodded. The marine's flak jacket was open, revealing a stomach tattoo of a human skull, its mouth wide open with a naked Endurian provocatively arching her back inside it. The marine nodded back, then fixed his attention on the jungle that sped by in a green blur outside the craft's open doors. The SLIC's passengers jostled and banged into one another from the turbulence of the flight.

A big mountain of a man with a strong cleft chin and a heavy full-auto blaster sat directly across from Wash. His face was smeared with greasepaint and a thin sheen of perspiration. He was working something over in his mouth—probably stim—slowly and methodically moving the round lump from one cheek to the other. The marine stared unblinkingly at Wash. Another admirer. Wash nodded, and was answered with a brownish-red stream of spit which landed just shy of his boots.

Berlin stood near the open door, right next to the SLIC's crew chief, holding onto a handhold, the wind blowing through his hair. He was following the gaze of the gunner, who vigilantly swept his weapon around in search of doro hostiles. But no dog-men seemed to be out. Berlin caught Wash looking and cracked a wide smile as if to say, "Isn't this great!"

Wash meekly smiled back. It didn't feel all that great to him. The rush of taking off and heading into the jungle had worn off now. As the marines eyeballed him, his mind ran through images of his CO launching a surprise inspection on the now-abandoned office hab. He could see his career circling the drain. Worse, he could see himself becoming the poster boy for everything wrong with this new program of appointed officers.

He shouldn't have come.

It had been foolish and rash, on more than one level. The most pressing of which was how utterly unprepared he was to be in the field for an undetermined amount of time doing jungle recon. He had just sort of assumed this would be a day trip. Maybe an overnighter. He didn't think Berlin would be keen on the weeks-long patrols that the Legion undertook. But Wash didn't actually know how long they'd be out here or what the mission entailed.

He had rations for three days and water for two, though he was comfortable in his ability to survive off the jungle if needed, and there were plenty of hydration options on Psydon. The whole planet was dripping wet. Charge packs might be sufficient for a few engagements—it would depend on how much he had to shoot. He had his knife and a med kit. But he wore no armor. If he had kitted up this morning, his decision would already have been made. He couldn't tell his friend no after that.

And along with the armor went other important items—like his ultrabeam, datamaps, and service pistol. As it was, he looked like some desk jockey who'd plunked down big credits to go on an exotic planetary safari. A wealthy wannabe traveling with experienced shooters boasting enough trigger time to keep him alive.

At least, in his Legion armor, Berlin looked the part of those operators, even if ultimately he was just another point, same as Wash. Truth be told, while Wash was feeling more and more like the SLIC's designated object of scorn, Berlin took on the air of the man in charge.

Wash thought about how often Berlin had skipped leadership and discipline classes during their time together at the Academy. This could all go real bad, real quick. He now hoped their foray into the jungle would be without incident. The exact opposite of everything he'd allowed himself to daydream.

Just let us get back to base without running into the doros.

"Dressed a little light, ain't ya, Leej?"

Wash pretended he didn't hear the marine as he looked out the open side door, watching the treetop canopy streak by between helmeted gaps.

"Hey." The marine's voice was louder this time.

Wash shouted back, "I'll be all right."

"Hear that, guys?" the marine said to his buddies. "He'll be all right. He don't need no armor or helmet or kit. Definitely never seen a leej go out on patrol like that."

The tattooed marine with the black hair sitting next to Wash picked up the conversation. The name on his flak jacket read *Haulman*. "You ask me? This guy ain't Legion."

Wash kept his face impassive, knowing that showing frustration would only cause a pile-on, and that laughing and playing the aw-shucks character would only earn him more scorn.

Haulman tapped Wash on the shoulder. "What you with? My bet is army intel. We takin' you to see something important close up?"

The marine on Washam's left, a man with cool, almost transparently blue eyes, and a sniper's notched long rifle cradled in one arm, chimed in. "He's a leej. Been around enough legionnaires to know how they hold themselves.

This one's got that legionnaire feel, even if the uniform says otherwise."

The rest of the marines paused to consider this.

"All right, let's hear it from the man himself," growled a sergeant, his eyes angry and full of experience, his helmet resting on the top of head, chin straps dangling unfastened. "You a leej or Repub intel?"

"I'm a first lieutenant in the Legion," Wash said, giving a fractional nod. "Just like the tab says."

"That's that," said the sergeant, whose name badge read *Shotton*.

The marine who'd started the conversation wasn't impressed. "I still ain't never seen a legionnaire go out into the field dressed as light as you."

The big marine sitting across from Wash shifted the wad of stim in his cheek before spitting another glob, this time away from Wash's boots. He wiped the dribble from his chin with a gloved hand. "You ask me, it don't matter what kind of outfit you wear as long as you smoke the other guy before he smokes you. That's one thing the leejes have right. That KTF junk they always spoutin'."

The sniper next to Washam—his name wasn't visible—leaned in toward the big man. "If that's true, Denturo, why do they all wear the armor?"

"How do I know why those pansies gotta wear protection?" The big marine swallowed some of his stim juice. "But it don't matter if you kill 'em all first. Does it, Lieutenant?"

Wash looked up. "It helps. Not a guarantee you'll get the chance when you're fighting that close... hence the armor."

Denturo stared blankly at the Legion lieutenant. "Bottom line. I don't need armor, and if some leej ain't quick enough to drop a dog-man before the dog-man drops him, he needs to stay the hell out of my way."

Wash shrugged, not knowing what to say.

"You can sign me up for some of that leej armor," chipped in another marine.

"Same here, man," replied Haulman, the marine to Wash's right. "But the Repub don't wanna pay to protect all its troops. Just the Legion golden boys."

"That's not true," Wash said, interjecting facts where none were wanted. "Statistically the Legion has a much higher casualty rate than the rest of the armed services combined. And since we got the armor, we're the ones sent into the meat grinders of the galaxy."

"Since *they* got it, Leej," corrected Sergeant Shotton. "Way *you're* dressed, you better watch out for spears and arrows."

"Either way," said Haulman, "I'll take me some of that armor."

Denturo dug his fingers into a pouch of stim and shoved several strands into his mouth, packing it so tightly in his bottom lip that it stuck out like a tumor. "Anyone who needs armor is a pussy. But you are kitted out way too light, Leej. Doros might not cook you, but they'll skewer you like a fish with some of them traps they got out there."

Wash smiled, which seemed to annoy the big marine, who spat again, this time closer to Wash's feet.

The marine sniper leaned over. "You'll be all right. SLIC's got extra flak jackets." He looked up at Wash's exposed head. "And that scalp of yours is gonna burn. We'll find something to cover it with."

Wash had a Legion-issued cap. Which he'd forgotten. He kicked himself inwardly. "Thanks."

As the sniper rose and moved forward to get Wash some kit, Berlin seemed to be in another world. If he heard the conversation, he hadn't felt the need to join in. He'd put his bucket on at some point while Wash talked with the marines, but the way he was standing made Wash think he was somewhere far away, mentally rehearsing stump speeches for his future political triumphs.

The crew chief looked up at Berlin and shouted something that Wash couldn't hear over the wind whipping inside the SLIC. Berlin nodded, then Wash heard his friend's voice come to life via the open comm relay in his ear.

"Two minutes."

"Two minutes?" shouted Sergeant Shotton, his dark eyebrows furrowed. "What happened to five minutes?"

Berlin didn't answer, and Wash at once knew that his friend had forgotten to relay the message, so lost was he in his thoughts.

"Two minutes!" the sergeant barked.

Marines strapped on helmets, checked charge packs, sealed up flak jackets, tightened down equipment, and otherwise readied themselves for the SLIC's landing.

Wash could feel those early morning cups of kaff dancing around bitterly in his stomach. He was thankful for having eaten a light breakfast. The last thing he wanted to do was run from the SLIC to puke.

"Thirty seconds!" Berlin relayed over the comm.

The SLIC was clearly decelerating. The blur of trees began to come into focus, and Wash could make out individual leaves and branches. The Psydon temperature, no longer blown cool by the wind speed, crept inside the vehicle, making Wash feel over-warmed and nauseated. The bird circled a landing zone, a wide stretch of prairie with tall grass, about a kilometer in radius and surrounded by jungle and a green, murky river.

Berlin was practically hanging out of the door as the door gunner looked for targets. Wash realized just how much he wanted to be in Berlin's place. It wasn't resentment, but a desire to make use of the training he had received. Already Wash was taking in the mistakes his friend was making. For example, Berlin hadn't clipped himself to the SLIC with a quick-release harness, meaning that if the craft had to make a sudden evasive maneuver, the recon team's commanding officer would most likely be flung out of the open door and into the hostile overrun jungle below.

Wash also realized that during the long flight, Berlin had not taken the time to review what their objective was upon landing. Maybe he'd gone over it with the marines before Wash showed up, but that seemed doubtful.

The SLIC continued its vertical descent until it was hovering mere feet above the ground. Long stocks of green grass bent over from the force of the repulsors, waving in radials as the gunner swept the horizon for doros. So far, so good.

As they hovered in place, it became obvious that everyone on board was waiting for Berlin to give the order to disembark. Berlin finally noticed this too, but a hair too late to save face. "Okay!" he shouted. "Let's go!"

He sounded confident, but it was clear from the way he stood blocking the marines that he had no idea how to properly execute a SLIC dismount.

Thankfully, the marines had done this before. As soon as they received the word, they hopped out of the craft, disappearing from the waist down as they waded into the waving grass to set up a defensive perimeter. It seemed the farther out they moved from the SLIC, the taller the grass was, until it reached chest height on the lead elements. Wash hoped there wasn't something nasty waiting for them below the surface.

He waited for his turn as the marines hustled out of the craft—the SLIC was a sitting duck should doro fire come their way—and spread out, weapons hot and looking for trouble.

The sniper slapped Wash on his shoulder and then left his seat, prompting Wash to follow. The two men jumped out of the craft, the noise and blast of repulsors hitting Wash like a physical slap against his whole body as he crossed the threshold. They moved into the reeds, Wash straining his eyes and keeping his head low.

An increased whine told Wash that the SLIC behind him was spooling up and taking on altitude, leaving the recon team at what appeared to be a secure LZ.

His ears ringing from the now-departed SLIC, Wash felt a breeze blow in from the river, carrying with it a foul, rotting-fish stench. The grass swayed with a gentle rhythm, reminding Wash of the waves outside his family's beachfront home. A place where he and Berlin had spent so much of their youth together.

That all felt so long ago. And now... now Wash felt alone, stranded and in danger. They all were. He kept his eyes on his sector, keeping vigilance with the other marines. Waiting for orders.

04

"What's the word, Major?" asked Marine Sergeant Shotton, a thick-necked man with a dark complexion that made his eyes and teeth look brilliantly white. Those eyes darted around looking for problems, but the landing zone appeared safe.

Although with the doros, you could never be sure. They were certainly giving the Legion a hard enough time out there. An impressive feat considering what many of these legionnaires, especially the older men, had gone through in the Savage Wars. But then, the doros, and most other sentient species in the galaxy, had gone through quite a lot too.

"Let's see…" Berlin began, sounding distracted.

Wash imagined that his friend was trying to navigate the intel maps and other features of his bucket. *Good luck.* The tech was great in theory, but in Wash's experience, the reality hadn't quite caught up. Berlin would be better off using the display hard-mounted to his forearm.

"We're… Let's head off into the jungle, men."

Wash winced, just for a moment. There was nothing confident about the way Berlin had issued that order. The Legion Academy had instructed Wash that spoken orders needed to carry with them command, authority, confidence, and knowledge. His friend sounded more like he was talking to a group of buddies as they figured out which trail would best take them on a hike to their campsite.

"Okay..." said Sergeant Shotton, obviously expecting something a little more substantial from Major Berlin. "Lotta jungle out this way, sir. You got a particular direction you want us to move?"

"Yeah... hang on." Berlin stood ramrod straight. He was obviously occupied with the small display in the corner of his bucket, and the rest of his body was freezing up as he focused his attention there. That was part of the problem with the design—it took too much effort to take in what the helmets were communicating. Maybe future models would be more effective.

The marines looked at Berlin with expressions of disdain and mistrust. Wash could see how quickly his friend was losing influence and control over the situation. And he knew the stories of incompetent officers getting fragged out on patrol, the doros always taking the blame. Something needed to be done.

So Wash acted.

"Sorry about that, sir," Wash said, pushing through the tall blades of grass to reach his friend's side. "I know I was supposed to upload the updated battle maps to your bucket's HUD, but I had some problems getting the interfaces to communicate."

Wash motioned for a gawking marine to turn around and fix his attention on what was happening outside this little circle of confusion, then Wash dropped to a knee, disappearing beneath the tall grass. With Berlin looking down at him, Wash motioned for his friend to join him beneath the grass sea. He didn't want the marines out there with them to witness their supposed hard-core Legion commanding officer having to be shown how to use his own navigational equipment.

Wash whispered among the singing grass so low that he could barely hear himself, trusting Berlin's audio receptors in that marvelous bucket of his to clearly hear every word. "Don't waste time trying to read the map in your bucket. Unless you've got at least a hundred hours with the thing, it'll get you killed. Use this." Wash took hold of his friend's arm, and with a few taps and access codes, he had the no-glare, low-illumination screen activated. "Once this boots up, we can see where we are. Where did you plan to lead us?"

"South," Berlin replied, not remembering to lower his helmet's local output.

"You say 'south'?" asked Sergeant Shotton. "We headin' south?"

Wash looked imploringly at Berlin to either confirm or salvage the situation.

The appointed major gestured with an open palm as if asking Wash to handle it.

"Ultimately, yes, Sergeant," Wash said, still hidden amid the grass. He didn't want to know what sorts of faces the marines were pulling right now. "But not straightaway.

I'm trying to bring up the map that plots our best course. We don't want to move in a straight line out here with as many doros as are suspected in this region. Too easy for one of them to sight us."

"Well, we ain't exactly well-hidden out here either," said Denturo, spitting more stim juice onto a strand of reeds. "So either hurry it the hell up or the dobies will smell us on this wind."

"That's a lieutenant you're speaking to," said Sergeant Shotton.

Denturo spat again. "All I'm saying is if the doros catch us out in the open… well, some of you queers are going home in a body bag."

Wash had no idea whether there were dog-men nearby or not. He barely had any idea where they even were in the jungle. And if Berlin knew, he wasn't doing a good job of explaining it. He needed to take off his blasted helmet so Wash could at least read his face. But then, Wash had a pretty strong hunch that his fellow appointed officer was teetering on the brink of panic. They were really part of a recon patrol moving through contested jungles. And if something as simple as orienteering was causing this much of delay, they were definitely in over their heads.

Or at least Berlin was.

Wash felt he could figure things out once his friend's hard-mounted mapping tech booted up. He just needed to know where they actually were.

"C'mon. C'mon," urged Wash as Berlin's wrist-mounted display screen communicated through a series of satellite and atmospheric relays, trying to get the information.

Finally, the map loaded and plotted their position, showing him a drift of a kilometer or less. Wash squinted at the grid coordinates. His stomach sank, and he could feel the blood draining from his face. The map had to be wrong. They were farther north into the jungles than any foray had previously gone. At least as far as Wash knew. This was practically in the heart of doro territory. Well behind enemy lines.

The Legion had been fought to a virtual standstill far south of here, giving it their all just to keep hold of its many firebases against nightly onslaughts. *If the Legion itself isn't able to roll this deep into the jungle, why the hell are we here?* It had to be some kind of mistake. The SLIC pilots must've gotten lost and put them down on the wrong LZ.

But if they acted quickly, maybe they could still reach them over comms and call them back.

Wash looked up at Berlin. He could see his own reflection in his friend's visor. "We're not supposed to be here," Wash whispered, tapping the display for Berlin to observe.

Berlin hunched over to take a look. "Yes, we are. This is the right place." He had remembered to reduce the volume on his bucket's external audio outputs so that his voice was a small hush. "We're going to find that doro artillery that's been wreaking havoc, and we're either going to destroy it ourselves, or plot TRPs so we can get someone else to do the job. We'll be heroes. Trust me."

Wash didn't know how to react. This was insane. It was suicide. It was the type of mission expected of Dark Ops kill teams. Only, Dark Ops wouldn't send its legionnaires without any intel to go by. They'd plan it. Sandtable it. Rehearse it. And then execute.

"Do you have some kind of reason for thinking it's even out this way?"

"Well," said Berlin, "we're deeper into Psydon than anyone. Where else would they hide it?"

"Berlin. No. This is a mistake. We need to scrub this mission now, because we *will* die out here. We need to call back the SLICs."

Berlin shook his head adamantly. "We're out here until the rendezvous. No turning back."

"Well, then, what do you suggest we do here? The Navy hasn't spotted the artillery through these canopies, and neither have fighter sorties. So how are *we* supposed to? And even if we did, they'll be guarded by a division of doros."

"Major. Lieutenant." It was Sergeant Shotton. "There a problem?"

"No problem," answered Berlin. "We're about ready."

"We're not ready," Wash hissed, for all the good it would do him.

Berlin tilted his head. "Wash, you're overthinking this. We've got blasters, explosives, and Republic marines. Worst-case scenario, we find the target, note its position, and then call in some crustbusters to take it out. Best case, we take it and destroy it ourselves. Big win. All is forgiven."

Wash opened his mouth to protest again, but Berlin was already rising to his feet.

"We're moving south, Marines," he said. And he led the way, leaving Wash kneeling in the grass.

The order was met with borderline sarcasm as the marines began to move out. "About time."

The heavy footfalls of Denturo approached Wash, stalks of grass bending and thrashing as the big marine approached. He turned his head and spat. "Dobies for sure to the south. You two homos better not have another lovers' spat and leave us hanging like that again. Or I'll do you both quick and painless."

05

The temperature of Wash's broken-down office hab was a longed-for, fond memory as the recon team moved through the sweltering jungle. The air was teeming with biting insects, whose chittering calls mixed with all the other hidden creatures to fill the air with an incessant, and hypnotically disturbing, noise. The air was so humid Wash felt like each breath sent more warm water than air to the bottom of his lungs.

If Berlin were to hand Wash a commandeered Legion bucket, he would take it in a heartbeat. Of course, the helmet would need the rest of the armor to unlock its full potential, and Wash felt more and more exposed without his as each sword-like leaf of the surrounding jungle slashed his exposed arms.

At least he wasn't wholly without protection. He had the flak jacket and the open-faced marine helmet from the SLIC. He again felt grateful to the marine sniper who had kitted him up.

Wash still had enough of his Legion Academy conditioning to keep up with the marines—more than keep up, really—but the march was difficult. The kilometer trek through the grass was followed by a tortuous six kilometers inside the tree line, with his heartbeat pounding the whole time in anticipation of a sudden firefight. There were no trails, so each man in the snaking reconnaissance column had to slither around obstacles, ducking spiked vines, odorous blossoms, and sticky, dripping mushrooms the size of hoverbikes. And Berlin's disregard for the Academy's conditioning was showing. The major trailed at the end of the line, clearly struggling with the relentless terrain. The climate controls probably helped him, and his bucket drowned out what Wash suspected was some heavy, labored breathing. It wasn't like Berlin was doughy and lazy, but he wasn't ready for this. He wasn't Legion, even though he dressed and looked the part.

Wash felt like a babysitter, hanging back to make sure his friend wasn't separated from the rest of the column.

As Wash reached a massive tree along the jungle floor, at least twenty meters in circumference at its base, he saw Sergeant Shotton waiting for him.

"Sergeant," said Wash.

"Your boy injure himself?" Shotton nodded back toward Berlin. "Moving awfully slow for a leej."

Wash turned and watched his friend. Berlin was taking his time getting down from a fallen tree that had blocked their route. He seemed oblivious to the fact that the rest of the men were outpacing him by a good margin.

"Uh, I think he turned an ankle," Wash lied.

"Guess he's hiding it all right, then," offered Sergeant Shotton diplomatically. "Well, it ain't like those artillery are gonna outrun us. We either gonna find 'em or we ain't." After departing the LZ, Wash had related the mission objective—such as it was—to the sergeant, who'd relayed it to his men.

"Yeah," muttered Wash.

"Anyway," continued the sergeant, "I told the men to take a break and grab some chow. But if the major can continue on with me to the front, I wanna figure out how we're going to handle this next stretch of jungle. It looks to open up a bit. Good place for a doro encampment... or an ambush."

Wash nodded and waited for Berlin to join them.

"Hey," panted Berlin. "What're we standing around for?"

He sounded like the out-of-shape friend on a hike who was doing his best to appear all in. Only Wash knew he meant it. He was giving it his all. Berlin wasn't a real legionnaire, but neither was he a quitter.

"Major," Shotton said, pointing ahead, "we've been pushing south for a while. My men have come up on an opening that just don't feel right. I need you to come forward with me, sir, and tell me if we're on the right course."

Wash followed the two men silently. He didn't like that Berlin was going to be the one deciding what came next, because he didn't trust his friend to make the best decisions when it came to keeping himself, and these marines, alive. The fact that they were in this sweltering mess in the first place was proof enough of that.

Of course, Wash's decision-making today hadn't exactly been exemplary either. He had only himself to blame for coming along. But for Berlin's sake, and for the sake of these men, he felt that his presence here was for the best. If he hadn't come, Berlin might've already been left by the marines to find his own way home.

It would be up to Wash to make sure they got back to base safely.

And if he could pull that off, it would then be up to Berlin to make sure their careers weren't ruined.

The trio passed marines resting on the jungle floor in silence as their brothers kept lookout. Denturo watched them pass by, and though he didn't spit in Wash's direction this time, he was staring daggers. "Took you homos long enough."

The marine with the black hair who'd been seated next to Wash on the SLIC—PFC Haulman—stood amid of tangle of hanging vines that secreted some sort of sticky substance that entrapped small insects. He waved for Sergeant Shotton and the legionnaires to come forward.

"What's up, Haulman?" asked the sergeant.

"Parker says he sees something," the marine answered in a whisper. "Thinks it's a dobie."

"Okay," Berlin said, "let's go check it out, Sergeant. Lieutenant Washam, you stay here and guard the... back."

"Yes, sir," Wash said, though he very much wanted to go forward.

He found himself in the company of Denturo and the other marines. He looked for the sniper whose name he still didn't know, but didn't see him. Perhaps he was the "Parker" that Private Haulman had mentioned.

Denturo, reposed in a thick patch of yellow-flowering vines, heckled Wash. "Solve an argument for us, Leej.

These guys here," Denturo spat in the direction of the other marines, "all say the major is gonna be the first one to die out here. But I say... it's you. So which is it?"

Wash walked over to the hulking marine, who was smiling at his own joke. He squatted down until he was looking Denturo straight in the eyes. "You're gonna wanna get up right now, Marine."

Denturo spat. "Yeah? Why's that?"

"Because those yellow flowers contain a nectar that doubles as a nerve-deadening agent. So I figure it won't be long until all you feel on your rear end is pins and needles."

"You an expert on that, LT?" Denturo asked. He was still defiant, but Wash saw a creeping concern in his eyes.

"I read the Psydon flora manual. Be a shame if you've gotta walk on numb legs through the jungle. Doros'll hear that for sure. Then I guess *you'll* be the first one dusted."

Denturo's face paled and he sprang to his feet, wiping the clinging flowers from his pants while his buddies did their best to stifle laughs behind open palms.

Wash turned, not bothering to hide the smile on his face.

Haulman was coming back in their direction. The marine signaled for Wash to follow, but to remain quiet. The other marines must've seen this too, as they all fell silent as a graveyard past dark.

Wash followed the marine, neither of them speaking, past massive, rain-catching leaves the color of emeralds. When they arrived at the foot of a small hill, Haulman motioned for Wash to go up, then the marine slid back into the jungle they'd come from.

At the top of the hill was another marine, crouched among odd, pink ferns. He pointed to Wash's left, indicating for the legionnaire to move down the other side of the relatively sparse jungle hill. It was sun-soaked, clear of trees, and covered with a season's worth of dried, decaying leaves and palms. Wash could see Berlin and Sergeant Shotton down there, ducking behind a massive fallen tree limb.

Dropping to his stomach, Wash slung his blaster rifle onto his back and pulled himself in a controlled low-crawl down the hill. At the bottom, he continued on his belly until he was covered by a vegetation line that allowed him to get to both feet and stoop.

There he found another marine stationed, this one with his arm up at a ninety-degree angle, a clear indicator for anyone behind him to stop. Wash stayed frozen for several seconds before the marine waved him forward to reach Shotton and Berlin. There was no doubt in Wash's mind that they had come across something that, if not outright dangerous, demanded extreme caution.

After passing several more marines, Wash finally joined Shotton at the edge of what seemed to be a small valley, though it was hard to tell with the massive tree limb obstructing his view. Berlin was obviously still breathing heavily, the way his chest armor moved up and down, but his helmet continued to drown out the noise.

"What's up?" Wash whispered.

Sergeant Shotton's head was barely peeking over the top of the tree limb. "Take a look."

Wash slowly brought his eyes above the limb to look down below. Doros—a species of vicious, dog-like pack warriors that could move on two or four legs—milled about in grungy fatigues. Each of the aliens had a beat-up looking blaster rifle slung over its shoulder. But with the exception of a few sentries, they seemed to carry about with a relaxed attitude. One group of the doros sat inside an open-walled structure with a corrugated metal roof, playing cards.

Wash dropped back down behind the tree limb and fumbled for his pack, retrieving his field macros.

"Wait a while," called a calm voice hidden in nearby foliage. It was the sniper—Parker. "Two of the guards are making their rounds facing this way. I'll tell you when they pass."

His back against the log, Wash looked from Sergeant Shotton to Berlin. "This what we came to find?"

"I sure hope so," said Berlin, his voice strong through his bucket's external speakers. He didn't sound all that winded.

"It's something, all right," said Shotton.

Wash couldn't get a read on the man, other than that he sounded like a professional confirming the facts of the matter.

"I didn't get the best look," Wash said, "but I'd say maybe... twenty, thirty dobies."

"Yeah," Shotton muttered. "'Bout what I counted, too."

"There's forty-eight," said Parker from the bushes. "About half of them are sleeping or playing cards. The rest are in two-man patrols or stationed in observation posts. It's safe now, by the way."

Wash crept up to have a quick second look with his macros. He skimmed the camp, counting concentrations of doros by sixes until he confirmed all forty-eight. He dropped back down behind cover.

"Forty-eight. Confirmed."

"That's more than triple our force," Sergeant Shotton said. "So what's the plan, Major?"

Berlin knocked on the chin of his helmet as though he was thinking the same thing. He rose up and placed both elbows on the limb, looking at the situation through the optical magnification his bucket's visors provided. The way he was holding his hands, he looked to Wash as though he was praying.

"We sneak into their camp," Berlin said, still watching. "I think we can get by 'em. Then we grab some intel and disappear back into the jungle. Easy."

Parker leaned his head out of the bush in order to exchange a look with Sergeant Shotton.

"All right," Shotton said, his face unreadable. "If that's the order, I'll get everybody up and in position. Unless you'd rather oversee that, Major?"

"Hmm?" Berlin sounded like he hadn't quite been paying attention. He looked over to Shotton, as if waiting for his brain to catch up to the conversation. "Oh! No, you're fine, Sergeant. You know what you're doing. Whatever positioning you set up is okay by me. As long as it works out, that's all I'm concerned with. I don't need the honor."

Wash drew his face back into a tight smile. That probably wasn't *exactly* leadership in action, but Shotton certainly was better suited to coordinate an infiltration on a fortified outpost than Berlin was. If anything, Berlin deserved a bit of credit for knowing his limitations. The way some of the other point officers talked, you'd think they were the second coming of General Rex himself. And that from a group of people who'd likely never even downloaded the tactical e-books required for their stint in the Legion Academy.

"Hey," Berlin said, as though he were talking to himself. "Where are they all going?"

Wash popped up and followed Berlin's line of sight with his field macros. Several of the dog-men were moving toward the edge of their camp in what looked like an orderly procession. They were speaking in their guttural language, but the distance was too great for any of it to be made out. Not that Wash spoke Doro. "They're definitely up to something."

"You probably can't see it," said Parker from inside his hide, "but there's a big old transport truck on the extreme edge of the camp. Sitting on a dirt road. That's where they're headed."

"Repulsor?" Wash asked.

"Nah. Tracks and wheels. Old. Probably running off of organics. Fossil fuels and the like."

Wash nodded in agreement. They hadn't seen much in the way of synthetic refineries in the doro cities. These more distant worlds still hadn't caught up to the full scope of tech enjoyed by the rest of the galaxy. And Psydon wasn't even really at galaxy's edge. Things were even harsher out there.

"We should blow it up," Berlin said decisively, sounding enthusiastic at the prospect. "We should destroy this whole camp."

"Sir, not that I'm one to turn down a chance to kill dobies... I mean doros, as per the regs," said Shotton, "but you just said our best plan was to sneak in long enough for a quick grab of intel. I thought our mission was to find those artillery platforms. We make a noise here, best believe that some doro running on four legs is gonna get the word out about us being in country. And that means all of us having to haul ass all the way to the LZ." Shotton added a final mumble, just barely audible. "Speaking of which, I wouldn't mind you sharing the location of our LZ with me, Major Berlin, in case something happens to you."

Berlin nodded. "Yeah, I'll tell you about it later. But if we were to take this place out... how can we take this place out?"

"We'd better do it quick," the sniper said. "That truck ain't just waitin' around for nothing. It's obviously getting ready to move."

Wash considered what was before them. It wasn't the artillery platforms, but that was a needle-in-a-haystack mission; the entire Republic fighting force hadn't been able to find and destroy those. Still, this *was* a doro outpost, and they had an opportunity to take it out. And Wash was confident they would be able to overwhelm the dogmen with a surprise attack.

And then he saw something that made the decision to take the camp mandatory.

"Sergeant Shotton," Wash said, almost surprised by the strong, Legion-trained tone of command in his voice. "Bring the rest of your men up. Let's get them into position to eliminate the sentries and move into the camp. We should be able to eliminate them in the confusion before they have the chance to raise an alarm and rally."

Shotton hesitated. He seemed both annoyed and reluctant to listen to the orders of this legionnaire lieutenant wearing a mishmash of Legion fatigues and marine combat greens.

Wash stabbed a finger in the direction he'd been looking. "*Now*, Sergeant?"

Shotton squinted his eyes, searching for what Wash was pointing out. Then his face lit up with surprise. "Oh, hell. Right away!"

The sergeant disappeared, leaving the two appointed legionnaires and the marine recon sniper as the only remaining vigil.

"Lieutenant Washam," the sniper said calmly. "I'm watching the truck through my scope, and it's a pretty narrow field of vision. You wanna share with me what got Sarge's panties in a bunch like that?"

"You got eyes on the truck's exhaust pipes?"

"Yeah."

"Scan twenty degrees. Your left. Beneath the camo cargo net."

Berlin, obviously struck with curiosity, began to look in the same direction. "What are we looking for here, Wash?"

"Holy..." the sniper said.

Underneath the canopy net—the type designed to stay hidden from the Republic's roving eyes above—sat a group of humans, their arms flex-tied behind their backs. The prisoners sat cross-legged, guarded by doros with well-worn blaster rifles at the ready, barking menacingly. The captives appeared to be Republic Army or Marines, but it was tough to tell from this vantage point.

"I'm willing to bet that's the cargo intended for the waiting truck," Wash said.

Berlin had finally spotted them. He placed both hands flat against the limb providing cover. "Holy sket! This is great! Wash, we've got to rescue them."

Initially, Wash had determined to argue against sneaking into the camp. Better to log its location and call in a bombing run once they'd returned to base. But now, seeing that the lives of fellow Republic citizens were at stake, the game had changed. Whether Legion or marine, you didn't leave your brothers to die.

The doros had them outnumbered, but a twelve-man recon team enjoying the element of surprise should be capable of securing its objective. So long as everything was done just right. The single biggest factor was time. Could they get themselves set up and in position before the prisoners were loaded into the truck and carried off to their next destination?

"Parker," Wash said, realizing as he did that he was only guessing that this was the sniper's name. He hadn't confirmed it.

"Yeah?"

"We can't let that truck get out of here. Do you have anything capable of stopping it?"

A full Legion team would have a heavy equipped with anti-vehicle weaponry. Wash wasn't unfamiliar with how a marine recon team was loaded out.

"We've got a portable launcher, but it's back with the others. I can make a shot though, man. Maybe clip the driver through the glass. Vehicle's too old to have anything thick enough to stop what we're bringing to the party."

Wash considered this. If the vehicle was moving, taking out the driver could be a bit of a wild card. If the dead doro were to get its foot stuck to the acceleration pedal or lean hard against the steering column, the truck could careen out of control. And if that thing rolled... well, you wouldn't want to be sitting in the back where the prisoners would be gathered.

"Roger that. Is that our only option?"

"Might be able to shoot out the engine. That is, *if* I'm right about how it's powered. That would stop the thing in its tracks."

Wash nodded. "Do whatever it takes. Let's just keep as many of our guys alive as possible."

Our guys.

Wash might be an appointed officer. He might never be accepted into the fraternity. But these were still his guys. And he was all in.

Sergeant Shotton returned, moving quietly ahead of the full grouping of marines. They joined the makeshift command center behind the fallen tree limb. "We're up. What's next, Lieutenant?"

Berlin seemed transfixed by all of this, watching both Wash and Shotton, waiting to see what would happen next. He made no pretense of wanting to give input.

"Gear up to take out the sentries." Wash pointed at two marines. "You two: move around the west slope and get your sights on the two doros patrolling the camp's perimeter."

The marines nodded and began to move. If they felt any hesitancy in following Wash, the commanding issuance of orders swept it all away. These marines were trained to fight, and they were being given orders regarding a fight that was about to go down sudden and quick.

Not wasting time with words, Wash gave silent instructions, pointing at teams of two and directing them to their objective. He trusted the marines to kill, the same as if they were Legion. They would slaughter as many doros as possible through stealth, and then get the rest of them once things got noisy.

With the marines moving out to eliminate sentries or to position themselves to send plunging fire into the camp, Wash spoke again in whispers to Parker. "Once they're set up, you have a green light. Take the shots you have to. But let us stay hidden as long as we can. Only... not at the expense of letting the truck get away."

"Copy that, Lieutenant."

Satisfied, Wash turned to Sergeant Shotton, pointing over the top of the limb with two fingers. "We're going down there. Gonna creep right up into the camp so we're in position to take those guards out once the shooting starts."

"All right," grunted Shotton. "Hopefully my knees don't creak so much they give us away."

"What about me?"

Berlin might not have wanted to be involved in the planning, but he clearly didn't want to miss out on the action. It didn't matter to him who decided how the fight went down, only that he was in it.

And Wash knew he couldn't cut his friend out. He knew that if he tried, Berlin wouldn't hesitate to use his rank. Berlin needed this fight; in his mind, his entire future life depended on it. And in a way it did.

"Blocking position," Wash said. "Call out targets for Parker, but be ready to cut off any doros if they try to climb up this hill."

"Right," Berlin said with a nod. "I can do that."

Wash nodded back. If there was confusion among the marines about which legionnaire was in charge of the mission, this interaction probably didn't help matters. Wash bumped a fist against Berlin's armored shoulder. "You got this, Major. Doros will probably run up this hill so fast once the shooting starts that you'll get more kills than anyone else."

"We ready?" asked Sergeant Shotton, who was staring at Berlin suspiciously.

"Yeah," Wash said. "Let's get into position."

"Hey," said Berlin, grabbing Wash's arm as he began to move by. "I'm seeing all these green dots moving around the perimeter in my helmet. What is... is that bad?"

"Oba," said a stunned Sergeant Shotton. Any doubt as to whether his commanding officer was capable had now been confirmed.

But Wash didn't have time to smooth things over between his friend and the sergeant. The marines would just have to accept that they were being led through the jungle by one of the Republic's shiny new appointed Legion officers. And anyway, Wash was going to show them firsthand that he, at least, knew how to KTF.

"Green dots are marines. Your bucket is tracking their embedded micro-transponders—part of their meat tags."

"Got it," said Berlin. "Green dots mean good guys."

Wash gave a wan smile. "Just don't even shoot in the direction of those dots. You see something over there, call it out to Parker and have him take the shot. Blocking position, remember? Don't leave the spot unless you're absolutely sure you're going to be overrun. And even then, don't run unless Parker tells you to."

"Shoot every doro that gets close," offered Sergeant Shotton, his professional cool taking over. "That's all we need from you, Major."

Wash nodded and looked to the sergeant. "Let's move."

06

Wash and Sergeant Shotton moved around the fallen limb and crouched in a patch of fragrant blooming plants that smelled of anise and vanilla. Wash held up a hand to tell Shotton that this was as far as they needed to go.

The marines were still stalking through the under-brush, closing in on their assigned kills. Most of the sentries were relatively exposed, but one pair of doros were emplaced with a heavy machine gun behind sandbags on a wooden platform. The dog-men were oriented to face the road, evidently feeling that it was the most likely direction of attack. Which made sense, because to date no one in the Legion or Republic had dropped a team in the middle of nowhere to blaze an alternate path through un-scouted jungle.

Only a point would be dumb enough to try that.

Denturo and another marine crept through the foliage, stalking the gunners in the nest like savage predators. With the camp distracted, the two marines were able to dash out of the jungle, taking cover on the blind side of the sandbags. They had their knives out, blades powder-coated black so as not to reflect the sun, and as they charged the emplacement, they thrust the blades into the doros' bark-boxes, sinking them to the hilt and holding the dog-men's muzzles closed with their free hands. Denturo lifted his doro's spasming body off the ground, keeping it from knocking around anything that might draw attention, until the dog-man went slack and was laid limply below the cover of the sandbags with an ironic and almost affectionate gentleness.

The big marine—whose cheek looked swollen with stim even from Wash's distant vantage point—held up a hand to let his sergeant know that they were now in place.

Shotton nodded and directed Wash's attention to the other machine gun nest. Again, it looked as though the recon team had arrived from the one direction the doros hadn't expected. They were ready for an attack coming from the Republic's lines, not from behind their own.

Berlin truly had convinced the SLIC pilots to go deep behind enemy lines. It was a wonder they'd done so.

With the doro machine gunners' backs turned—exposed to Shotton's recon patrol—two marines Wash didn't know moved into position. Unlike Denturo, these men wouldn't have the opportunity for a silent takedown. Not without being seen. They held grenades, which would be the smartest and—for them—safest way to take out their target.

Sergeant Shotton held up a hand, telling the marines not to throw them yet. There was one more important takedown needed before the big boom: the guard tower, which Haulman was going after. He was by far the most exposed marine as he climbed, even with his buddy watching his back from a covered spot on the ground below.

Haulman slowly climbed up rung by rung, moving precisely, painstakingly slow, so as not to make any noise. A single doro sentry atop the wooden structure looked out casually at the jungle, facing opposite his enemy. He leaned against one of the support beams that held up a canvas providing shade to his canine-like head.

Haulman paused at the top rung, ready to slip inside.

"Tell them ten seconds once we reach the hut where those doros are playing cards," Wash instructed Shotton.

The sergeant conveyed the order in three sets of hand motions. They had short-range comms, of course, but the intensity of the situation was such that no one wanted to speak. And the doros were known to listen in on the open military comms—all save the Legion's ultra-encrypted L-comm. It would all be easier with Legion helmets, but they were doing it the old-fashioned way. Knife work, and a bloody business at that.

Wash found it both exhilarating and terrifying to watch. He pushed aside his emotions—pushed out any thoughts about what might happen to him if the doros were to capture him, or any of them. With Sergeant Shotton at his side, he began to quietly move down the depression, creeping toward the camp, trusting the sniper and Berlin to keep them safe. Trusting that the other marines poised to storm the camp would do their jobs when the time came.

Just inside the camp, they came upon the small shack with a single wall where the dog-men were playing cards. Wash had been counting down in his head, knowing that the sentry in the guard tower should be dead soon, and then the machine gun nest would be grenaded.

Making a split-second decision, he grabbed a fragmentary grenade of his own, setting it to explode two seconds after he released the kill switch.

Looking toward the prisoners' holding area, still distant, Wash made eye contact with one of the captives. She was an Army basic, arms tied behind her back and wearing the standard fatigues of a supply soldier, stripped down to pants and the standard-issue tank top. Claw marks on her arms, right below the shoulder, suggested her jacket had been ripped away. Her helmet was missing, and her black hair rested messily on sunburnt shoulders, making her already deep brown skin appear that much darker.

The prisoner shook her head, not removing her gaze from Wash as if to say, "Don't."

But there was no turning back now.

Trusting his mental countdown, Wash tossed the explosive inside the doro shack.

It landed in the middle of the pile of credit chips, adding an ante to the pot that none of the players wanted. The dog-men froze for a second, and then at once began to bark. They jumped to their feet, but the grenade detonated before any of them could take a step. Shotton and Wash turned away from the blast, remaining hidden behind the shack's single wall.

Not a full second later the twin booms of two grenades erupting in the last machine gun nest sounded out across the jungle soundtrack. No sooner had that blast subsided than Wash could hear a pained yelping and whining above the din. He turned and saw the doro sentry flailing in free fall from the guard tower. The dog-man hit the ground hard, sending up a cloud of unsettled dust.

Then all hell broke loose. Dog-men pawed for weapons as high-cycle blaster fire from the marines stationed around the base began to rain down, ripping holes in the alien warriors. The doros scrambled frantically, but got cut down the moment they found themselves out in the open.

Wash and Shotton moved at the low, heading toward the impromptu POW holding area. The prisoners were ducked down, as if in some prayer of obeisance, trying to stay low while their confused doro captors snarled and barked threats. One of them, a larger member of the pack, raised its rifle menacingly, its vicious-looking snout curled back to reveal white dripping canines and raw hate foaming along the muzzle. He was going to kill the prisoners.

The doro's head then simply vanished in a mist of red blood and gray brain matter, fragments of skull and skin plastering the stunned prisoners cowering before him. The electric crack of Parker's sniper rifle told Wash everything he needed to know as the doro's headless body fell on the ground and poured out blood.

"Go!" shouted Wash as he and Shotton moved forward. The sniper had saved the prisoners with his first shot, but it would be up to Wash and Shotton to stop the other guards from carrying out the massacre.

They ran hard, raising their rifles and dropping a guard. They turned their rifles on the two remaining doros, but not before the dog-men opened up with their decrepit-but-far-too-lethal weapons, laying waste to the hapless prisoners in a sudden blur of automatic blaster fire.

"Sons-a—!" shouted Sergeant Shotton, even as he expended a full blaster pack in cutting down the murderous dog-men.

The battle continued on, getting in the way of their progress. A doro appeared from around a corner, snarling and shooting blaster bolts at Wash and Shotton. The two soldiers hit the dirt, rolling to return fire, only to see the dog-man's chest explode from another of Parker's shots at distance.

Wash scrambled to his feet, looking in the direction the doro had come from, just in case it had any buddies following. A concussive blast—another grenade—boomed near the building, causing its flimsy wooden reed door to fly open. Inside was another dog-man. It wasn't armed, but what it was doing was just as dangerous. Coiled over its canine-like ears was a modified comm headset, and the alien was clearly barking frightened messages into a mic.

Nothing good would come of that.

Wash raised his blaster rifle and thumbed the selector to full-cycle fire. He sent bolt after searing blaster bolt into the comm shack, punching holes through the wooden structure, which splintered around the smoking, black-charred rings. The doro danced in a seizure of pain as the bolts tore into it, the comm equipment going up in sparks and flames.

Wash's charge pack went dry. The comm shack was a ruin.

"We gotta hurry up," he shouted to Shotton, who was firing on a fleeing doro. "Chances are they've called for help."

They continued on to the site of the slaughter. The blood of the doros mixed freely with that of the butchered army basics, soaking the dry, leafy ground red.

"See if you can get a medic down here," Wash ordered the sergeant. "And watch for visitors."

"Rog, Leej," answered the sergeant.

Leej.

The marines—the sergeant at least—thought of him not as a point, but as a legionnaire.

But a real legionnaire wouldn't have let those prisoners get done like that, would they, Wash?

Wash stepped over corpses, making sure to put a blaster bolt into the head of any doros lying around—whether they looked dead already or not. Just to be sure. Then he shouldered his rifle and surveyed through the deceased prisoners. The effect of heavy blaster rifles at close range wasn't pretty. The bolts made a scorching entry wound, but the close-proximity fire allowed the kinetic energy of the bolt to punch right through so fast that little was cauterized, making the whole area looked like some sort of gory barbecue pit, with pieces of cooked and raw flesh intermingled with hair, bone, and unit patches.

Wash examined each prisoner for vital signs, his hands growing progressively slicker from blood as he went from one neck to the next. His mind told him that there was no chance of someone surviving, and to give this up and find some dog-men and make them pay real bad for what they'd done. But in his heart Wash felt that this was what he owed these soldiers for failing to save them. He had to at least try to find one alive and get them to hang on until the team's medic could be brought down.

Is this what you wanted, Wash? Would you have still gotten your feet wet if you knew it was in the blood of all these soldiers? Dead because you weren't leej enough to get the job done?

And yet, in spite of all the death all around him, Wash had never felt more alive in his life. Each blade of dead grass was revealed in a hundred different colors. The air tasted of burnt ozone, and sounds were sharp and clear. He felt a sense of shame over this. The Legion Academy had covered a litany of useful subjects, but dealing with these dueling feelings of elation and sorrow... that wasn't one of them.

Finally, he reached the still face of the woman he'd locked eyes with before everything went down. She was practically buried under her fellow soldiers, her head resting in the guts of some poor guy who'd been nearly shot in two, like some macabre pillow.

Why had she warned him off? Was it because she knew this would happen? Had the guards told her what would become of them if they tried anything, and had Wash forced their hands?

Or maybe it was a *fait accompli*. The guards had acted as though they already had orders. Perhaps the truck wasn't waiting to transfer them to another holding area— perhaps it was just waiting to carry their dead bodies to some mass grave deep in the jungle.

Wash picked his way through more dead. He saw other unit patches but nothing combat. No frontline soldiers. No marines or legionnaires. Just unlucky Republic Army soldiers who'd been captured trying to move food, water, and other supplies in the repulsor convoys needed to keep the various firebases equipped. Places too hot for a slow-moving shuttle entry and swarming with doro forces that would likely get to, and booby-trap, any orbital drops in the nearby jungle before the intended recipients ever could.

The sudden report of Sergeant Shotton's blaster grabbed Wash by the collar and shook him out of his thoughts. He looked up to see the marine drop a pair of doros running past the POW netting, cutting them down with a three-shot burst.

"Lieutenant, they're fleeing from this end of camp and making for the truck," Shotton growled, scanning for more targets and sounding just as angry as Wash felt. "All due respect, but the dead ain't goin' nowhere and we need to snuff these doros out before they get the chance to tell someone about it."

Wash felt another flush of shame, this time because he'd let his situational awareness be virtually eclipsed by the task of going through the dead. Something that could have waited, like the sergeant said. He looked around. The marines had poured down into the camp, pursuing the remaining doros, seeking to trap them against the truck like a hammer coming down hard on an anvil. The truck's driver didn't seem keen on waiting for his comrades to arrive.

He was already moving down the road, picking up what speed his massive rig could muster.

"Make sure that truck doesn't get away!" Wash shouted.

"Parker'll stop 'em," said Shotton with smug relish.

A sharp, intense blaster bolt backed up the sergeant's claim, slamming into the truck's engine compartment and sending a shower of sparks and smoke heavenward. The truck seized, stuttered, and stopped. The driver jumped out of the cab and was promptly turned into cooked meat by a follow-up shot that tore out the dog's long throat in a vapor puff of red mist. Then the sniper began picking off the other fleeing doros, causing them to stop and turn around in the chaos. Causing them to be dead a second later.

With no harm in using the comms, now that surprise was achieved, Wash called out a warning to his friend. "Berlin, they're coming your way!"

"I see 'em," Berlin answered, sounding positively ecstatic.

But the legionnaire's blaster fire didn't come. The doros were running on all fours, clawing their way up the hill and getting closer and closer to Berlin and Parker.

Something was wrong.

Berlin came back on the comm, his voice heavy with concern. "Blaster rifle isn't firing! They're gonna be right on top of us!"

The sniper fired again, but there was no way he could pick off the mob of rapidly approaching dog-men. And then Wash heard Parker's voice shouting over the comm. He was screaming at Berlin. "Is your damn selector on safe?"

Whether Berlin's gun truly was just in safe mode, or whether it was a bad pack jamming the weapon, Wash didn't know. But soon Berlin was sending down a stream of blaster fire into the advancing doros. The dog-men were struck on their heads and shoulders as they ran up on all fours, taking the hits at point blank. Searing blaster bolts from Berlin's weapon pounded into them. The doros couldn't move up, couldn't move to the side—they could only fall back or die right there.

And that's what they did. They just... died. It was like some galactic hit man lining up rival gangsters in a dirty back alley and cutting them down in cold blood. The doros fell down the hill, and what survivors there were now ran frantically in the direction of Wash and Sergeant Shotton.

"Fantastic!" Berlin shouted in triumph. "You see that, Wash? They're coming your way now!"

Wash raised his blaster rifle and added his blaster bolts to those of the marines, cutting down the remaining panicked doros in a final one-sided showdown that left the camp totally in control of the Republic.

07

"Status reports!" shouted Sergeant Shotton into the comm. "Everybody all right?"

"Haulman got hit, but nothing bad. Doc's patching him up now."

Shotton looked to Wash. "Not bad, Lieutenant."

"Yeah," Wash agreed. "Your men did fantastic work."

"They did their jobs."

Wash turned back to the executed prisoners, thinking to check again for any life, or information. "I don't think we'll want to stick around long enough to bury these guys."

Shotton grunted. "Shoulda kept a couple of doros to dig a grave for all these... plus one for themselves. I'll set up a perimeter, but, yeah, let's boogie when we can, sir."

What the sergeant suggested was technically a war crime according to the Republic, but Wash kept to himself. He understood where the man was coming from, and if he was honest with himself, the doros responsible for what had happened deserved what Shotton described.

As he began to pick over the dead again, he became aware of just how much blood was on his hands. He tried to shake the blood free before finally wiping his hands off on the uniforms of the deceased. And then, when he couldn't find uniforms of the dead not soaked, he wiped them off on his own uniform. So much so that it began to feel like a wet towel that would no longer hold any moisture. He must look a mess.

For all his efforts, there were no survivors. They were stone dead, every last one of them.

Wash stood up just as Denturo arrived with some other marines. "I don't know about the rest of you homos," Denturo spat, "but that was better than sex."

No one answered the gregarious hulk of a man, but that didn't seem to bother him. He spit fresh stim juice into the dried leaves and then looked around the ruined camp. "That can't be all of 'em. I got a whole lot more dobies to kill before I leave this jungle today."

Wash resisted the urge to shake his head. The marine sounded like something straight out of a cheesy action movie. "We'll find out from Major Berlin if this is it or if we're moving on to another target."

"Yeah, well, tell the major to set up more doros, and I'll knock 'em down straightaways. Thank Oba the marines taught me how to squeeze a trigger. I damn well could kill every dog-man, woman, and child on Psydon if they'd turn me loose."

"You just talking through your ass for fun, Denturo?" Sergeant Shotton asked, eyeing the big marine with a mix of hardness and approval. It was clear to see that the marine recon team enjoyed Denturo's antics. "Or is this one of those situations where you won't shut up until one of us admits that you could've killed everybody on your own?"

"Damn right I could've killed them all on my own, Sarge. Didn't even have to use my big gun. Give me a few extra charge packs and I'd have dusted every dobie in this camp. That ain't bragging. That's a fact and—holy sket!"

Denturo jumped in surprise, both feet almost leaving the ground. So did Wash. So did all the marines. They were all equally alarmed by the sudden, otherworldly gasp that came from what had been, to them, a corpse only moments before.

The woman Wash had locked eyes with had just loudly sucked in a lungful of air, as though resurfacing from a deep dive. As though her spirit had just returned to her body. She then fell instantly back into unconsciousness.

If Denturo was set to lose any macho points for jumping, Wash canceled it out. The surprise knocked him on his rear as he took an involuntary step back and tripped over a dead soldier. He grabbed frantically for his fallen blaster rifle, pointing it at the revitalized basic before realizing that it was only her.

"Looks like we got a breather after all," Sergeant Shotton said. The fright had turned his dark skin pale. "Need a corpsman here!"

The sniper, Parker, arrived in their midst, leaving Major Berlin to struggle down the hillside on his own. "Pretty good day when it's not just about the killing. Always fancied myself a hero. Shoulda been a fireman."

Wash felt hope kindle in his innards. What had happened to all the others was terrible, but it was... *good* to see that at least someone had survived the rabid executioners. But would she be all right?

Wash moved toward the woman to take a closer look. Her eyes popped open, and she screamed.

"It's okay!" Wash shouted back, immediately regretting the volume of his voice. He repeated himself, calmer now. "It's okay."

Taking care to keep his hands open and assume a non-threatening posture, he continued toward the woman. Her chest was heaving, and Wash felt as if he could hear her heart thumping from inside her body. Her eyes looked around wildly as though her mind hadn't caught up fully with what had just happened to her. And to everyone who had been alive and most likely known to her only a few minutes before.

"Hey. Hey. We're on your side." Wash spoke gently, dredging up the reserves of polite respectability that his civilian station had drilled into him as part of his planet's elite class. Why else would he have been chosen for the appointment program, if not good breeding? "You're safe. The doros are all dead now."

The survivor shrank back from him, pushing herself against the corpse of a fellow soldier until she was literally sitting on top of that other dead body. "Legion and marines, sweetheart," Denturo said, spitting after for good measure. "We look like dog-men to you, honey?"

Wash gave the marine a detestable look. That wasn't going to help things. But when he turned back around, he found that the big marine's words had gotten through.

The survivor looked less fearful, her eyes no longer wide with panic.

"You got a name?" Wash asked.

The woman licked her dry lips with an equally dry tongue, which stuck to the skin for a second before retreating back into her mouth. "Tierney. Tierney Behrev."

Wash put his hand on his chest. "First Lieutenant Scontan Washam, Fifth Legion." He inclined his head toward the watching marines. "These are all hullbusters. Don't worry about their names—none of 'em are worth getting to know."

The joke drew approving snickers from the marines, even Sergeant Shotton. Only Denturo seemed to take offense. "Up yours, Leej."

"Listen... *Tierney*," Wash said, moving closer and feeling more at ease when she didn't flinch or attempt to further retreat. "You're safe here, but that doesn't mean you're okay. We need to check you out, and then we gotta go. We're taking you with us."

"Where the hell is Corpsman Hellix?" shouted Sergeant Shotton over the comm.

"Sorry," replied the corpsman's voice over the open comm channel. "Just finishing up with Haulman. These jungles breed infection, and he needs to be sealed up before we start walking again."

"He's all right, though?"

"Yes, sir. Just a glancing blaster bolt."

"Well, finish up and then double-time it over here, Marine. I want the survivor cleared to move, and then I want us gone before the ants return to the picnic table."

"On my way, Sergeant."

The corpsman arrived not long after, cutting through the crowd of marines. He paused at the sight of all the bodies—all those prisoners shot down like vermin. Mouthing a silent prayer, Corpsman Hellix moved straight to Tierney, kneeling down at Wash's side.

"Okay, soldier," said the corpsman, "tell me your name."

"It's Tierney," Wash answered.

The corpsman gave a look that clearly told Wash to shut it. He then looked back at Tierney. "Sorry, what was it again?"

Wash felt like an idiot. The marine didn't care about her name. He was trying to get her talking to make sure she was all right. Hoping to see any signs of a concussion or any other problems that could be more easily identified through direct communication.

"Tierney," said the survivor.

She sounded a bit loopy. Maybe there was a concussion after all. Maybe she was losing blood.

Maybe… she wouldn't make it.

"Okay, Tierney," the corpsman said, looking her over and gently exploring her with his hands for any obvious wounds. "You hurt anywhere in particular? Were you hit?"

Tierney shook her head as though she was struggling to find her thoughts. "Feel a little sore… but… I don't think I got… don't think I was hit. Just… all… everyone crashed on top of me all so fast."

Hellix nodded. "I need to lift up your shirt, okay? These guys won't watch. Turn around, guys."

Such acts of modesty were generally considered misogynistic on the core worlds. Why would the corpsman ask this woman something he wouldn't have asked a man? But Wash found himself appreciating the care Hellix was showing the injured survivor.

Wash turned his head just as the tank top was lifted up, revealing the lower half of her body right up to a sport bra. Her ribs were bright red and already showing signs of significant bruising.

"Does this hurt?" the corpsman asked. "Are you having difficulty breathing?"

Wash looked back, his curiosity getting the better of him. The corpsman had his hand pressed firmly against the woman's ribs.

Tierney breathed in, clearly pained. "It doesn't hurt except when you're pushing on it," she said through gritted teeth. "It feels fine when you're not touching it."

The corpsman removed his hands. "Okay, so let's not touch it. How about your legs? Do you have feeling in them? Can you stand up?"

The woman nodded. "I can feel them. I can stand."

Using the bodies around her, she pushed herself up into a sitting position, using them further to rock forward into a squat. She stood with some effort, Wash and the corpsman holding their hands out to offer her help with balancing.

Tierney wobbled slightly before nodding that she was okay. "I'm fine. Just a little lightheaded."

There was a story here. Some tragedy—beyond the POW massacre—that had brought this soldier so deep into the jungle. But finding it out now wasn't a luxury Wash or the marines had. They needed to move.

Denturo spat a fresh stream of mouth juice. "Can the basic walk? 'Cause we don't need to be slowed down out here."

"Stow it, Denturo!" snapped Sergeant Shotton.

Wash was thankful for the rebuke, and not just because it meant he wouldn't have to poke the tigrax again. They were all supposed to be in this together. Now was the time to think about how to get a fellow member of the Republic military machine safely out of this jungle hellhole and onto a medical SLIC. Her nightmare—and what else could it feel like but that?—needed to end.

"I can walk," Tierney said, taking a few tentative steps as if to prove it. She shot a dirty look at Denturo. "But thanks for the concern."

Wash and the corpsman walked out of the carnage by her side, each ready to catch her should she stumble.

"So what's the plan, Sarge?" asked Parker. "I mean, other than her, the camp is empty... not sure we'll find anything of value."

The sergeant looked over to the major—who was still milling about by the hill he'd defended, counting the doros he'd killed—then sighed and looked at Wash. "Well, how about it, Lieutenant? Anything left for us to do here?"

Wash thought about the doro he'd killed working the comm relay. It was unlikely the alien was simply catching up on the Republic's constant counter-propaganda feeds. Wash had to assume that a response of some sort was coming, and while the doros' air and space forces were destroyed on day one, they knew their way through the jungle terrain and could move on foot almost as quickly as a truck or sled could arrive by snaking through hastily cleared jungle roads.

"We gotta go," Wash said. He offered Tierney an apologetic frown. "I'm sorry, we can't stay here. No time to bury the dead. That's... just the way it is."

The woman nodded, an unspoken acceptance of the grim fate in store for those exposed bodies. The jungle would reduce them to skull and bones in a matter of days. By month's end, there would be no trace.

"Major Berlin!" Wash shouted, cupping his hands around his mouth.

The major looked up and jogged over to his friend. He slowed at the sight of all the dead captives. It was as if he hadn't realized anything that had happened beyond his narrow cone of KTF.

"Sir," Wash said on Berlin's arrival, "I think it's time we made our way back to the SLIC LZ for exfil."

Berlin looked from Wash to the other marines. He drew a foot back, dragging up the dead leaves as he did so. "Uh, well... I didn't think we'd get something done so fast. The landing zone is the same place we were dropped off. But I told the SLICs not to come back for two days. We'll just have to hang out there until then."

The marines began to protest at this, swearing as only a marine can. There was no way out—the comms wouldn't reach an orbiting destroyer or a base—not this far behind the doro lines while competing with jammers and every other hack the dog-men used to keep the playing field even.

"Stow it, marines!" Shotton snapped, quieting his men down. "All due respect, Major, but there is not enough cover or fortification to simply wait in that tall grass for *two days* until the SLICs arrive."

Wash sighed, feeling betrayed by his friend, and yet... what did he expect? There wasn't a single part of him that believed Berlin was a capable strategist. He'd simply allowed himself to be caught up in the excitement of getting into the fight, and now his life, as well as the lives of the marines and this surviving POW, were in his hands. Hands covered in the blood of the POWs he had failed to save. If he had wanted to serve the Legion, he should have stopped this before it started. All that was left now was to lead the team to safety.

"We can't go back anyway," Wash said, chewing on his lip. "The doros are elite trackers. They'll find our trail and follow it to where we landed. We have to move forward, stay ahead of them."

"So we're walkin'?" Shotton asked.

Wash nodded. "Through the jungle, yes. Until we either find an elevated location suitable for a general comm transmission, or until we reach our lines."

The marines groaned.

All save Denturo. "Good. Said I wasn't done killin' dobies. Now I don't have to be."

"All right, marines!" Shotton yelled, circling a finger in the air as he turned toward the jungle that lay between them and the nearest Republic firebase. "Let's move out!"

08

Republic Army Firebase Hitchcock
Middle-of-Nowhere, Psydon

For Sergeant Major Boyd, being a legionnaire, one of the Republic's elite warriors, one of the best soldiers in the galaxy, was all he'd ever wanted. And he was a damn good legionnaire at that. But after six years in the Legion, an even greater opportunity came along.

Dark Ops.

Darks Ops was the Special Forces branch created by General Rex... before Rex was killed or thrown out, depending on whom you believed. If the Legion was Boyd's coming-of-age, his boyhood, Dark Ops was where he became a man. It had gotten him his nickname—Subs—as well as sharpened his already lethal skills into something downright... mystical.

But now, as he sat in the sweltering, sun-drenched firebase under command of the Republic Army, Subs felt more like a fish out of water than a man. He didn't belong here.

Subs was a Dark Ops legionnaire with no teammates, no Dark Ops commander... no purpose.

It all went bad a year before, during a Legion indigenous training operation gone terribly wrong.

The Legion was a strictly human force. That wasn't because other species weren't capable of forming elite fighting forces—anyone who'd ever faced a quad-wielding Tennar in a firefight, or tangled with a brutish Drusic in close quarters, would never again question their combat ability. It was because a humans-only approach was both efficient and effective. It allowed for standardization of equipment. It meant temperaments and motivations were reasonably aligned. It eliminated friction and made for more easily formed, stronger bonds, and greater camaraderie.

In short... it worked. And when you were knee-deep in some backwater jungle, facing hostile forces, and the only thing between you and a quick death were your brothers-in-arms... that was all that mattered.

But the Legion *was* active in training other species to form their own fighting forces, each different in its own way, as suited the species' temperaments and abilities. Subs and his team had personally worked with a number of local planetary militias to make them better able to defend their own planets. The Legion couldn't be everywhere, and having local, loyal forces that knew how to KTF was Legion Commander Barrow's strategy for containing the brushfire conflicts erupting in the shadow of the Savage Wars.

So when the tall and slender Ukos—members of a Republic world brought in during the Savage Wars—were facing a hostile rebellion by decidedly socialist and anti-Republic revolutionaries, Subs and his Dark Ops team were sent in at the Republic's behest to teach the Ukos how to shoot straight, how to move and think tactically, how to… KTF. All within the confines and limitations of the Ukos' culture and physiological ability.

Unfortunately, one of the Ukos they trained—an alien who had supposedly been vetted at the highest levels—wasn't actually interested in protecting his home planet. He was interested in killing legionnaires. In scoring one for the revolutionary guard. And so when Subs turned his back on that alien, mere moments after giving thirty Uko commandos instructions on how to fire a fully automatic blaster rifle, the traitor in the ranks used that leej-acquired knowledge, along with the Republic-supplied weapon, to fill Subs's back with blaster bolts.

Subs's partner, who was watching Subs's back even as the rifle was raised, dropped the Uko an instant after the betrayal had started. But not before what was done was done.

Subs didn't blame his buddy. That's how life went sometimes.

What followed were hours of surgery and months of rehab, only to be told at the end of it all that his time as a legionnaire was finished. Subs was medically unfit for combat—and in Dark Ops… fighting was expected.

That didn't sit well with Subs's commanding officer, who passed his concern up the chain of command. And each time Subs's case reached the next level, it didn't sit well there, either.

Once it reached the sector Legion commander's desk, arrangements were made. Subs was less than a year away from retirement, and it was decided that he would wind out those last few months in the Legion, until his Republic pension activated. No combat, of course—someplace out of the way of all that. And yet, someplace close *enough* to the fight that he'd get over the threshold required by the House of Reason for time served in war zones. Which meant a bigger pension, something that would make civilian life just a little bit easier.

Because, as far as the men running the Legion were concerned, a man like Subs deserved that much. And if the Legion wouldn't take care of him, then who would?

It really was a beautiful thing.

But if Subs had known that it meant being stuck in a sweltering Republic Army forward supply base, one that smelled constantly of urine and jungle rot, he probably would have told his CO to frag off.

As it was, he'd thanked the man profusely, and now here he was, out of uniform, sitting on the edge of a rifle pit that had been dug out along the base's perimeter, his legs dangling into the foxhole.

He looked out past the mile-wide zone of cleared trees—the jungle was struggling to regrow in between defoliation drops—and into the swaying tree line beyond. Just passing the time.

The kids were out there. In the jungle. A bunch of fresh-faced basics patrolling in a part of Psydon where dying wasn't so common. Which was why Subs was there, too. They didn't want him to die, not after pulling all the strings needed to keep him in.

He'd taught the basics how to do what they did better. Partly because he had nothing else to do, but also because he'd grown attached to them, and he wanted them to come back from their patrols in one piece. Since he couldn't go out with them—he had explicit orders not to leave the wire—teaching them was all he could do. So he told them all the things that their R-A drill instructor left out. Showed them how to move through the jungle quieter, quicker... deadlier.

Sometimes they went out and returned just fine, and he was proud of them. Told them they were learning how to KTF, and that the doros would tuck tail and run if they ever made the mistake of mixing it up with them.

Other times those boys and girls would come back, but not whole. The patrol would return with the medical bot pulling a stretcher behind it. Sometimes with a dead basic... sometimes with a basic whose life had just been changed forever. And on those days, he wondered if he could have prevented that if they'd let him go out with them.

He thought so.

He was waiting for the platoon to return. Smoking a cigarette and looking through a haze of blue smoke for that first basic to emerge from the thick jungle. But Psydon's tropical sun was waiting out there with him, and its heat was oppressive against his leathery tanned neck.

Subs took a final drag of the cigarette and flicked the butt into the rifle pit. He watched the red glow of the cig wink down there in the shadows and decided that it might not be so bad to wait awhile in the shade the pit provided. But as he looked down, he saw something else. A glimpse of his stomach, visible past the marine-style flak jacket he wore open.

It was the first time since he'd been a young boy that he couldn't see any abdominal muscles. He wasn't fat, not by any stretch; even at thirty-eight, his body was better than those of the basic teenagers running around on behalf of the army. But there was no denying the fact that life on the firebase wasn't doing him any favors. Without other leejes to push him, without those long, grueling operations that were achieved through tenacity, heart, and determination... he'd grown soft. At least a little.

And a little was too much.

He could get fat when he officially retired. Until then, it was time to kick his own ass.

Subs slapped his stomach. There wasn't enough fat there to ripple. "Sit-ups, Sergeant Major Boyd. Sit-ups."

Sergeant Major Boyd.

That was another thing about being stationed alone on an army base. In the Legion, he'd been given the call sign Razor because of his penchant for shaving the entirety of his hair and eyebrows with an old-fashioned straight razor. It made him feel clean and cool inside his bucket. Then in Dark Ops, he got the nickname Subs because he seemed able to fill in for any job on the team that needed doing. And he did it well.

But here... everyone referred to him as Sergeant Major Boyd. And now he was calling *himself* Sergeant Major Boyd. But he was Subs. He was Dark Ops.

Sergeant Major Boyd was what they would refer to him as during processing when he retired in three months.

But he couldn't be a Sergeant Major Boyd—not yet. Not while he was Dark Ops.

At the noise of an incoming SLIC, Subs looked up from his perch at the top of the foxhole. The aircraft flew directly overhead, making for the firebase's only landing pad. He looked back to the jungle one more time. Still no sign of the kids returning. *His* kids, as he'd begun to think of them.

"Guess I'm staying out in the sun," Subs said to himself as he stood up and dusted off his hands, not at all looking forward to the long walk in the harsh sun to reach the landing pad. But... maybe he could be of use. There was no reason for anyone to make a stop here, at Firebase Hitchcock, unless it was an emergency.

After a few steps he decided to jog, heat be damned. Then he decided to sprint.

Blame it on his disappearing abs.

* * *

When Subs got within five hundred meters of the landing pad, he decided to slow his pace so as not to be huffing and puffing on arrival. The SLIC's two pilots were already out of the craft, stretching, while maintenance bots rolled around the vehicle. There was no sign of the door gunner, which meant the poor marine had probably been shot while ferrying troops somewhere in the Psydonian jungle.

Subs looked around, wondering what was taking the medics so long to reach the craft. He quickened his pace, again hoping that he could be of some use. He'd been trained as a medic while in Dark Ops. At least at a rudimentary level. They all had.

But as he drew near, something about the pilots threw up a flag. Their demeanor, the way they held themselves... it seemed off. And then the door gunner appeared from the other side of the SLIC, emerging from beneath the vehicle's shadow. He walked over to his crewmembers and began speaking to them, swinging his arms behind his back and then forward in an exaggerated clapping motion.

His mind still on injury and triage, Subs thought that if the door gunner wasn't wounded, that only meant some kid was on board, all shot to hell from a trip into the jungle, and needing immediate medical attention. Even a small forwarding operating base like Hitchcock had enough stasis bubbles and med bots to at least keep a soldier from dying until they could get further treatment. They might end up a cyborg if regenerative medicine couldn't be applied right away, but at least they wouldn't die.

Yeah, some wounded legionnaire or marine probably explained the SLIC's arrival from the jungle. As for the flight crew's casual demeanor... maybe they'd simply gotten used to the sight of young Republic citizens with missing limbs or holes burned into their bodies. Psydon was that kind of war. And while Subs wasn't crazy about the featherheads being so cavalier, he didn't begrudge them their behavior. You had to do what you had to do just to deal with it all. And they'd done what they could in getting their SLIC down onto the landing pad.

Subs sprinted the remaining distance. The heat beat down on him from above as he moved, then greeted him from the ground up once his feet landed on the hot dura-crete pad.

It felt good. Doing something. Running. Getting shot and a year's worth of rehab made you grateful for movement.

Subs reminded himself not to take it for granted. There would be a time when he could run no longer.

He slowed to a stop, breaching the flight crew's bubble of conversation. They'd been watching him sprint toward him, looking confused as if trying to figure out what was so important.

"How many wounded?" Subs asked, pleased with how little winded he was. "What's taking the med team so long?"

"Cool your thrusters, Leej," said one of the pilots, friendly enough.

Subs had no idea how they took him for a legionnaire. His jungle camo pants were standard for the Republic soldiers on Psydon, and his open vest was marine-issue. Subs looked down, remembering his open vest and the large Legion crest tattoo on his midsection, the hilt of the blade at his chest and the blade running down to his navel. Yeah, that was a pretty good giveaway.

"No wounded here," added the other pilot, a handsome man with a movie-star smile. "If there were, you'd see us doing everything we could to keep 'em alive—with or without a med team present."

Subs nodded, relieved to hear that—happy that he'd misread the pilots and their gunner as men too jaded to care any longer. But he still didn't understand why they were landing on this firebase that *no one* visited unless ordered to.

He examined the SLIC. It wasn't fitted for med duty, but it was stocked with a payload of missiles—not a full attack bird, so probably a craft outfitted to insert troops rather than a full-on gunship. There was no visible damage to the craft suggesting she needed to make an emergency landing, nor was there any trail of fluids or smoke suggesting a technical problem. But maybe the jungle humidity had simply taken its toll. There were sensitive pieces of technology on board that may as well have been magic to an old legionnaire like Subs. And maybe the pilots simply got too nervous to keep going without getting on the deck to see what the matter was.

Evidently, the crew picked up on Subs's confusion. That, or his examining stares.

"We're just stopping to refuel is all, Sergeant Major," offered the crew chief.

Refuel? That was... odd. Subs had been inserted by SLIC countless times, and while he couldn't spout off the exact fuel capacity nor the precise number of miles a skilled pilot could coax out of the craft, he'd developed something of a gut feeling for how long a SLIC could stay in the air before going down. He'd been on ops requiring a stopover for refueling. He'd been on ops where the SLIC could no longer run on fuels and was forced down. He knew how far and how long a SLIC could go on a round trip, and how long it could hover on overwatch before having to break and return to base. And for this crew to have to land *here* of all places suggested that they were a long way from home.

The only thing Subs could think of was that the crew had done an insertion much deeper in the jungle that what he was aware was authorized. It was possible they'd been holding an overwatch position to pull security over the firebases in the region, but that was a pretty thin explanation. The big ships in orbit had taken over responsibility for keeping an eye on the battlefield after the doros started to get adept at shooting up SLICs.

"Where did you take off from?" Subs asked.

The pilot with the movie-star smile tried to dismiss the question out of hand. "Can't really say, Leej. Classified."

Subs smiled back, hoping to express his amusement at the flight crew. He pointed to the identification chip tucked beneath his skin where sternum met collarbone. His meat tag—a backup identifier just in case he was removed from his armor and killed. "See, I'm Dark Ops. And that means there is nothing that the regular Legion does that I can't know, too."

The three crewmen looked from one to another as if playing hot potato over who would answer the man who'd just revealed himself to be a highly skilled Legion-trained operator standing in their midst. The two pilots stuck together, staring at the crew chief expectantly, though they were officers and he an enlisted man.

The crew chief just shrugged. "Hell, don't look at me. Tell 'im."

The movie-star pilot, pearly white smile and thick black hair—the kind you'd expect to see flying space fighter in one of the entertainments—gave Subs a charming, easy grin. "So it's like this. Some leej major comes to the hangar and sees that we're not on the duty roster."

"Off day," chimes in the co-pilot.

"Off day. So anyway, he orders us to fly him and a team of marines out behind the doro lines. Deep."

"How deep?" asked Subs.

The pilot's smile broadened, as though he was particularly proud of the answer he was about to give. "The deepest I've heard. All the way back past the Cuchin Valley."

Subs looked down, processing this information. The Cuchin Valley was *well* beyond the edge of any mission he'd heard of. Even the Dark Ops raids in search of those infernally evasive artillery batteries hadn't gone so deep. Or... so Subs had heard from the sidelines. This SLIC had gone a full thirty kilometers beyond the deepest probe the Republic had managed.

"Was this major leading a Dark Ops operation?" Dark Ops was the only answer that made sense to Subs. Only his brothers in the black armor would be crazy and capable enough to try such a thing.

"No," answered the co-pilot, shaking his head congenially. He was a slight man with a mid-core accent. "The major was regular Legion. Same armor as the rest of the legionnaires. And then... the marines."

Something was up. A single legionnaire and a SLIC full of marines heading out deep behind enemy lines for who knows what. Highly developed warning bells were ringing.

"Did they say what the mission was?" Subs asked, making clear with his tone that he was being very serious.

The three-man flight crew shifted uncomfortably, clearly not liking the direction this once-pleasant conversation was heading.

"No," said the co-pilot.

"Is there anything else you can tell me about them? It was just a single legionnaire major and a squad of marines?"

The pilot with the movie-star smile looked nervously at his co-pilot and gunner for a second. "Yeah. I mean… that's all I saw."

"Me too," confirmed the co-pilot.

The door gunner pressed his lips into a tight smile, his pencil-thin mustache almost disappearing inside his mouth. "No, there was one other guy."

The two pilots looked to their gunner as if this was news to them.

"Yeah," said the gunner, talking to his pilots more than to Subs. "But he wasn't dressed for battle. Just Legion fatigues. No armor… or helmet for that matter. He had a blaster rifle and a ruck, but that was about it." The gunner pointed to the pilots, snapping his fingers as if helping them recall. "He was the reason we touched down again before we went out over the jungle."

"Oh," said the pilot. "Yeah, the major said it was part of his final preparations. I didn't realize he'd brought someone back on board with him."

The gunner nodded.

"You guys are sure of this?" Subs asked. Sweat rolled down his back, adding to the swamp inside his pants.

A trio of nods answered.

"Nether Ops," Subs said, to himself mostly. "I'm guessing your last-minute rider was Nether Ops."

That piece of information didn't seem to sit well with the flight crew. In fact, Subs had probably just rocked their world by confirming that Nether Ops, which at best was a shadowy dirty whisper that reached them as scuttlebutt among pilots, had now been confirmed by someone who would know.

"Is that bad?" the co-pilot asked.

Subs shrugged. "For the legionnaire and the marines, probably."

Subs had never actually worked firsthand with Nether Ops. He knew they existed to serve the House of Reason, designed to be the equal of Dark Ops, only under the heel of the politicians. The contention among those who'd retired before he had his papers in the queue was that the House of Reason got a real hard-on for their own deep cover state agency of killers once General Rex refused some mission they'd wanted executed.

The old man got offed for his trouble. Or disappeared. It depended on whom you talked to.

But it wasn't unheard of for Nether Ops to do joint operations with Dark Ops. And it also wasn't all that uncommon for marines and legionnaires to be under joint-force missions under the command of the Legion Special Operations Command.

Subs considered all this. He was still a part of the inner circle of Dark Ops, but this wasn't his business. He was only on Psydon because his commanders wanted to do him a good turn. He needed to trust that they knew what they were doing, and let it go.

He smiled, feeling his sunglasses slide on his cheeks from the constant humidity and perspiration. "You know what, guys? Forget I said anything."

The pilot with the megawatt smile held up his hands in a defensive manner. "Whoa. Dark Ops, listen: we were all just following—"

The pilot was interrupted by the arrival of a Republic Army maintenance tech and two bots. Subs knew the kid was surly and lazy. He didn't like him.

Unkempt, with a gut and a stained uniform—and not grease stains, more like some kind of powdery confection—the tech paid no mind to the men standing in conversation. The two bots, both a meter tall and on tracks with manipulative claws, stood by as if waiting for orders.

"Well, there it is!" shouted the maintenance tech, kicking one of the bots in its side and causing a hollow-sounding gong. "Hurry up and get going so we can get back into the shade, you dummies."

The bots rolled forward and began to remove the SLIC's fueling covers.

The tech looked at the pilots through one squinting eye, the other shut tight against the sun. "Won't be long. Maybe five minutes. There's a flight lounge out of the sun where you can wait if you want."

He pointed to a shanty-like building with an overhanging roof and three walls that only kept about twenty percent of the interior shaded thanks to the direction of the sun.

"That's fine, thanks," said the co-pilot through gritted teeth.

The tech shrugged and left, apparently counting on his bots to finish the job without his supervision.

It was clear to Subs that the crew was concerned with being in hot water. Which wasn't at all the case. But that didn't mean he couldn't maybe use that fear to get a little more information. He knew he *should* let it go... but it wouldn't rest well with him during the heated nighttime hours while he lay sweating in his hooch.

"So about this insertion," Subs began.

"We're not in trouble, are we, sir?" the pilot asked.

That was rich. Subs was being called "sir," in spite of being an NCO, all because of his Dark Ops mystique. He didn't mind it, though. Didn't correct them either.

"No. You're not in trouble."

"Because again, we were following orders. The major said—"

"Yeah, I get it," Subs said. "What was the major's name?"

"Uh..." the pilot looked up, trying to remember.

"Berlin!" supplied the crew gunner.

"Major Berlin. How many other SLICs went in with you?"

"Just us."

"Just you. When's the exfil?"

"He said to come back to the same spot in forty-eight hours."

Curiouser and curiouser. Out there, way behind the lines... it didn't make sense. That's not how Dark Ops would do it. They wouldn't double back upon finishing an objective and be picked up at the same place they were dropped off. The only time anyone used the same LZ was when the exfil vehicle was waiting for them to do their business right then and there.

Subs sighed.

This needed to be looked into.

"Okay, guys," he said, shaking each man's hand. "You've been a big help. Make the pickup as ordered, but I want you to stop in and ask to see me on the way out. I may need to come along."

He turned to see about finding a Republic Army building with some air conditioning. The comm room was usually cool… when the parts were working.

"Wait!" called one of the pilots. "Who do we ask for?"

Subs turned back, not breaking stride. "Me. I'm the only Dark Ops on this base. They'll know."

09

Wash held his blaster at the low ready as he took a turn leading the column of marines through the thick wild jungles. A howl that sounded every fifteen to twenty minutes and seemed to consist of a guttural roar and warning hiss pierced the air, causing all other animal life teeming within the jungle to hush into sudden silence.

"There it is again." Berlin had been more occupied with the source of that predatory howl than with navigating through the jungle itself, often stumbling and steadying himself against tree trunks to stop and listen for it.

One by one, the animals of the jungle added their voices, until the jungle again was filled with a cacophony of sound.

"Probably a dreex," Wash said, ducking beneath a leafy palm, looking for signs of doros. It wasn't uncommon for the dog-men to lay traps in the jungle, but that was usually closer to the Republic's bases, or the trails favored by the marines and basics. Wash, by contrast, was blazing a trail straight through solid jungle, legionnaire-style.

"How could you possibly know that?" asked Berlin.

"I actually read the flora and fauna manuals." The Legion had provided the electronic booklets to all soldiers, to let them know what was on the planet that could kill them—other than the doros. "Biggest land-based predator on Psydon."

"That's cheerful to hear."

Wash smiled. "Don't worry. Biggest doesn't mean that it's colossal—it's all relative. The doobers back home could eat these like snacks."

"A doober could eat us both in one bite. That doesn't help me, Wash."

"It's probably only a threat if it can corner you without your blaster rifle ready."

Berlin gripped his weapon at the words.

Sergeant Shotton broke through the palm leaves Wash and Berlin had just passed through, catching up. "You talkin' 'bout the dreex?"

"Yup," Wash said.

"Ain't no thing. We ran into one last month. They can't stand up to a single rifle, let alone a patrol-ful. They're drawn by blood—probably our friend Tierney. She's soaked in it."

"Well," said Berlin, "I guess that means we're safe tonight. Might want to have someone guard her, though."

Wash nodded appreciatively at his friend's remark. It wasn't exactly selfless, but he was at least thinking of others. He wondered if Berlin would use this encounter during his political campaign tours. He was poised to tell quite a tale—the battle at the doro outpost where he singlehandedly killed ten doro insurgents... His leading the party through pristine jungle wilderness as a bloodthirsty predator stalked them for kilometers…

Wash chuckled to himself. *Hell, that would get my vote.*

"Who's coming up behind you, Sergeant?" Wash asked, realizing it had been too long since they'd had the chance to speak. They needed to figure out how they were going to get out of the jungle.

"Haulman," answered Shotton.

"I want him on point so we three can have a talk."

Shotton gave a whistle that blended in well enough with the jungle sounds, and soon Haulman was up. "Take point," Shotton said. "We're talking."

"What do we need to talk about?" asked Berlin.

"How we're going to get out of this jungle," said Wash.

Shotton grunted his agreement.

"But you're the major," Wash said to his friend. "You can stay with us and have a chat, or you can keep your ears open for the dreex."

Berlin shrugged and joined Wash and Shotton as they moved back along the column, Shotton giving instructions to each marine they passed on how they could better button up and meet marine standards.

"The way I see it," Shotton said in between soldiers, "we keep moving, staying ahead of any doros, until we get to friendly lines. That's a long hike through this jungle, but I think it's our best move. Maybe as we get closer, we'll be able to reach 'em on comms and find a place for a SLIC to pick us up."

Wash nodded. "Trouble is, unless we find an unmapped clearing on the way, it's all treetops. SLICs won't be able to get down low enough to pick us up."

"I could've told you that," Berlin chimed in. "That's why I picked the clearing we landed in. It's the only place SLICs can touch down beyond Poro-Poro Peak and the valley— and the doros have that valley locked in for artillery fire."

The conversation halted, as did the three men, as they reached the corpsman who was keeping close to Tierney.

"How you doing, Private?" Wash asked.

Tierney managed a plucky smile that did little to hide the obvious pain she was in. "I've been better."

"She'll be okay as long as we don't set a pace much faster than this," Corpsman Hellix supplied.

"We've got lots of time," Berlin said casually. He clapped the former POW on the shoulder. "So take it easy and we'll get you to a field hospital. Soon you'll be back on your feet and into the fight in no time."

Tierney didn't look enthusiastic about that. "Thank you, Major."

"Don't mention it."

"There was something I wanted to speak with you about."

Berlin removed his helmet and flashed the smile that would win him a seat in the House of Reason someday. "By all means. What is it?"

"Were you all... looking for us?"

Berlin looked sheepishly from Shotton to Wash. Both men only shrugged.

"Well..." Berlin said, "not exactly. But once we found you, there was no way we were going to leave you. Sorry about... about the others."

Tierney nodded. "You were coming for the artillery?"

Shotton raised an eyebrow.

"I really can't say..." began Berlin.

"I really can't believe I'm about to say this," Tierney said, looking at the jungle floor as she spoke. "But I feel I owe it to the Republic and to the ones who—well, so they didn't have to die for nothing." The woman sucked in a deep breath, as though she were about to take a jump off the high dive and was afraid of heights. "Okay, here goes. The artillery is close. Real close. It was right down that road leading out of the camp... maybe ten kilometers."

"That kind of information would have been useful *earlier*, soldier," scolded Shotton.

"I know that, sir. I... I just have been using this time to build up my courage. I don't want to go back." Tears welled in her eyes. "But we have to, don't we?"

Wash wasn't so sure. If they were all in the vicinity, they could still return to a firebase and call in the location. If the bombs came quick enough, surely the Legion would get 'em.

He was surprised when Berlin gave his opinion. "Absolutely. Take us there."

* * *

"They would transfer us here for interrogations and then back to camp," Tierney said to Wash and Berlin as they looked at the distant platforms through their macros. "Usually they don't move, but when they do—they make a lot of noise."

The doros' mobile artillery platforms weren't just hidden by the jungle—they *were* the jungle. The front of the platforms contained something like a beveled plow blade that scooped up the jungle—trees and all—and carried it over the top of the platform, its big guns retracting when something too big got in its way. It was like the artillery platforms were burrowing beneath the surface of the jungle, and as it moved, what it had dug up was planted back behind it. The platforms were slow and noisy—they could be heard from three kilometers out—but they moved through the jungle without a chance of being spotted from watching ships orbiting above.

"That's an engineering marvel," said Berlin. "I would never have guessed the doros were capable."

"I don't think they are," said Wash, no less impressed by what he saw.

Sergeant Shotton dropped his head behind a toadstool-infested log. "Whether they are or aren't, we didn't pack near enough explosives to stop even one of those things. So if taking them out is still our primary objective... I'm telling you our little recon team can't get it done."

"I thought you said your team was capable of operating as sappers," said a crestfallen Berlin.

Shotton stared blankly at the major, but his tone bore no insubordination, just an NCO telling it like it is and letting the chips fall where they may. "Yeah. For stationary pieces or the kinds of guns towed by trucks. Not for something like this."

"Okay, so what do we do?" asked Berlin. "We can't just do nothing."

"No, we can't," Wash agreed. "Our priority now has to be getting the location of these guns to Legion command."

"That means marching back to base," said Shotton. "Guns might've disappeared by then. Not that they look like fast movers."

"I agree," said Wash, taking Berlin's wrist to bring up his hard-mounted display map. "Figure a two-day march back to our firebase."

"At least. Remember, we're bringing along wounded."

Tierney shut her eyes and looked down.

"I think she'll hold up fine," Wash said. "Two days' march to get to a place where we can pass the info along."

"Or we can wait two days for the SLIC to come back where I told them to," Berlin suggested.

Wash ignored his friend's comment. "But if we move to Poro-Poro, we should be able to do an all-hail comm relay and get heard from somewhere by someone."

"What's an all-hail?" asked Berlin.

It was something that Berlin should absolutely have known. It was covered in his Legion training. Covered again during patrol protocols upon arrival on Psydon. In fact, it was common knowledge for anyone holding the rank of private and above. The only ones on Psydon who didn't know were probably the points.

"It's our best chance of getting out of here and getting these guns wrecked," Wash said.

Shotton nodded once. "Yeah... unless we stumble on some kind of secret Dark Ops base, that's our best option."

"Dark Ops would probably kill us before we could get too close."

Berlin drummed his fingers on a mushroom.

"Careful," warned Wash. "That's poisonous."

Quickly removing his hand, Berlin said, "Okay, but why don't we simply wait at the landing zone for a couple days?"

Sergeant Shotton showed remarkable cool in giving Berlin an answer. He had to know by now that he was dealing with an appointed officer who knew next to nothing, but Berlin *had* fought earlier. And clearly that meant something.

"We have to assume, sir, that the dog-men are already out looking for us over there." Shotton inclined his head to Wash. "Is Poro-Poro high enough for something like that?"

Wash tapped his finger on the display. "It only shows a rise in elevation. The southeast slope is about forty clicks from us. But seeing as how this map was probably made from a satellite flyover with the usual jungle obfuscation, we aren't really going to know until we get there."

"Obfuscation?" asked Shotton.

"It means obscure or unclear," said Berlin.

Shotton shook his head. "Glad they had time for vocabulary lessons at the Academy."

Wash and Berlin smiled as the artillery platforms continued their slow, rumbling progress through the jungle.

"That's a long march just to be disappointed," Tierney said.

"Especially with the jungles and doros," said another voice.

Wash turned to see that Parker, the sniper, had sidled into their midst. He stared at them with his pale eyes and said, "Looks like a foot patrol is headed up in our direction. So we either need to prepare to put them down, or we need to disappear before they get here."

Shotton looked to the officers.

Wash nodded. "We've got what we can from this place. Let's move out."

10

Wash and the marines had traveled twenty kilometers before Corpsman Hellix told them they had to stop. Tierney could go no farther. Not without taking a long break.

Denturo was nearby when the word came in. "That's just great. We save her life and she repays us by getting everyone killed. I say leave her."

"We're not leaving her," Wash said, looking up to the darkening jungle canopy. Night was coming soon, and with the number of depressions, logs, and massive tree trunks around them, it was as good a place as any to rest. "Sergeant Shotton, let's find some high ground and wait the night out."

"Yes, sir." Shotton began stirring his marines up like a kid kicking over an anthill.

"Thank you, sir," whispered Corpsman Hellix before leaving to return to his patient.

Wash nodded. He wanted to sit down—he felt the day's fatigue all the way down to his bones—but he couldn't. Not until the marines, the enlisted men, were off their feet first.

He looked over to Berlin, who had practically collapsed on a bed of moss at the base of a vine-entangled tree.

One of the artillery guns boomed in the distance.

The doros were firing with the fall of night.

As tough as things might be for Wash and the recon marines after a day of fighting, marching, constantly watching for doro traps, and contending with the jungle, things were even harder for the frontline legionnaires and marines right now, as heavy metal rained down on them from the night. They would be ducking in rifle pits and foxholes waiting for the barrage to end, knowing that the moment it did they'd probably be swarmed by waves of yipping doros emerging from the jungle to give them hell all night long. Fighting hard to get into the pits and make it up close and personal with knives and gnashing teeth. The doros were willing to spend lives in bulk to get close enough to stick a knife in a legionnaire.

It had been that way for months. When the Republic began showing in force to deal with the Psydon rebellion, things had started off well. Spaceports were taken on day one. Major cities fell as the Legion battled its way across the planet. But then the doros fell back into the jungle, and there, amid the creepy-crawlies, they were able to do a number on the Legion with a combination of hit-and-fade guerrilla warfare and those ever-hidden field guns.

Legion recon had been looking as deep into the jungle as they dared—some never returning. And here Wash, an appointed officer, the last person the Legion would want in this situation... he knew where the guns were located.

He only needed to make sure they got back to tell someone about it.

"Lieutenant Washam?"

Wash looked up, hoping that his name hadn't been called more than once while he was lost in his thoughts.

"Yes, Private Haulman?"

"Sarge has us set up with shifts covered. Says you and the major should try and sleep through the night if you can. We've got this, sir."

Wash smiled. "Thanks. But I'll at least take last watch. Send someone to wake me up."

"Yes, sir." Haulman disappeared into the jungle, but not before adding, "Watch out for those big cats, sir."

His feet heavy, Wash walked over to where Berlin was lying at the base of the tree. The major looked as though he was already asleep. Not wanting to wake his friend, Wash settled down quietly.

It felt good to be sitting. His back and feet rewarded him by hurting slightly less than they had a moment before.

He thought he would fall right asleep, but he found himself wondering just what it was that had had him so amped up to go out and experience war firsthand that he'd left his post.

Fortune and glory.

Heartbreakers and life-takers.

That was supposed to be the life of a legionnaire. Was missing that opportunity what had made Wash do it? And would it really have been so bad to have never fired a shot in anger?

He imagined most of the other appointed officers would've been fine never coming up against the doros.

But not him.

He was a real leej.

Wash looked over at Berlin. His friend was pretty damn close to the same, in his mind. He'd killed doros, acted bravely in combat. They were the two best points in the Legion. For whatever that was worth.

Wash was thankful for his friend. More than that, he was proud of him. Because even though Berlin wasn't worthy of being an officer of the Legion, not by any stretch, he'd done better than any of his appointed colleagues—any civilian—could ever have hoped to in the situation. And the Legion was lucky to have him. Berlin could have stayed home. Rich and living easy. But he signed up. Came here. He was a good man.

Sleep was still a ways off, but close enough to whisper to Wash about the coming of dreams. His thoughts shifted as they so often do in those moments before slumber.

He thought of his family back on Spilursa.

Mom and Dad.

He hadn't thought much about them since he'd joined the Legion. He hadn't written home while undertaking Legion training. He didn't long for a home-cooked meal; his mother never cooked anyway. That's what servants were for. And real servants, not bots. Anyone could invest in a bot, but employing real, organic beings to do your bidding... that was wealth. That was status. And Wash's family had it in spades.

Wash didn't know why his family was now in his thoughts. He wondered obliquely what they might say about the events that had occurred this day. Not that he needed their approval, or had any illusions about receiving it. They'd made their thoughts about him joining the Legion quite clear on the day that he and Berlin were told that they were House of Reason Delegate Roman Horkoshino's selections.

Mr. and Mrs. Washam were more than unhappy at their only son going down such a *vulgar* path. It was all fine and well for the Berlins to send their eldest off to war—that family had always been something less stately than the Washams, in Wash's parents' minds. The Berlins were actually richer, by far, but theirs was a newer wealth—one that could only be traced back a mere handful of generations. Wash's family had landed on Spilursa centuries before, during the Great Migration. They'd built a fortune from the ground up. A fortune that had withstood the test of time. Starting out with noble occupations and cultivating the natural resources of their planet so it could develop to its rightful spot as one of the shining jewels of the galactic core.

Good, honest money.

Not like those Berlins, who had more money than they could possibly need, money that was obtained in the lowest of ways. Everyone knew a galactic-wide shipping company was only a couple of steps above outright piracy.

Wash found it all funny. He and Berlin. Their parents. Everyone was a case study in opposites. Wash wanted the Legion's glory. Berlin wanted the House of Reason's power. Wash's parents wanted political power for their son. Berlin's wanted their son to give back to a Republic—and a Legion—that had been so good to them.

"If you want a career in politics," Wash's father had lectured him when word of his appointment came out, "then you need to follow in your older brother's footsteps. Find a nice neighborhood on the cusp of a major housing boom. One of the hip districts that used to keep the lower types sheltered. The sort of locale that's attractive to all the young people who want to play at being urbane and sophisticated."

Wash smiled at the memory of his starched father using words like "hip."

Wash hadn't told his parents—or anyone, other than Berlin—that he'd applied to be an appointed officer. They didn't learn the news until after he was chosen. And even then, Wash's father assumed it was all merely an angle for him to move up politically. A foolish angle.

"Make yourself a community activist," Wash's father had said. "Get a name for yourself. Live in the biggest house on the block. It'll still be affordable when you move in, and you'll be doing just fine when you sell it later and move to the capital after the district elects you for local office. It's that simple. Just repeat until you climb each rung. Make the right friends, say the right things, and then you get a shot at the House of Reason. That's the respectable way to go about this. Not running off to join the damn Legion like some kind of testosterone-fueled trigger monkey."

Wash's mother was no less disapproving, but for different reasons. "I don't care if the House places you in protected roles. The Legion is always fighting. Always getting shot at. I don't want to see my little boy blown to pieces."

Wash smiled at this too. The risk of being blown to pieces while fighting with those testosterone-fueled trigger monkeys was the only reason Wash had taken the opportunity. It was the only thing that could have moved him to absorb the scandal of walking out on his family and joining the Legion Academy.

Because the Legion was different. The army, and to a lesser extent the marines—the navy especially—had all had appointed officers for some time. And those were viewed as respectable paths to power. They were part of an established gentry. But the Legion... that was an unruly and completely different animal. If anything resembling a well-groomed officer class was to come from the Legion, it would be viewed as a shock by many in the core.

"Hey, Berlin," Wash said in a whisper, venturing to see whether his friend was sleeping lightly enough to wake up.

Wash felt like talking.

He wanted to know how Berlin felt *his* parents would handle what had happened today. The Berlins had been thrilled when their son was accepted as an appointed Legion officer. Though Berlin's father didn't serve—not beyond lending several of his ships to the Legion for combat refitting during the end of the Savage Wars—the rest of the family, from grandfather to several great-grandfathers, had all served. Some even as legionnaires.

"Yeah, Wash?"

"What do you think your parents would say about today?"

Berlin didn't stir, he just spoke. "Wash... they'd be so proud."

Wash smiled.

"How 'bout yours?" Berlin asked, his voice distant, as though he wasn't quite awake. But he was doing his best.

"They'd never forgive me."

Berlin laughed. "That's probably true."

Wash waited a long moment before asking his friend, "Do you think... Do you think your parents would be proud of me too?"

Berlin's only answer was a light snore.

Wash realized that he was growing melancholy, which led to thoughts of loss and death. He'd seen no shortage of that today. And what about him? Would he soon face the unimaginable... the hereafter? What could be worse than if there simply was no more life?

You can die out here, Wash. Easily.

And...

Do everything as though your life depends on it.

Wash didn't want to die. And yet... he was out here to kill. To make sure that life stopped living.

But those were just doros. And if they didn't want it, they shouldn't have started it. Wash was only killing those who wanted to kill him first.

His eyelids tugged at him, and he felt the heavy promise of the rapture of sleep. It was probably a good idea to doze off. He didn't want to spend the next several hours in a steamy distant jungle lying wide awake and thinking about his own inevitable death.

He hoped it would be quick. His death. That it would just... happen before he had a chance to know it was about to occur. Because that was the worst part. Knowing it was coming.

Probably why we all try to drive the thought far from our minds, Wash.

Truth be told, it was a big part of why he'd signed up for the opportunity to serve the Legion. It was why he'd gone through the grueling trials of Legion training instead of taking a pass.

He would die someday, and some complex and quiet part of him wanted to live so seriously and so dangerously that when that day came, he would feel like he had cheated death long enough. Like his dying was part of the bargain. Like it was only fair to the rest of the galaxy that a man who had lived so hard and so fast should finally catch up to the rest of the lost souls.

That fight today... It was exactly what Wash wanted to do for the rest of his life. It was what he hoped he would die doing. He hoped he would die fighting.

He hoped he would die a legionnaire.

* * *

Wash woke up to the sound of the sniper hissing his name. "Lieutenant Washam."

Though Wash's eyes opened, they still felt thick with sleep. His tongue didn't feel fully functional. He didn't trust himself to modulate the volume of his own voice. He reached into his nostril, pinched his fingers around some nose hairs, and yanked them out violently for the sudden waking jolt it brought about. "Time for my watch?" he asked.

"No," the marine answered urgently. "Dobies."

11

Wash jumped to his feet, rifle in hand, ready at that moment to engage in a firefight.

But the sniper waved him down. "They're not in the camp. But not far enough away, either. Saw 'em close enough that I know they're tracking."

Of course they aren't in the camp. You would have heard the blaster fire if it were otherwise, knucklehead, Wash yelled at himself.

"Okay," he said in a whisper, giving a slow, deliberate nod to let the sniper know that he understood the situation.

"Sarge is asking me to go through and get you up first, then the others. He wants to see you." In the sparse moonlight penetrating the jungle canopy, the sniper's face was painted a ghostly blue, and his eyes looked like they had no color.

"I'll wake up the major," Wash said. "You go on ahead. Thanks, Marine."

"Yes, sir."

Wash gently pushed on his friend's shoulder. "Berlin," he whispered urgently. "Buddy, wake up."

Berlin stirred, then faced Wash, blinking in the darkness. "It's not morning."

"I know. A scout spotted the doros and they might be on our trail. We need to get up and be ready for whatever comes next."

The seriousness of this statement prompted Berlin to rise up, but the sleep wasn't fully gone, and he did so clumsily, making quite a racket.

"Shhh!" Wash put a finger to his lips. "Wake up all the way, then let's go. We need to talk with Sergeant Shotton."

Berlin let out a yawn and stretched his arms as though he'd just woken up from his plush point bed in his special Legion quarters. His rank got him perks a first lieutenant didn't see. "I was dreaming about my parents. Funny."

"I know. That's because we were talking about them right before we went to sleep."

"We did?" said Berlin. "Huh. They'd be proud of us, Wash."

"I know."

The two points moved past bleary-eyed marines. It was evident that the sniper's rousting had come much too quickly for all their tastes. Tierney, still accompanied by Corpsman Hellix, looked as though she'd need an injection of narco stims to ever get up again.

They found Shotton quietly directing Denturo and a few other marines on where to set up. The men hastily and dutifully moved off to their positions as Wash and Berlin arrived.

"Is it still too early to say good morning?" Wash asked the sergeant. He'd barely been asleep for an hour before Parker roused him. Dawn was still a long ways off.

"Don't know about the protocols in all that, but so far, things ain't lookin' very good."

"What's the situation?"

"Parker says a team of about eight dog-men are about a kilometer back that way." Shotton hitched his thumb to point in the direction from which they'd marched. "Doros had their noses to the ground, so it's a good bet they're tracking us."

"Only eight?" Berlin said, sounding optimistic. "We can handle that many."

"We can *handle* a good deal more than eight," the sergeant replied. "My concern is whether there aren't more of 'em out there than what Parker saw."

"Either way," Wash said, wanting to cut to the chase—there was no telling how much time they had before the doros arrived—"I take it we're making a stand here?"

Shotton nodded. "This is as good a spot as any if it comes down to it. Better than most, actually. We can execute an effective ambush on anyone who follows us into this little defilade. How's that for fancy words, Academy?"

Wash smiled. "Nicely done."

"But what if there are more than eight?" Berlin asked. "Can we hold back a division, if that's what the doros throw at us?"

The thought was ridiculous. Of course they couldn't. But perhaps Wash's friend was thinking of a platoon rather than a division. That would still be tough, but not nearly so impossible.

Rather than correct Berlin, Wash said, "If it comes down to fighting, we'll know how many dog-men there are before too long. Let's hope this is only a small scouting party and that the main force—if there is one—is still a good deal behind."

"So that's the plan in action," Shotton said, crossing his arms. "Unless either of you have a better one in mind."

Wash rubbed his chin. "I don't see an alternative strategy to the one you've laid out, Sergeant. Where would the major and I be of the most use?"

"I got my marines arranged in a little V-shaped flytrap. If the dog-men keep coming from the direction Parker saw them last, they'll walk right into it. But if they decide to go around the long way... bad news. I want you set up to watch our flanks and rear."

"We can do that!" Berlin said eagerly. "And if we get the chance, we'll open up on the doros as soon as we set eyes on them."

Wash held out a staying hand. That was a perfect way to ruin an ambush. "*Only* if they approach from the direction we're assigned to cover, Major. If they move into the ambush zone, it's critical that we wait for the marines to take the shot."

"Yeah. Of course," the major agreed. Only Berlin would be so affable in being corrected by a junior rank. And Wash loved him all the more for it.

"All right," Shotton growled, showing a certain relief in his eyes that the two appointed officers knew enough not to spoil the ambush. "Now it could be that they don't actually have our scent. We've all got the funk of these mushrooms on us, and though the doros got better noses than us, they ain't that much better. If that's the case, I'd rather we sit tight and let them walk on by. If we can keep them guessing about where we actually are... that's better'n dropping a few."

Wash hitched his rifle over his shoulder. "Agreed. If we can keep our whereabouts hidden, let's do it. Berlin and I will go set up. KTF, Sergeant."

Shotton winked. "Ambush. That's the idea."

* * *

It was Denturo who first opened fire, though he hardly had a choice in the matter. The dog-men had moved quietly into the kill zone, but not in a single file. Instead, they had fanned out, walking abreast of each other, sweeping through the jungle like an advancing line of infantry.

There didn't appear to be more than a dozen of them once they drew close enough to be viewed through the single optic starlight scopes the marines—and thanks to a friendly borrow, Wash—had attached to their helmets. Berlin, of course, had even better night vision in his Legion bucket. But without anyone to speak to over the L-comm, he was unable to communicate in the tense silence beyond elbowing Wash, pointing out new targets for him to spot.

It was hard for Wash to keep his eyes on his own sector when the offending doro—the one that forced Denturo to fire—crept toward the ambush line. The dog-man moved so close to the big marine, lying flat on the jungle floor, buried beneath a layer of dried leaves and rainforest moss, that if Denturo hadn't fired, the doro would have stepped right on him.

Blaster fire erupted, lighting up the night and flashing in technicolor relief against the exotic plants of Psydon. Small creatures scurried into the underbrush as blaster bolts slammed into the doro trackers, catching them in a deadly field of converging fire.

The dog-men weren't even afforded the chance to shoulder their blaster rifles, let alone return fire.

"Cease fire!" shouted Sergeant Shotton.

The call was picked up and repeated by marines in the ambush zone. The last blaster shot echoed its wayward report, sounding like a last bit of applause that had gone on just a little too long and was now awkward.

"I said cease fire, dammit!" Shotton yelled.

The jungle seemed to hiss as smoke rose up from the torn and charred bodies of the destroyed trackers. Tree bark and leaves smoldered as the heat from the blaster bolts slowly extinguished.

Everyone lay still for several moments. Listening. Straining their ears for some indicator of what to do next. Trying to determine whether more doros lay ahead, or if perhaps some dog-men had managed to avoid the ambush and were now scampering away in the jungle to acquire help.

But nothing moved. Nothing made a sound. Not even a groaning or whining among the dog-men who had been so thoroughly and ruthlessly cut down in the ambush. They were all stone dead.

Still the marines waited, listening in the predawn darkness.

Wash looked over at his friend. The two legionnaires had done their duty. They had refrained from firing and had protected the marines from any flanking maneuvers. Wash was proud of the self-control Berlin had shown. It probably wasn't easy for him to just sit there, knowing he had the opportunity to rack up a still-higher kill count. Because the bigger he could make his legend on Psydon, the more likely he was to actually pull off his little trick of forcing his way into the House of Reason before the gatekeepers told him it was his time.

After several minutes of silence, Sergeant Shotton crept over to Berlin and Wash. "I think we've got the jungle to ourselves again," he said, looking around as if to confirm the statement. "I sent Parker and Haulman out just to make sure. But if they come back and tell us that no one is around, I think we need to get moving."

Wash agreed with this. Whether they'd encountered a probing scouting party attached to a larger force, or whether that small band was all the dog-men had for them in this section of the jungle... that wasn't something they could know. Not until it was too late, anyhow. Staying around would do them no good.

"I'm with you, Sergeant. I don't think anyone is going to get much more rest after this—"

"Speak for yourself," interrupted Berlin.

Wash ignored his friend's comment. "And all these dead doros are only going to attract more attention, either from their dog-men friends or from those dreex that have been stalking us. We should get a move on."

"Yep," said Shotton, gently patting his knees as he stood up from crouching. "I can't do this crap forever. Fightin' is a young man's game."

Shotton stretched out his back. He suddenly looked ancient to Wash.

Hoping to encourage the sergeant, Wash said, "We made it halfway to the peak before we stopped. Let's see if we can get the other half done before sunup."

12

Republic Army Firebase Hitchcock
Middle-of-Nowhere, Psydon

Subs was cooking in his portable, supposedly climate-controlled hooch. The air conditioning was broken, and all he could do was sit and sweat. Back in the day, he'd have seen this heat as an opportunity to abuse himself—to see how well his body could handle wind sprints and endless burpees as the temperature rose. But now...

He slapped his belly. Yeah, it was a belly, but there was a layer of rock-hard muscle below the surface. He'd be all right. He just had to tell the little bird that sat on his shoulder telling him to eat that extra slice of bread or drink that beer where it could stuff its feathers.

He wanted to find out more about this Major Berlin. Ideally he'd get the scoop from his friends on Psydon, see if any of them had heard of the guy. But unlike virtually every moment of Subs's life since he'd joined the Legion, in this moment there was no fellow leej to be found, and his long-range comms weren't working. As a last resort, he'd tried to pull up his local copy of the Legion database on his datapad, to at least pull up the major's basic details. But he couldn't even do that, because his access code was out of date—and he couldn't get the new code without speaking to another leej, none of whom were at hand.

Subs became overwhelmed by a sudden urge to stand, if not work out. He tossed his datapad aside and lunged out of his chair, his hot skin sticking to the leather-like material. He held sweaty arms out at his sides as if taking an air bath. All he was wearing was a pair of skimpy, black satin shorts affectionately called "silk diapers" by the legionnaires who wore them. And now the basics called them that, too, thanks to their exposure to Subs. Some had even ordered pairs of their own.

It wasn't always a pretty sight around Firebase Hitchcock.

But in the Psydon evening's oppressive humidity, Subs wished he weren't wearing even the scant silk diapers. If it weren't for his hooch's location on the base's main thoroughfare and the number of female officers who walked by his very see-through windows—these were unsealed and rolled down, since the climate controls didn't work— the Dark Ops legionnaire would likely be strutting about with nothing but his complexion and his little leej to keep him company.

Not that the female officers would necessarily mind. He'd seen a few of them taking a lingering look at him even as he was dressed now. But the last thing he needed was to get in the doghouse during the final months of his tour because the wrong officer saw the wrong side of him. So Subs walked around in his silk diapers, strutting like a supermodel—even if his gut *was* a little too round. At least he still had his biceps. It would take a lot of carbs to cover up those rocks.

He decided to put a call into the base's comm center. He'd made friends with the army comm tech who seemed to be always on shift.

"Hey, Alistair, you working tonight?"

It wasn't the most professional way to communicate, but in a place like Hitchcock... things got a little lax.

"Oh, hey, Dark Ops!" came the reply. "Yeah, I'm here. Because... *I'm always here.*"

Subs smiled. The sarcasm felt good, like an old friend. Alistair was about the only person who didn't tremble in awe at the sight of the mighty Dark Ops warrior on base. He regularly gave Subs a hard time, treated him with disrespect, made him feel like an idiot whenever he could... it was a lot like being with other legionnaires.

"You sound surprised to be on duty. Right now. At this exact time," Subs said. "In the Legion, we check the duty rosters so that when our shift starts, we're actually ready for them."

"You're hilarious. Really. Hey, when you get a chance to talk to all those legionnaires who kicked you out of their club and made you hang out with basics, will you ask them"—here, Alistair began to shout into the comm—"*what's the point of having duty rosters is if you're the only comm tech on the whole stinking base!*"

Subs laughed.

"Let's see," Alistair continued, "what day is it? Tuesday! Double shift! But that's okay because on Wednesday and

Thursday, there are more double shifts, which will set me up for the double shift on Friday. Then, on the weekend, a double shift!"

"Sounds like you're afraid of a little hard work."

"Oh, no. That's not it. I just don't know how to properly express my awe and appreciation over officers with such an amazing penchant for administrative genius."

"Oh yeah," said Subs, playing along. "I forgot that the Republic has had points in the army for years."

"They're the best. Bet you can't wait for them to show up in Dark Ops."

"Nah. They won't show up there. Too easy to get dusted while assaulting a house."

Now it was Alistair's turn to laugh. "The frightening thing is, you're probably serious."

Subs was.

"So what can I do for you, brother?" Alistair asked.

"My long-range comms aren't working. I've been waiting for them to come online for hours to reach a buddy serving at Legion Camp Roode. I was wondering if—"

"Wonder no further," interrupted Alistair. "It's not an issue with you, but with the base. Long-range comms are down, no matter how many happy thoughts I throw to the relay room. You'll have to wait for Specialist Bucholz to get back from patrol."

Subs walked around the room. He could actually feel the warm air passing between his toes. "Yeah. Speaking of which, I kind of expected them to be back by now."

Alistair's voice went small. "Oh. You didn't hear?"

"Hear what?"

"They're dead, dude."

"What?"

A burst of laughter erupted from the comm. "Oh, Dark Ops! You were so earnest. I'm wiping away tears. You must really love all the little basics running around under your wings."

Subs frowned. "You're a jackass, Alistair."

"I won't let on about how much you really care."

"So they're all right?"

"Yeah. They're fine. I talked to 'em on the short-range not long before you called. Should be here in under an hour. Just lots to do today."

Subs ran his hands through his hair, pushing off sweat until his hands came away dripping as though he'd just stepped from the shower. "Well, I guess you'd better let me go. I've got a lot of waiting and doing nothing planned for tonight."

"Roger that, Dark Ops. Me? I'm hoping that *this* double shift is the one that makes the army really proud of me."

There was a time, when he was fresh out of the Legion Academy, that Subs wouldn't have been caught dead joking around with a basic. The Legion was its own breed, the heartbreakers and life-takers, and everyone else wasn't worth your time. But as the years passed, Subs came to realize that, regardless of which military branch they served, people were either cool or they sucked. No amount of Legion training could make a legionnaire who sucked fun to hang around with, even if he could KTF with the best of them. And the basics at Firebase Hitchcock... they were all pretty cool. Truth be told, Subs felt more of a kinship with guys like Alistair than he did with Legion command.

But what Subs had failed to tell his comm tech friend was the real reason he needed long-range comms: to ask his buddy for the Legion access code so he could look into this Major Berlin the SLIC pilots told him about. The Legion net had changed passkeys, and Subs was probably the only legionnaire with sufficient clearance who hadn't been given a heads-up. His name had been dropped from the update list when he'd gotten hurt, and it had never been added back on. Which wouldn't be so bad if he could just ask a leej buddy. But when he was out in the kingdom of the basics... that kind of oversight stung a little bit. Like he was forgotten. Like what Alistair had teased him about held more truth than was intended.

Subs looked over to his bed, which was made with drill instructor precision. It always had been, but it was easier to keep it that way now, given there was never a need to get beneath the covers—not in the Psydon heat. At the foot of his bed, in his trunk, was his legionnaire armor. He hadn't worn it since first arriving at camp. He felt like a fish out of water among the basics as it was, and insisting on keeping in his uniform when he couldn't even leave the wire wouldn't win him any favors. It seemed like a prime way to get off on the wrong foot and make running down the clock on retirement more miserable than it needed to be.

Sure, the cooling system would be nice. But a little suffering along with others did wonders for harmony.

"I wonder if..." Subs said to himself.

He opened the trunk and retrieved his bucket. It was the built-in L-comm he was after.

Republic techs were always trying to expand the range of the proprietary communications network. Budget requests predicted that someday in the not-too-distant future, a leej's bucket would be able to communicate with every other legionnaire on the planet so long as he had the right L-comm frequency. Not to mention constant contact with their supporting battleship overhead. The L-comm would be immune to jamming altogether. Someday.

It would be a welcome addition.

But for now, the best the L-comm could do was supply an ultra-secure private comm connection with any other L-comm device in range. That was better than what Subs had now over the base's short-range comms, but still not enough for him to reach his buddy at Camp Roode.

But maybe...

He put his bucket on over his head, keenly aware of how ridiculous he must look: a half-naked man wearing only a silk diaper and a legionnaire's helmet. Like some high-end advertisement for an overpriced cologne.

Subs spoke into the L-comm. "This is DO-13. Anyone have a copy?"

A hum, then a voice from somewhere on the other side. "I hear you. Challenge key?"

Subs recited the key—more of a pass phrase, really. "Six rendered truces wattle shellacked ruby nine."

The doros couldn't passably pronounce these phrases, no matter how much they wanted to. They'd proven surprisingly effective in keeping security tight over comms when needed.

"That was last week's challenge."

Subs shook his head. "Yeah, well, that's kind of the reason why I'm reaching out, Leej. I'm stuck in one of the regular army's corners of Psydon, and I've got no long-range comms to reach someone in Legion command who can help me."

"Listen, buddy," said the legionnaire voice at the other end. Subs could hear SLIC engines in the background. This legionnaire was probably either flying in, or more likely, coming out of a fight. "I'm not gonna broadcast the leej access code, even if it's over L-comm."

"No, hey," said Subs, eager to clarify what he wanted. "That's not what I'm after."

"What was your identifier again?" asked the legionnaire.

"DO-13-RD."

"Dark Ops, huh?" Subs detected a mix of respect and suspicion in the legionnaire's voice.

"Yeah. How about you, what's your identifier? Who'm I talking to?"

"LS-517-VC."

Usually when legionnaires exchanged identifiers, their helmets, or just the general knowledge of the operation, allowed them to just give their specification—such as LS for Legion Soldier, or DO for Dark Ops—and their number. Legion command rightly presumed that you'd know which company you were serving with. But when talking on a wide battlefield such as Psydon, it was necessary to add the last two letters. There were scores of LS-517s on Psydon, but only one was in VC.

"Victory Company!" said Subs. "I've done some ops with you guys. Years ago. Still know how to KTF over there?"

"Hell yeah. Still the best in the One Thirty-First."

Subs chuckled. "So, like I was saying, I don't need any special access codes. I don't need any classified information. In fact, just talking to another leej has me feeling pretty good right now."

"So what's up then, DO?"

"I need a little bit of... scuttlebutt. Need to know if you've heard anything about a name. It's like I said, I'm out here on my own with the army."

"What's the name?"

"A Major Berlin," answered Subs. "You or any of your buddies know him?"

There was a certain disdainful strain of incredulity in the legionnaire's voice. "Know him? Thankfully, no. But I've heard of him. Guy's one of those new appointed officers. Freshly sent by the House of Reason."

"A point?"

"Yeah. But don't let *them* hear you call 'em that. Otherwise you're working like a bot to clean latrines."

"All right," said Subs, not really sure what else to say, though he did enjoy talking. "I guess that's all I had. You boys keep your chins tucked and gives those doros hell."

"Roger that, DO. KTF."

"KTF."

Subs removed his helmet and stared at it, the visor lifelessly returning his gaze. "A point."

Well... that was that. He wasn't going to get mixed up in that political wormhole. If the SLIC pilots actually did come back the next morning, maybe he'd see about getting them to fly him to Camp Roode for a visit. It's not like anyone would notice he was gone.

The legionnaire bucket continued to stare up at Subs. He was going to miss being in the Legion. He had a wife to go home to, a pair of sons who had mostly grown up without him. A job waiting for him on Teema with his father-in-law. But somehow, deep down in the darkest reaches of his being, where the truth is always shining, he knew that none of it could ever be as fulfilling as the Legion. And that thought brought up emotions he didn't know how to deal with.

He placed his bucket on top of his footlocker. The air in his room suddenly felt too thick and oppressive to endure any longer. There was no breeze coming from the windows. A sheen of sweat covered his body. He stretched and reached his fingers to the top of his hooch, where the air felt even more stifling.

He needed to step outside. Not that it would be any cooler. But... maybe. He'd taken his pills to protect against Psydon's bloodsuckers, so he might as well try.

Flinging open the hooch's door, he emerged into the night. The only real light came from low-energy illum-poles stationed sporadically along the main thoroughfare. Not enough to light up the whole way—just enough so that you'd pass from dim light and back into shadow as you walked.

But maybe the dim light made it better. Because you could still see the brilliant canopy of stars overhead. That was the one thing Subs loved about being deployed: he was usually somewhere away from the light of a planet's cityscape. Dark Ops did its work on the worlds where things still got really and truly dark. Where you could look up and see that great glittering galaxy with your fellow leejes and point the stars out one by one.

What about that fight on Linton?

Remember the time on Rrrddat?

Subs knew he would miss the Legion. But maybe… maybe he could convince his wife and sons to move away from the promised job in the city. Maybe they could find a plot of land somewhere in the country. Or in the wilderness.

And then he could stand out in the dark under all those stars with the fledgling men he'd missed so much time with and say, "Did I ever tell you about the time I was there?"

And maybe in those nights his boys would grow to comprehend all the turmoil in the galaxy that had kept their father away. And they'd all appreciate just being home. Together.

13

It was a relief to Subs when the patrolling soldiers began filing back into Firebase Hitchcock.

He roused himself from a heat-induced torpor and hefted himself out of his synthetic leather chair—his skin peeling away from it like the film protecting a new data-pad. The first few soldiers in the platoon trudged by the hooch, not bothering to look anywhere but down.

They were bushed.

Subs went back out into the night air, oblivious to the cloud of pestering insects that hung thick overhead.

"Lookin' good, Subs," said a soldier shuffling by, a cigarette hanging loosely from his mouth.

Subs looked down, remembering only then that he wore nothing but his silk diaper and a pair of running shoes. Oh well. Nothing to do now but ride it out. "Yeah, well, I knew you basics had a long march today, so I wanted you to have something good to see once you got back to Hitch."

Those nearest him laughed as the platoon continued marching by. Their uniforms were soaked in sweat and stained from their time out in the bush. They trudged onward, no doubt wondering whether the showers were working, or if anyone had stuck around to keep the chow warm... but most of all hoping no one would stand in their way from racking up and going lights out.

Subs looked over the lines like a vulpine she-bear watching her cubs. He eyed every passing soldier, looking for signs of injury. He craned his neck for the med bot pulling a stretcher with wounded. Or worse... body bags. But all looked well.

The platoon's captain, Robert Garcia, approached Subs, walking tall among his men. For a basic, the captain was all right. Serious about his job, cared about his soldiers. But he was also military, and might not be thrilled at the example Subs was setting in his state of near-undress.

Subs met Captain Garcia's eyes. "How did it go?" he asked, careful to sound earnest and inquisitive. He was, after all, an enlisted man, even if he *was* Dark Ops, and while Garcia wasn't a point, he cared enough about the distinction in rank that he might take offense.

Ranks didn't always carry the same weight from the other branches to the Legion. You had to earn your respect from a leej. That was something all sides were aware of, and that the Republic armed forces bristled over. It wasn't unheard of for a leej to tell a Republic Army general where to stuff it. And so long as the general was relying on those leejes to complete his objective... he couldn't do sket about it. But Subs was a different breed—a unique case. No one on Hitchcock actually needed him; he was ornamentation. So yeah, he was respectful to Garcia.

"All in all, I'd call it a good day," Garcia answered. His only comment on Subs's appearance was a quick downward glance at his silk diaper. "We got three listening stations set up pretty deep out there. Once the link is made, we should have some better insight about what the doros are doing beyond the wire."

"I take it that's what took you all so long out there?"

The listening stations were cleverly camouflaged to look like desiccated tree stumps rotting in the jungle. They weighed a ton and would definitely slow an expedition down as they were humped through the uneven terrain. The trouble was, these big stations had a design flaw that allowed water into their inner workings in Psydon's unreal humidity. They had to be replaced all the time.

"No, not this time," Garcia said. He sounded upbeat; he must have been feeling good about what his platoon had accomplished. "We planted some new devices—essentially bots but small... look like local insects. R&D developed them for Dark Ops is the word, and now they're making their way into the main branches."

Subs nodded. He knew the devices Captain Garcia spoke of. They didn't have the same range, but they were so inconspicuous that they made up for it. Also, they weren't prone to malfunction. "Those are a whole lot easier to hump than what you had earlier."

"You got that right."

"So how far did you go?"

"Dropped them off at some predetermined spots on the grid. But farther than any patrol I know of before."

Subs gave an appreciative nod. "Nicely done, Captain, if you don't mind my saying so."

Garcia smiled. "I appreciate that, Sergeant Major."

Now that Subs had a good rapport going with Captain Garcia, he wanted to get down to the last order of business. "Captain, when you have the opportunity, could you do me a favor and have Specialist Bucholz report to the comm station? I'm not relaying an order or anything, but long-range comms are down again and Alistair says she's the only one with a hope of getting them back online."

"I think there's a resupply flight coming in tomorrow," the captain replied. "We're supposed to be getting a redundancy relay for the long-range comms."

Subs nodded. "Yeah. That's why it's a favor. I need to look into the Legion net—something's digging at me and I want to research it—only I'm getting denied access."

"Did the last all-pass turnover skip you?"

Subs sighed. "Yep. Best not to grow old and forgotten, Captain. It kind of sucks."

Garcia chuckled. "Well, the only way to follow that advice is to die young. Not sure I'm looking for that."

And yet in Subs's experience, a lot of the best men he knew had done just that.

"I'll have Specialist Bucholz report to the comm station. I wanted to go there anyway to make sure the uplink with the listening bots worked. You should come and see how these new bots work out. Well, new to us, I guess."

"Sure thing, Captain. I'll come. Call it professional curiosity to see how this version compares to what I used to deploy. Mainly we just snuck in literal flies on the wall to know when our target would be home for our surprise visits."

The pair began walking toward the comm station, cutting through the still-shuffling platoon returning for the field. Captain Garcia halted abruptly. "You... you aren't *really* going to go inside the comm room still wearing a silk diaper?"

Subs looked down as if he was unaware. "Oh. Sure. I mean, why not? What are they gonna do? Kick me out of the Legion?"

* * *

The comm center was built like virtually every other comm center in use by the Republic military machine. It was the most secure building on base, created from modular printed walls that fit together to form a tight seal— much nicer than the mobile hab units doled out for most administrative purposes, and a whole lot better than the lousy hooches and tents given to the soldiers.

What was better still was that the comm building had functioning climate controls. Granted, they didn't work all that great, but *not all that great* was still far better than *not at all*. It was noticeably cooler inside the building, and the humidity was drastically reduced. That alone made them popular locations on Psydon, and any time anyone could wrangle an assignment in the comm station or received orders to report to the comm center... they were happy.

In fact, Subs thought, *that's probably why Alistair always takes those double shifts without complaining. Not that complaining would do him any good anyway.*

Still in his silk diapers, Subs sat on a desk, his legs dangling, as Alistair, his comm tech friend, worked at his station to get the listening bots connected to Hitchcock's systems.

Subs noticed that Alistair kept casting sidelong glances in his direction. "What?"

"Oh, nothing," Alistair said through gritted teeth. He went back to his work for a moment before turning back. "It's just that... you're all nasty, and I *use* that desk."

Subs looked around. The desk looked clean and neat. It certainly didn't *look* like his friend made use of it. "I'm cooling off, thanks to the climate controls."

Alistair gave a tight smile. "Yeah, sure. Whatever." He went back to work, swiping across his displays and bringing up various subroutines. Then he turned back again and shouted, "Could you just sit somewhere else!"

Subs laughed and hopped down off the desk. He moved to stand next to Captain Garcia, who had been busying himself with incline pushups, using another desk for that purpose.

"Aren't you tired from the patrol?" Subs asked.

"My legs are," said Garcia. "Arms didn't have to do much."

Alistair was out of his seat and standing in front of the desk Subs had just surrendered. "Ahh!" he screamed. "I can see the sweaty imprint of your butt and nuts!" He scrambled back to his desk, grabbed a can of disinfecting spray, and doused the entire area with a carpet bomb of pine-smelling particles.

Subs gave a deep belly laugh. "It'll dry off. You're overreacting."

Alistair looked up at the Dark Ops legionnaire, his finger still depressing the nozzle on the sprayer. "I *eat* at this desk, man. Not cool!"

"When you're done," Captain Garcia said, as if none of this conversation had even happened, "I'd like to know how long until we can expect an uplink. Is that something Specialist Bucholz has to make happen? Because if those bots find some doros, I want to make sure we can organize a reaction force to wipe them out before they get away."

Subs often felt like the regular Republic Army was too stuffed with regulation- and career-minded officers to truly bring the fight to the enemy. That was the legacy of the appointment program that he was sure would eventually poison the Legion as well. It seemed like all the branches, except the marines, relied too heavily on the Legion to bring the actual fighting. But Captain Garcia was a good reminder that there were still some soldiers and officers who remembered that the primary specialty of an army was killing. No matter how socially taboo that might be to say out loud.

Alistair put down his can of disinfectant and dropped into his chair, folding his arms so they rested on his stomach. "Okay, so to properly answer that question, sir, I have to address a number of different items. In no particular order..." The comm tech began to count on his fingers. "One: we do need Specialist Bucholz. Two: but not to see the data. Three: we need her to get the long-range comms up, so that if we find something, you can actually call in a mission to get it taken care of. Four: I don't know when she'll show up. Five: what Sergeant Boyd did was inexcusable, and I want to file a formal complaint for him *literally* sweating his ass off on my workstation. And I want it filed like that verbatim and sent to the Legion commander— not the sector Legion commander, the big daddy."

"He wouldn't listen to a basic," Subs shot back.

Garcia let a slight smile curl up the corner of his mouth. "The data. We can listen to that right now?"

Alistair nodded. "The firmware for the bots you implanted is only a variation of what's used for the bigger, tree-stump varieties. So since we had those synced into our system, I was able to migrate the newer listening bots by looking at the two source codes. It's essentially a redundancy of what's already in place, so it didn't really need a full install, which would take an hour or so. I did a couple of tweaks and… boom. We're up."

"Okayyy," said the captain, drawing the word out as though he didn't understand most of what he'd just been told, but was ready to move forward all the same.

Subs leaned against Alistair's desk, arms crossed and looking down at the tech.

"Dude!" shouted Alistair, his eyes fixed on Subs's silk diaper leaning against the edge of the desk. "Would you, for the love of Oba, remove your *sweaty keister* from my *workstation*? You're on my datapad, and you're already fogging up the screen!"

Subs looked down. There was indeed half a data-pad trapped under one of his cheeks. He hopped off the desk. "Sorry."

"You Dark Ops have no respect for the rest of us," said Alistair haughtily.

"That's not really fair," protested Subs. "It's not just Dark Ops. *No one* respects basics."

"Yeah, yeah," said the comm tech. "No one respects the basic. Not even our girlfriends. Not that I *have* a girlfriend, mind you. But if I did, there would be no way she'd respect me."

"So how long until we can find out what's on these things?" asked Captain Garcia, steering back to the business at hand.

A chime sounded at the workstation.

"It's ready now," said Alistair. He leaned into his console, running his fingers across the various transparent displays, expanding, collapsing, rotating, twirling, and skewing various symbols. Executing directives and commands until a notification bar that read "Bug One" appeared. Directly below the bar was what looked like an audio wavelength. "Play findings for bug one."

A soft, feminine voice came from the workstation. "Listening post bug one has twenty-seven seconds of potential audio interest."

The track played, beginning with the gentle swaying sound of jungle leaves in the wind and insects playing their arms and legs like stringed instruments. The symphony was drowned out by a piercing howl—a cross between a guttural cry and a mouthy hiss. The howl sounded twice more before the computer announced, "End of log."

"Well, that was terrifying," said Alistair, looking between Garcia and Subs. "Either of you have any idea what kind of monster makes a noise like that? Because it didn't sound human or doro."

"Not sure," answered Garcia. "But I agree it's not human or doro."

"It's a dreex," Subs said matter-of-factly. He saw Garcia and Alistair looking at him in surprise, and explained, "The Legion gave a dossier to all legionnaires. What not to eat and what might eat you. A dreex is the thing most likely to eat you."

"Well," said Alistair, "suddenly I don't feel so bad about hanging out in a climate-controlled room behind the wire. Okay, actually, I *never* felt bad about hanging out safely behind the wire. But I'm sure that *you* could wrestle one of these things to the ground and snap its neck if you had to, Dark Ops."

"Probably."

Alistair smiled as he went back to manipulating his screens. "So cool," he muttered in genuine admiration. For all the kid's sarcasm, it was obvious he looked up to Subs.

It was true... everyone wanted to be a legionnaire at some point in their life.

"How about the other stations?" Garcia asked.

"Let's see..." The comm tech moved through a myriad of submenus. "Nothing from bugs two and three. Four has something. So does five."

He opened bug four. "Play current file and skip the introduction."

The computer began to play the track. It started off much the same as the other, capturing the sounds of the jungle, but distantly. It went on like that for nearly a minute, ending without any other noise of interest.

"What's that supposed to be?" Garcia said.

Alistair shrugged. "I don't know. The algorithm picked up something it identified as an anomaly. Maybe the general noise of the jungle didn't line up with the rest of the data. That happens sometimes when the sample size is too small. Did you notice anything, Subs?"

The Dark Ops leej shook his head no. But not because he'd heard nothing—rather because he needed more. Something was gnawing at him. Something about the way the recording ended. "Let's hear five."

The comm tech brought the last file on-screen. "Let's hear bug five, computer. And skip the intro unless it has analysis marked critical."

"There is no significant recommendation or observation attached to this recording."

The clip played, sounding much the same as four. It was a bit louder, but nothing stood out.

"Another nonsense track," Garcia said.

Subs wasn't so sure. "How far apart did you place four and five?" he asked the captain.

"Not far. Maybe a kilometer? Less than that. Three quarters of a click. One and two were replacements for malfunctioning units—the stumps—closer to Hitchcock. We dropped them first, then planted three through five to form a sort of isosceles triangle. Intel designed it to be a surveillance zone capable of pickup up anything happening inside."

Alistair chimed in. "Word among the comm techs' gossip circle is if these work, we're going to be setting up zones like this through the whole jungle in preparation for a massive push to find those artillery platforms."

Subs nodded, trying to get an image of the setup in his mind. "So three and four—I'm guessing you set those up in straight line at the farthest edge of your patrol? With the triangle's point somewhere below?"

"Yeah, that's it," Garcia confirmed.

"You said you went far. How far? Did you get close to Cuchin Valley?"

"Actually, yeah. Pretty close. We didn't cross it, but we snuck right up next to it."

Subs ground his feet. A terrible realization was beginning to form in the pit of his stomach. "Play me four again."

Alistair did as he was asked. They sat in rapt silence as the track played out.

"Still sounds like a lot of nothing to me," said Garcia.

Alistair rubbed his eyes. "Yeah, me too."

But something didn't sit right with Subs. The way the track ended… He thought he'd heard the same thing at the end of track five. Like he was hearing the same thing from two different angles. A stereo recording, but only one isolated and decayed channel at a time.

"The tracks the computer selected from bugs four and five," Subs said. "Were they recorded at the same time?"

Alistair entered a few commands. "Huh. Yeah, actually, both tracks are from the exact same time. Just minutes ago."

"Can you play those two tracks together? Have the computer sync them up?"

The comm tech looked up. "Yeah. What did you hear, Subs?"

Subs pinched the bottom of his lip, thinking. "I'm not sure. But I want to hear them both together."

Alistair gave the computer its instructions. "Here we go," he said.

The screen played the synthesized file. All was still quiet and faint in the recording, and the three men strained to hear.

"Turn that up loud as you can," Subs said.

White noise hissed, filling the digital void. The recording played to the very end, where a tiny *timp, timp, timp* could be heard.

"Okay, I heard that," said Garcia. "Any idea what it is, Sergeant Boyd?"

Subs leaned in to examine the display, looking at the minuscule jumps in wavelength that marked the almost imperceptible sounds. It seemed obvious now—a noise he'd recognize from anywhere.

"Yep," he said. "That's a firefight."

14

Near the Cuchin Valley, Psydon

Wash had set a blistering pace through the jungle after leaving the ambush site. He had been told to do everything as though his life depended on it. And right now, that meant *marching* like that was the case. Because something told him that it was.

But the marines—not to mention Berlin and Tierney—were lagging behind. Only Parker, the sniper, seemed capable of keeping up.

"Let's hold up," Wash said to Parker.

He could hardly fault the others. They were doing their best, even Berlin. It was a matter of just how much you were capable of with your life on the line. That wasn't a universal.

Eventually Sergeant Shotton hobbled up, his grimace visible in the moonlight. "Not all of us are as conditioned as you, Leej. Especially my old butt."

"Sorry," Wash said. "I just wanted to put some distance between us and those dead doros. We can take a breather now."

"Well, a breather might not be enough. What we need is a *rest*. Let me set up a perimeter to watch for any dog-men, and then let's take some time. I'm thinking we've got, what? Six hours until dawn? We can still get a move on before the sun rises and brings the heat."

Wash comprehended everything the sergeant was saying. And it was the right call for the marines. Still, he felt like he was making a mistake by not pressing on. Alone, he was confident he could reach the base of the peak before the sun came up, which would give him the cover of night to scale it and call in his all-hail. But with the rest of the team—especially Berlin and Tierney—they wouldn't make it by then.

So what do you do? Stay with your team, or leave and let Shotton and Berlin handle things? And if you left... would you be able to find them again after separating? Both choices carried risks.

He decided to stay with the group. It wasn't because they couldn't get on without him; Shotton, if not Berlin, was a capable leader. But staying together had the best odds. They'd press toward Poro-Poro after a rest. They'd send word about the guns and their location... and everything might turn out all right.

"We haven't seen any signs of the doros out this way," Parker said conversationally as three men began backtracking to rejoin the main element. "I think we're the only thing that can use a blaster out in this neck of the woods. At least in a long while."

"How about you, Sergeant?" Wash asked. "Have you gotten any sense that there are any of 'em on our trail?"

"If I did, I'd still be runnin' to keep pace with you. Nah. I think if any of 'em were after us, other than the ambushed suckers, they must have zigged instead of zagged."

"Why do you think that is, Sarn't?" asked Parker.

"Because of where we're headed," grunted Shotton. "You gotta be a fool to go out of the jungle and right down into that valley, with no cover, clear as day for all those deep-brown puppy-dog doro eyes to see. Not where *I'd* go. Unless I absolutely had to."

"And we do," Washam insisted.

"Yes, sir," said Shotton. "Just worried that the doros are gonna find them dead scouts and put two and two together and come up with us out here wanderin' around. They don't gotta chase us down if all that needs doing is an artillery strike once we're caught out in the valley."

This was the first time Sergeant Shotton had articulated any misgivings about the plan.

"It's a definite risk," Wash said, feeling that engaging with the sergeant's comments would be a better leadership move than ignoring or berating the man, though part of him wanted to ask why he was bringing this up now so long after they'd committed to the march. "But Poro-Poro remains our most direct opportunity for extraction and the best chance to get those guns before they disappear. The audacity of going straight for it is to our advantage. We could take the long route and snake through the jungle, but something tells me the doros will find us and catch us before we ever get there. Increasing time out here favors the odds of that scenario."

The three men carried on in silence for a time before Wash added, "Although, I'm open to suggestions. If you have any, now is the time to voice them."

"Nah," Sergeant Shotton said. "I don't have any better idea. I just don't like what we're caught up in as a whole. But if our options are a game of hide-'n'-seek with the doros in this jungle, or a flat run for the peak... then let's run."

Wash nodded. The reality was, hide-and-seek wasn't their only concern. The marines lacked the food and water necessary for prolonged exposure to the jungle. They could live off the land, but not without slowing down considerably.

"My only request," Shotton continued, "is that when it's time to run, my men are rested enough to have a chance if we get into a firefight. Being dog-tired ain't gonna increase our odds or improve our skills."

"Roger that," said Wash.

He was about to say more when something caught his foot, and he pitched forward. Parker and Shotton threw out their arms to catch him, but Wash felt himself slip through their grasp, and the ground came up to meet him.

Hard.

"Hey, you all right, man?" Parker asked.

"Yeah," Wash managed, the wind nearly knocked out of him.

The impact with the ground was much greater than he would have expected from soft jungle floor. And as he shook his head and pushed himself up, the ground beneath his hands felt firm. Like... rock. And not a misshapen boulder either, but a smooth slab.

He brushed away dried leaves and jungle debris. This was definitely some kind of large paving stone.

"You just gonna lay there all day, Leej," asked Sergeant Shotton, "or do you plan on getting up?"

Despite his casual tone, they all spoke in hushed whispers, on heightened alert after the noise of Wash's fall.

"Yeah," Wash said, pushing himself to his knees, then slowly standing. The jarring impact still hurt. "Something snagged my foot."

He stepped off the slab and once again felt the spring of the jungle floor. Turning back, he pressed his foot on the stone. "I think this is a... walkway or something. You guys know of the doros building any fortifications in the jungle?"

Wash was worried he might have stumbled upon some kind of doro pillbox, or the outskirts of a reinforced bunker. And that the doros were nearby, if not watching them right now.

"Not that I know of," said Sergeant Shotton, testing the stone slab with the toe of his boot. "Once we pushed the doros out of the cities, their fixed defenses were pretty flimsy. The sort of thing we saw back at that camp. Tin and scrap wood."

Wash looked around through the single optic starlight scope attached to his helmet. During his rapid march with Parker at his side, the surrounding jungle had looked pretty much the same everywhere, a nondescript blur. In fact, if he hadn't been orienteering with a compass attuned to Psydon's magnetic poles, he wouldn't have been able to tell whether he was making progress or only going in circles—things looked that similar. But now, as he stopped and looked around, he saw a distinctive shape a short distance to the west. It looked like a vine-covered hill rising up from among slim trees with broad, bowing leaves. A small structure stood at its crest.

"What do you make of that?" Wash asked, pointing out his find.

Parker let out an impressed whistle. "Surprised we didn't see that before. We were moving pretty fast, though."

"I want to take a look," Wash said, already feeling more at ease. Whatever was in front of him, it didn't have the look of a bunker or a doro pillbox. He started toward the shadowy mound, and under his feet he felt the firmness of more covered paving stones.

"Seems deliberate," Shotton said as he followed Wash down the path. "Somebody laid these stones to lead where we're headed."

Wash thought the same thing.

Sure enough, the path led right up the hill to the structure. Up close, it looked like a ruined temple left forgotten in the jungle, fighting a last stand against the creeping foliage. Four stone walls protected a spire of some sort within, and stone stairs led up to a great entryway. If there had ever been a door, it had rotted away long before.

The trio stopped at the bottom of the steps, staring up and into the darkened ruin. Though aged, the stones seemed sturdy and the foundation strong. There was some crumbling, some decay—most of which was caused by the relentless and intrusive vines pushing their way between the rocks. In a few spots, they'd succeeded in making a spire fall over or to pull down one of the uppermost cut stones at the top of the wall.

"This place looks like something the Ancients left behind," Parker said.

Wash's mind was on more practical concerns. He quickly realized that with the height of the building's stone walls, its defensible entryway, and its position on high ground... this ruin was probably the best defensive position in the entire jungle. It was a sure sight better for the weary marines than just lying among the leaves.

"How much farther behind is everybody?" he asked.

"Closer than they were," Shotton growled. "I told 'em to keep movin' until we were all reunited."

Wash nodded. "This looks like a good spot to get some rest. We can set up shifts with some men up on the walls to keep lookout. It's a defensible position in case the doros are out there tracking us."

Shotton nodded. "Yeah. It'll do. I'll go get the men."

"You want me to stay here with you?" Parker asked Wash.

Wash thought about that. He wouldn't mind the company, but he'd rather the sergeant—tired as he seemed—have someone with him. "No. Go on with the sergeant, and I'll stick around here to flag you down in case you have trouble seeing the place on the way back."

Shotton and Parker hustled off into the jungle without another word.

Wash had no idea how long they'd be gone, but he felt it would be a good use of his time to poke around the temple a bit. As he climbed the steps, he felt a cessation of the light breeze that drifted through the jungle, carrying a scent of jasmine and fig.

The inner courtyard was a perfect square, made of the same stone as the walls and ziggurat—and probably the same stone as the path leading here. The whole thing was likely carved out of some mountain ages ago. Which made Wash wonder how far it had been carried and who had cut it and put it into place. The architecture certainly didn't match a style popular with the doros—at least in their cities—but what did he know about dog-man prehistory?

Hidden inside the temple walls, Wash turned off his night scope, plunging himself momentarily into deep blackness, before switching on the flashlight attached to his rifle rail. The beam lit up the dried leaves, rubble, and other detritus gathered in the corners. Wash blinked several times, his eyes struggling to adjust to the sudden radiance.

Slowly he crept along the walls, listening for any signs of the marines approaching and looking for imperfections that might be exploited if they did fall under attack. Everything looked to be in good shape. The walls had a sort of parapet that could be reached by stone staircases that began in the middle of each wall and rose up to the corner.

Whoever built this temple, they'd built it to be defended.

Wash had inspected half the square, working his way around the ziggurat, which seemed to be purely ornamental—no stairs or doors were visible—when just beyond a blind corner, he heard a rustling sound. Wash's heart rate spiked so suddenly he could feel his blood pumping in his throat. With his rifle up and at the ready, he quickly turned the corner.

His light fell upon a small, fox-like creature with gray fur and a black tail.

The animal froze in place, its eyes reflecting back a ghostly green. Then it opened its mouth, emitted a small shrill scream—revealing three rows of needle-sharp teeth—and quickly scurried away. It disappeared around the ziggurat and presumably out of the temple faster than Wash was able to follow with his light.

Wash sighed, feeling the tension escape from his shoulders and detecting the arrival of a slight headache at the base of his skull.

As he continued with his reconnaissance of the temple, he heard another sound-—and this sound was definitely not made by another of those fox creatures.

Footsteps approached.

Wash switched off his light and ran up the nearest set of stairs. He was amazed at how solid they felt given how many centuries, if not millennia, this temple had likely stood. As he reached the parapet, he drew down his night scope and looked out into the jungle to see who was coming to visit. It was probably the marines, but if it wasn't, Wash wanted to be ready for them. Even a single-man ambush from this position could be devastating for whoever it was.

It was just the marines. The column came into view led by Parker, who looked as though he would walk right by. It turned out to have been a good idea for Wash to stay behind; even with the benefit of night vision, the old ruin was too well hidden among the trees and vines to be easily spotted. That gave Wash some comfort. He realized that he'd spent every moment in the jungle sure that the doros were only a short distance away, waiting to discover them. But maybe the doros would miss the temple just as easily.

"Parker," Wash whispered.

The sniper swung his rifle toward the disturbance in the split-second where reflex is faster than thought.

A voice from behind the sniper asked, "What is it?"

"Nothing. This is the place." Parker ushered everyone toward the temple.

Sergeant Shotton emerged from the column to take the lead and move up the temple stairs first. In a low voice, he directed his warfighters to different points throughout the temple. They took off so fast, clearing each corner and making their way up the steps to the parapets, that Wash didn't have time to tell the sergeant he'd already cleared most of the area. The men moved busily, expending those final bursts of energy before a promised rest.

Shotton looked up at Wash from the temple floor. "You coming down here, LT? Or do these old knees have to come up to you?"

"It feels cooler up here than down there," Wash answered.

There was something stifling about the temple floor that Wash had only realized when he reached the parapets. As if all the jungle's heat and humidity got trapped inside the structure, conspiring with the vines to better decay the stone.

"My knees can handle it if that's the case." Shotton moved up the steps, not quite hobbling, but also not showing a full fluidity of motion. The hard marching, hard fighting, and jungle conditions were obviously taking a toll on the older man.

"How long you been in, Sergeant?" Wash asked when the marine reached the top.

Shotton shrugged. "Could've retired last year. 'Cept we keep finding wars to fight in, and the marines know the value of a good NCO. They're sort of like the Legion that way."

Wash nodded. "You ever think about hanging up your helmet and blaster?"

"Lately that's *all* I think about. These knees won't stop remindin' me. But I don't want to leave my boys, not yet. Not until Psydon is all over and put to bed." The sergeant leaned against the parapet, resting his elbows on the top. "See, if I get pulled out of the lines for a few weeks to get my knees fixed, well, I can all but guarantee you they won't put me back in. Nah. The next shuttle I'd take after that surgery would be straight back home. They'd make sure I retired."

"So you play through the pain."

"Comes with the job."

"Marines are lucky to have you, Sergeant."

Shotton looked Wash directly in the eyes. In the moonlight, he looked grave, concerned, and sincere. "I sure hope that's true, Lieutenant."

Denturo bounded up the steps, his gear jingling as he skipped two at a time. "Hey, Sarge, Corpsman Hellix wants permission to bring the girl up. Says it's too stuffy for her down below. You ask me, that's why you should only bring men into combat. You don't hear any of us whining about the heat."

"She didn't choose to go into combat, she was dragged into it," Wash said. "She and the rest of those basics got ambushed and captured, remember?"

Denturo spat on the stones. "Same thing."

"Have Hellix bring her up," said Shotton. "And I want you and Haulman up here with them. This is your overwatch."

Denturo nodded and left to pass on the orders.

"All right," Shotton said to Wash. "I'm gonna find a corner up top to lie down."

"I'll stay up for the first watch, Sergeant." Wash was still amped up from the hike. It was as if the distance he'd covered in the hard march from the ambush site had woken up all the muscles in his body. He felt as though he had enough energy to go on for days nonstop. Like he was just floating above the surface. He looked across to an opposite parapet and saw Berlin already lying down. Probably asleep.

Wash wouldn't be able to sleep tonight. He knew it.

"Well..." grumbled Shotton. "Get yourself some rest. You're a legionnaire, not a war bot. And even *they* have to recharge their systems from time to time."

Wash nodded and moved to the far end of the parapet, not wanting any further conversation. Particularly if it came from Denturo.

* * *

Twenty minutes passed with nothing to remember them by.

Wash kept vigil on the jungle ahead of him, overlooking the terrain he and the marines had traversed. If the doros were out there and tracking, that's the direction they would likely come from. Of course, some entirely different element of dog-men could show up, in which case there was no telling where they might appear.

But all four sides of the temple were guarded by vigilant marines that night while their comrades slept, or attempted to. Despite their exhaustion, the men trying to sleep constantly stirred, rolling over and readjusting themselves in an effort to find that magic position that would let their discomforted bodies find rest. Some of them gave up trying and whispered soft conversations instead, their backs pressed against the ziggurat.

Tierney was one of the ones who couldn't sleep—even though Wash imagined she must be the most exhausted of all of them, given the condition they'd found her in. Corpsman Hellix had wanted to give her a sedative, but she'd turned it down, explaining, "I don't want to have to rely on someone to carry me if it comes down to it."

That invited a comment from Denturo. Without taking his eyes off the jungle, he spoke out of the side of his mouth. "We saved your ass from the doros once. No guarantees we do it again."

That jab effectively killed the small talk on Wash's parapet, leaving Wash, Haulman, and Denturo to watch the jungle while Corpsman Hellix slept on the stone.

Tierney leaned against the parapet wall, her back to the jungle, arms crossed, head down, seemingly lost in daydreams. Maybe that was why she wouldn't go to sleep. You can at least control the dreams that happen while you're awake. After what she'd been through... Wash figured she was due for some nightmares.

The jungle had grown relatively still, as though it sensed the hour required a certain quiet and peace. The pulsing hum of background noise that you stopped hearing once you were in it long enough was still there, but the loud, distinct calls of the bigger animals or birds... insects—whatever—had died down.

That was the case until a sudden fluttering, like the buzzing of a large winged insect, sounded from out in the jungle. The buzzing came closer, and the bug zipped right over all their heads.

"Must be one hell of a big bug," said Haulman, breaking the silence.

Wash couldn't count the number of times he'd heard some strange new animal sound during his time on Psydon. This one sounded like an odd mix of a buzz and a whirl. And evidently there were more creatures where that one came from. Another buzz zipped toward them.

Without warning, Tierney collapsed, falling in a heap on the parapet stone.

Denturo was the only one who might have done something about it. Wash and Haulman were too far away, and

Corpsman Hellix lay sleeping in between where Tierney and the big marine had stood. Denturo looked down at the passed-out basic, spat a stream against the stone wall, and called out, "Hellix, wake up. Heat was too much for your patient and she passed out."

The corpsman roused himself and moved over to Tierney. "She's not my patient, she's a soldier. And honestly, Denturo, you should be a little more concerned when someone faints. Maybe—I don't know—try and help her?"

Denturo spat over the side of the high temple wall. "I ain't in the habit of concerning myself with dead weight."

"Oh no," the corpsman said, rubbing his hands on his uniform and holding them up to the moonlight.

"What is it?" asked Wash. "What's wrong?"

"She must've hit her head. Her hair's all bloody, and I—" The corpsman cut himself off.

Denturo snorted a single chuckle. "Be some tough luck to get rescued from the doros only to kill yourself by banging your head on the ground."

Corpsman Hellix shook his head. "Something's wrong. There's a hole in the back of her head."

He sounded concerned. Highly concerned.

"What?" asked Wash, feeling dumb for not thinking of anything else to say.

Another of the buzzing, fluttering insects came in from the jungle.

Haulman pitched backwards with a grunt, tumbling off the parapet and down to the stone temple floor below.

"Sket!" shouted Denturo. "Gotta be dog-men!"

Not waiting for orders, he began to fire his weapon into the jungle shadows.

"Doros!" someone else shouted.

Wash didn't know if it was a guess or if someone actually saw advancing dog-men. But it didn't matter. The marines were sending blaster bolts into every nook and cranny in the jungle.

The jungle started to fire back.

Denturo's intuition had been spot on.

Shotton, Berlin, and the rest of the sleeping warriors rose up and joined their comrades in firing their weapons in response to every muzzle flash and incoming blaster bolt they could see. The old temple was peppered with blaster fire from all directions.

As Wash gritted his teeth and sent torrents of hot bolts into the doros, he let out a primal scream to warn the dog-men that only death waited for them inside the forgotten ruin.

15

Republic Army Firebase Hitchcock
Middle-of-Nowhere, Psydon

"A firefight?" asked Captain Garcia. "You're sure?"

"Yeah, I'm sure," Subs answered, feeling annoyed that the officer would question him. "I know the sound. It's a blaster fight. A hot one at that. How recent did you say these timestamps are?"

Alistair looked up with concern. "This is happening *right now*. Well, as of two minutes ago."

Subs felt a knot of concern grow in the pit of his stomach. "So right now, someone is in a fight within the listening radius of those two bots."

"If that's what you say those sounds are, then yeah," confirmed the comm tech. "They have an effective listening radius of twenty kilometers for something as loud as blaster fire, taking into consideration the baffling caused by the jungle. So if you're hearing blasters..."

Captain Garcia held up a cautionary hand. "Let's hold on a bit here. We don't know it's a fight. I'm not disputing your expertise, Sergeant Major, but if it's blasters, how do we know it's not some doros taking late-night target practice? Just because blasters are being fired doesn't mean there's a firefight."

"I know what target practice sounds like, too." Subs was rapidly tapping his foot on the floor. There was combat happening within his area of operation, and he felt the overwhelming urge to do something about it... not that he could leave the base. "Listen: I've got a good idea that this fight involves a small recon team made up of legionnaires and marines."

"How do you know that?" Garcia asked.

"I got word from a SLIC crew that came into Hitch to get refueled earlier. They said they took two legionnaires—points—out on a recon patrol way deep, past the Cuchin Valley. If they've been moving back toward friendly lines, they could be within range of your bugs."

"So they're in trouble?" Alistair said, leaning forward in his chair.

"Well, there's a whole lot more doros out there than Republic."

Alistair swiveled around in his seat, working his datapad. "I'll see if I can't get Specialist Bucholz in to work on long-range comms."

Captain Garcia crossed his arms, nodding approvingly. "Good. We need them up ASAP."

"If she can't fix them," Subs said, turning for the door, "make sure she explains very clearly how long it'll be until they're back up."

"Where are you going?" asked Alistair.

Subs paused long enough to say, "Don't worry. I'll be back."

* * *

Subs returned to the comm station looking a far cry different than he had before. He'd swapped the silk diapers for Dark Ops armor. He'd actually psyched himself out prior to putting it on, thinking that during his time on the base he'd gotten too soft. Too puffy. That the armor wouldn't fit.

It fit just fine. Just like he remembered.

He felt alive in a way he couldn't describe. It was a feeling that all legionnaires knew, one that was communicated with a simple nod: *I'm one jocked-up, lethal, ready-to-KTF son of a kelhorn. And I didn't forget nothin'.*

And God forbid you're the one standing in the way.

Specialist Bucholz sat with a frown on her face on the same desk Subs had… *occupied* earlier. Only Alistair didn't seem nearly as bothered by her presence. Of course, she was dressed a good deal more modestly—though Subs couldn't help but think that Alistair wouldn't complain if the specialist were wearing a pair of her own silk diapers.

"What's the word?" Subs's voice carried with it a confidence and command forged in the intense fires of combat. He had fought, killed, and seen men die. But never him. He was untouchable. Dark Ops. Legion.

And he sounded like it.

"Word isn't good," answered Captain Garcia. "We aren't seeing comms anytime soon."

Alistair was staring at Subs in his armor, his eyes wide. The kid had always idolized Subs a bit—a fact the legionnaire kept in the back of his mind. Things like that brought with them a sort of... responsibility.

"You look dangerous," Alistair said. "But if you're thinking about doing your KTF thing to the comm relay, I'm sorry, but electronics repair doesn't work that way."

Subs didn't so much crack a smile. Which seemed to bother his friend. But the legionnaire didn't have time for that either. Because the reality was that in spite of Captain Garcia's conjecture that the blaster fire they heard might not have involved any Republic personnel, Subs knew better. Those two points had gotten themselves into a hornet's nest. And it was going to take the iron fist of the Legion to get them safely out of it.

"Have you been monitoring the bugs?" Subs asked Alistair. He had questions for Specialist Bucholz too, but first priority was to get a clear picture of what was happening in the jungle. As clear as possible. "Now that you know what to listen for, are you still hearing the blaster fire?"

The comm tech seemed pleased to be asked. "Yeah, they're still reporting in, and we're still getting the same signature we saw before. Just from those two bugs. So I guess that means the fight's still going on?"

"Sounds like it." Subs looked directly at Specialist Bucholz. "When Captain Garcia says 'anytime soon,' what does he mean?"

The tech brushed a strand of oily hair away from her face. She looked tired, her eyes baggy. No doubt the result of the day's march. "Simply put, a critical component has failed," she said. "We don't have a spare, and it's not something I can jerry-rig out of something else. Long-range comms will be down until that replacement part arrives. Which, thankfully, is scheduled to be tomorrow at oh-nine-hundred."

"Appreciate your conciseness," Subs said. He felt like he was running a mission planning meeting with his old kill team.

But no long-range comms. That increased the suck by orders of magnitude.

Sometimes these things couldn't be helped in a theater of war. Machines and men alike broke down. Flanks and bases were occasionally left unprotected. It was the nature of war.

Republic Army command *should* already know that Firebase Hitchcock's long-range comms were down. Failure to check in would have tipped them off. They'd have an observation drone or orbiting ship watching the base for signs of combat—exchanges of blaster fire in the darkness, things like that. More importantly, this meant that the scheduled resupply tomorrow morning would absolutely happen. Normally, that was never a guarantee. Schedules changed. But under these circumstances, unless there was some kind of mass casualty event that required the use of every SLIC in the area, that part would come in. Even if it meant canceling the flight of some colonel looking to make his rounds.

That much was good.

What was bad was that the fighting was happening right *now*. Maybe the marines were holding up; maybe the doro force wasn't very large. But out there, behind enemy lines... it could grow quickly.

Subs shook his head at Bucholz's report. "Let's say you get the part at oh-nine-hundred hours tomorrow morning. How long to fix it?"

"Maybe thirty minutes?" guessed the specialist.

"So oh-nine-thirty we got long-range comms. Best case. Which means maybe within an hour of that a SLIC gun run or Legion QRF gets into the air."

It would all be easier if Subs could reach another legionnaire flying close enough for L-comm range like he had earlier. He'd been trying, but he kept coming up empty.

Captain Garcia looked down, his face grim, shaking his head. "Thinking it might be too late by then?"

"For a couple of points and a handful of marines? Yeah. How long did it take you to march to the location of bugs four and five?"

"Maybe six hours."

Subs nodded, his face not betraying the momentous internal decision he'd just made. "All right. I'm heading for their location now. I'll try to reconnoiter where the fight is happening. It'll probably be over, it'll probably be too late. But in the event that they hold on, I might be able to make a difference."

The captain's mouth fell open. "You're not actually thinking of going into the jungle by yourself to get mixed up in this firefight?"

Subs gave a mischievous smile. "I don't have to go by myself. You can come if you're up to it, Captain."

A part of the Dark Ops legionnaire did want an extra hand. Every blaster rifle wielded in battle was a force multiplier in the hands of a legionnaire. Subs had been in enough fights where that one blaster rifle was all that made the difference.

And it was part of the Legion code. *Everybody* fights. He'd stressed that to the basics on Hitchcock repeatedly.

"You know I can't do that, Sergeant Major. I would if I could. But I can't leave my command, and I can't take my soldiers back out into a fight. Not on foot."

Subs nodded. "Just giving you a hard time, Captain."

Alistair was looking more alarmed by the second. "Wait, Dark Ops—this is crazy. Think about this for a minute. You've told me—*complained* to me—a hundred times that you have orders from Legion command not to leave this base. And now you're talking about running out into the jungle—at night, I might remind you, in case you forgot—to go get into a blaster fight at the bleeding edge of where the Republic has managed to push. That's insane, man."

Subs unholstered his pistol and checked the charge pack. It was full, like he knew it would be. But that doesn't mean you don't check. "Yeah. But that's what I gotta do."

"Okay, but why? They're *points*. You said yourself that they'll be the ruin of the Legion. So if they got themselves into trouble... I mean, oh well, let them get themselves out of it. And if they don't, well, then maybe the stupid House of Reason will leave well enough alone when it comes to the Legion. They've already messed up the army, Oba knows."

Subs shook his head. "Can't do that either. First, because whether I agree with them or not, they're still legionnaires, and my duty to the Legion requires me to protect my fellow legionnaires to the last. And more importantly, it's not just them. They've got a team of marines with them. And now those marines are looking death in the face because of two men wearing *my* Legion crest. I owe it to them."

What Subs left unsaid was that, if those marines were his sons—his precious boys—if *they* were the young men out in the jungle on some godforsaken planet that only mattered because the government said it should... if *their* lives were on the line, and the Reaper was coming close and there was someone, even one person, who was in a position to do something about it... Subs would want that person to act.

You don't leave someone to die like that.

You don't stand down.

"Captain Garcia," Subs said, taking up his helmet in both hands and placing it over his head. "Once those comms are up, do everything you can to get help up there. Lie. Threaten. Call my old Dark Ops unit and ruin my career by reporting my AWOL. But get it done." He paused, then added, "Sir."

Alistair rose to his feet. He looked pale and unsteady. His hands were shaking. "Then, if that's the way it is... I'm coming with you."

At that moment, Subs's heart broke. For the naivety. For the gesture. For the love just shown. "Absolutely not."

"You're my friend, Dark Ops. I can't let you go out there alone. And you said it over and over again in all your *endless* Legion stories that every rifle matters. Well, I know how to use a rifle. I spent that week in Basic on the range. I'm coming."

"No." Subs moved for the door.

But Alistair was persistent. "You can tell me no, but you can't stop me. I'll follow you if I have to."

"I could break your legs right now."

"I'd crawl."

"I could kill you."

"That seems a little extreme."

This was wasting time. Subs needed to get on the move. He had hopes of reaching the listening bugs just before sunrise. With any luck he could track down the marines, or what remained of them, before the first SLIC arrived in Firebase Hitchcock.

"Captain Garcia, I hate to ask this, but put my friend in the brig. Make sure he doesn't follow me."

Alistair walked aggressively toward Subs. "No. No, no. That won't work either, because next to you the bots on this base are my best friends, and I happen to know how to get them to let me out."

Subs noticed that Specialist Bucholz had slipped out of the tension-filled room. He could hardly blame her.

He looked to Captain Garcia as if to ask such a thing were possible.

Garcia only shrugged.

Subs didn't have the time to argue this, and he wasn't going to shoot his friend in the leg to keep him on base. He shook his head. "Fine."

"You know," Garcia said, "you're a popular guy around the base. I'm willing to bet a lot of other soldiers beyond Alistair would want to come with you. If they're up to it, I won't stop them. Every rifle counts."

Alistair nodded enthusiastically. "Yeah. Totally. I'll go get them." He ran out the door like a kid ready to go to the zoo.

"Five minutes, and then I'm leaving!" Subs called after him.

What had he ever done to end up in a situation like this?

Oh yeah. He served the Republic.

16

Subs was surprised at the number of basics who mustered to go into the Psydon jungle with him.

Alistair was beaming, the weak light of the camp's illum-poles casting shadows across his face. Clearly, he was proud of the half dozen soldiers who had gathered with rifles in hand. A couple of them Subs recognized as having already been on patrol earlier in the day. They were tired, but committed. To him. Ready to undertake an all-night hike through the dangerous jungles and deep into enemy territory.

Or at least they thought they were ready. Subs would make sure.

"Sorry," panted Alistair. "This was all I could get in the time you gave me." He swung his blaster from his shoulder to the ready position.

Subs nodded. "I'm gonna say one thing and then I'm going to leave. Because I don't want to be misunderstood."

The waiting soldiers eyed the imposing legionnaire, kitted out fully in his armor, practically blending in with the shadows. A ghost among mortals.

"Your basic buddies who opted to stay behind: they're the smart ones. This trip isn't going to be safe, and it damn sure won't be easy. You want to come along and join the fight, I won't stop you. But I also won't wait for you. Which means you've gotta keep up. Fall behind, and you're finding your own way out of the jungle. Sorry if that sounds harsh, but I can't play hide-and-seek."

Subs crossed his arms and stood with his feet spread wide apart. "So if there's *any* doubt in your mind about whether or not you can do this"—he looked directly at Alistair, who only shook his head defiantly—"then you should head to your bunks, rest up, and see if you can get a spot on tomorrow morning's SLICs to join the fight then."

For a second, everyone stood in place. Nobody wavering. Nobody wanting to move first.

But then a fresh-faced private who'd only arrived at Hitchcock five days earlier—one had grown paler the more Subs had spoken—took a step backward.

Another followed his lead. With heads down, the two basics turned and walked back to the barracks.

And with that, the rest of the line melted away. Each soldier turning and leaving. Some with apologies, some with a shame that Subs knew they would feel for the rest of their lives, unless tomorrow really did bring a way for them to get in the fight. But it was the smart thing to do. And Subs didn't blame them. He'd hardly given a pep talk.

"Hey!" called Alistair after them, watching in dismay as his hastily gathered support team evaporated. "C'mon, guys!"

"Let 'em go," Subs said. "You should join them, but we're not going to get into this. You jocked up to KTF?"

Alistair nodded, swallowing hard. Maybe the reality of what he'd gotten himself into was catching up to him.

Subs looked over the comm tech's gear, tightening down ties and checking his ruck for sufficient charge packs and water. There were drinks to be had in the jungle, but that would slow them down. Best to pack in your own.

"Okay," Subs said. "Now jump."

Alistair looked quizzically at Subs for a moment, then left his feet, jingling as he came back down.

Subs produced a roll of tape. "Everything that made noise needs to be taped down. We're not going to let the doros hear us coming."

Moments later, Alistair repeated the exercise. Subs's handiwork had done the trick—only the sound of the comm tech's boots landing could be heard.

"I... brought grenades," Alistair offered.

Subs nodded. "Good."

A mechanical voice spoke to them from the opposite direction. "Sir, if it's not too late, I've been instructed by Captain Garcia to accompany you on the mission."

Subs turned to face the voice. One of Hitchcock's medical bots was walking toward them on spindly legs augmented with shock absorbers and stabilization gyros—special modifications to help the bot navigate the tricky jungle terrain. The machine stood around six feet tall and was painted a dull green. The only indications that this was a medical bot were the portable stretcher attached to its back and the red-stenciled cross on its arm—a symbol of medicine since a time no longer remembered, and for reasons long-since forgotten.

"Not too late," Subs said, surprised and pleased that the captain would be willing to spare the bot. These things could be lifesavers in a firefight. Their medical programming, toolkits, and modest-but-effective armor were often enough to keep soldier in the fight. And instead of a basic having to stabilize a wounded buddy with the doros bearing down in an attack pack, a med bot doing the job allowed every gun to keep firing.

"I am pleased to hear that, sir." The bot looked around Subs to Alistair. "With your leave, sir, I will download your team's most current medical files so as to be prepared for any casualties."

Alistair swallowed.

"Be my guest," said Subs.

"Thank you, sir." The bot's optics twitched as its lenses changed focus, taking in Alistair from head to toe. "I have completed analysis." The bot faced Subs. "I would like to have your medical records as well, sir. In the event that—"

"Sorry to be a spoilsport," Subs interrupted, "but I can't access the Legion database until the base's long-range comms are fixed, and that's not going to be until tomorrow."

"I see, sir. In that case, it is my professional, medical recommendation that your operation be delayed until proper medical records can be downloaded. That is, if such a delay is possible."

"Afraid it's not," answered Subs, not at all annoyed by the machine. Bots, like soldiers, followed the programming they were given. Once you understood that, they became a whole lot easier to coexist with.

"In that case, I shall do my best should any unfortunate incidents take place."

Subs nodded. "Thanks. I'll do my part, too."

The bot inclined its head with a mechanical whir. "Your part, sir?"

"I'll make sure the doros don't hit me." Subs walked past the bot, trusting it and Alistair to follow.

The bot's receptors studied Subs as he moved by. Finally it straightened. "Oh, yes. I see, sir. Yes. Please do avoid being hit."

* * *

The darkness of the jungle wasn't a problem for Subs. His helmet provided him night vision, and his audio sensors alerted him to potential threats thanks to an algorithm that had examined recordings of other legionnaires in ambushed in combat and had crunched the data to key in on telltale noises—or the lack thereof.

But Alistair didn't have anything like that. Nor did he have a starlight scope. All he had was a red-lensed headlamp just powerful enough for him to see what was directly in front of him.

Subs would have told him to put it out, but with the way the med bot's eyes were shining in the darkness, he didn't see what good it would do. Maybe that was why the marines and Legion preferred human medics and corpsmen to these machines. Useful as the bots were, in low-light conditions, they might be just as likely to *get* you shot as save you from dying.

But there was no turning back now, and they'd made respectable if not blazing time. They hadn't been forced to stop, though Subs could tell from his friend's breathing that he was nearly at the end of his wind. He slowed the pace, not particularly out of mercy, but because he didn't want the basic's exhalations to add yet another clue that they were out in the jungle.

"Oh, good," panted Alistair, who wasn't fat by any stretch. Just... not in shape. "Are we close?"

"No. Sorry."

The tech's head drooped.

At least the bot had been able to keep up. The engineers who'd designed the stabilizing exoskeleton around its legs deserved a pay raise. Nothing seemed to slow it down.

"Sir," the bot said, its voice modulating to a low volume befitting the mission. "I am noting a significant increase in heart rate from your assault team."

"Shut up, bot," Alistair said, hands on his knees.

"I thought you liked bots," said Subs. "Thought you said they were your best friends other than me."

"Yeah. But not this one."

Subs squatted down to look Alistair in the eyes. "Listen. I can't slow down any more after this. Lives are depending on it. Now, you gave it your all, and it wasn't enough. There's no shame in that. But you need to head back for Hitchcock and do what you can from there. Take the bot with you. You'll both be all right. There aren't any doros that I've detected."

Alistair shook his head. "No. I can keep up. I can go." He straightened himself, making a show of being ready to hit the trail again. But it was clearly an act.

"Sir," said the bot, "I believe I have a solution. I am more than capable of carrying your assault team on my stretcher until we arrive at destination. And unlike a biologic, I will not fatigue from the rapid pace."

Alistair looked at the machine and shook his head as if insisting he do it alone. But then he stopped. "You know what? Sure. I'm not too proud. The bot can carry me into battle. We'll get there faster that way."

Subs wondered how he'd gotten himself into all of this. *You're too soft. Like your gut.*

He had let his time on Firebase Hitchcock dull his body and his judgment. He could have shut this down before they'd ever left the wire, but he'd been led by a sense of compassion and a desire to keep his friend happy—to let him know what it was like to be a war fighter. Maybe even to let him see Subs in action, a real Dark Ops legionnaire.

Which meant it was his fault. Which meant he owed it to Alistair to keep him safe. Just like he owed it to the marines to get there in time to help them.

When the bot had secured Alistair, Subs bounded down the trail with the machine right on his heels.

They made good time.

17

Jungle Ruins
Near the Cuchin Valley
Psydon

The firefight raged on for over an hour, its intensity never slacking. Marines were interspersed along the temple parapets, sending fire into the large pack of doros attacking from the cover of wafting, leafy palms and spiked tree trunks. The doros' attacks were focused on the three big walls of the ruin; they were evidently unaware of the open stone steps leading inside.

Wash had Berlin guard the entryway. The major knew how to shoot a bottled-up pack of doros. Experience had shown that much.

It was difficult to say how many dog-men were out there. Wash guessed as many as fifty, judging by the amount of blaster fire that was scorching in from the jungle. The exact number didn't matter too much at the moment. What mattered was that the marines were clearly outgunned and were barely holding their own, even with the blaster-impervious stone cover they enjoyed.

The marines had other advantages. The darkness. Their starlight scopes. But Wash didn't know how much damage they were doing—or how long they could keep it up.

Occasionally the wounded yelp of a doro casualty rose above the din of fire. But it all felt tenuous. Wash was convinced that doro reinforcements and a strong doro push would result in the ruins being taken. Once the doros discovered the entrance, that was.

And that was Wash's big concern. It was a hard fight, but if there were enough dog-men out there—or if a larger element arrived, perhaps detached from the mobile artillery group they'd seen the day before... well, there would be no holding back such a wave.

Wash feared that he'd led the marines into a defensive rock that could easily double as a death trap—and a part of him sought to lament the decision he'd made. But Legion training told him to kill that part and move forward, recalculating to determine the best course of action for complete mission victory.

A doro blaster bolt struck the lip of the temple wall, sending up dusty stone fragments into the face of one of the marines. The man dropped below the parapet line, grabbing his face and swearing while a buddy called for Corpsman Hellix.

This man wasn't the first to be wounded in such a way, and attrition was taking its toll. The doros hadn't managed to get any direct blaster shots on the marines, but collateral incidents like this one had been happening all along the wall, requiring Hellix to scurry along below the cover line like a space rat, going from one marine to the next. He would bandage the small cuts on their faces and use some of their water supply—precious and dwindling—to flush out the rest in order to get the marines back on their feet.

To their credit, every marine stayed in the fight. There was no sitting this one out.

"Sergeant!" Wash yelled to Shotton, hoping the marine could hear him above the noise.

The sergeant ran low toward him. "Yes, sir?"

"Get a man down by Berlin. I'm worried about the doros finding our back door."

Shotton nodded and slapped a marine on the shoulder, sending him down to support Berlin.

Wash spotted a doro crouched in front of a fern pocked with globe-like flowers that seemed to glow in the night. He dropped the dog-man with a short burst. "Keep pouring it on!" he shouted to the marines. He wanted them to know that he was in the fight right next to them.

Another dog-man ran across the jungle terrain. The area he was leaving was heavy with flashing blaster fire, and he was making for an isolated but equally hostile area. Probably a messenger. Wash tracked the alien and brought him down with a full-auto squeeze. The doro lay still among the leaves, and Wash searched for his next target.

The incoming blaster fire intensified. Bolts sailed above the marines' heads or crashed into the stone walls harmlessly, scorching where they hit and sending up puffs of smoke that smelled chalky and stale. Wash was again impressed at how this temple was built. The marines' firing angles were superb, and the doros' were terrible. For the dog-men to get a shot on a man, they had to be lucky—

which, unfortunately, was sure to happen given enough time—or they'd have to possess the pinpoint accuracy of a rifle-qualified marksman. In the dark. Whether the doro possessed such shooters, Wash didn't know.

But he felt confident the doros could be held at bay for as long as blaster packs could be found.

Or until the doros broke contact and stormed the open stairs.

Something sailed through the air toward the temple. Wash tracked it, realizing with a pang of adrenaline that it was a grenade. But the trajectory was too low—it wouldn't make it over the wall. Doros didn't have particularly good arm strength, and would have to get a good deal closer to get a grenade inside the temple. And they'd be dead before they pulled back their arms if they tried it.

The grenade bounced off the wall about halfway up, dropped back down, and detonated, sending a spray of rich black soil and shredded vegetation into the air, where it hung like a filthy mist in the jungle humidity.

"I'll show you how it's done!" shouted a marine, who promptly pulled a grenade from his flak jacket and tossed it in perfect textbook form out into the jungle. Its explosion caused a volume of incoming blaster fire to wink out as the doros nearest where it landed scattered.

"All right, Marine!" shouted Sergeant Shotton.

It took Wash several seconds to realize that the grenade had caused more than a lull in the incoming fire; for the moment, it had stopped altogether. He sent word for cease-fire all along the parapets.

Panting, sweaty marines waited, their rifles resting on the tops of the parapets, still pressed firmly into their shoulders as they hunched down searching for targets through their sights. The men were covered with grime and dirt and sweat—they looked exhausted—but their professionalism never wavered. They stood there, victorious sentinels listening to the pathetic whimpers and whines of their vanquished foes. Their thoughts, Wash knew, were not on the doros' suffering—let 'em rot—but on the unsettling, almost frightening growls of the living doros who had retreated farther into the jungle.

"Headin' down," Wash said, moving down the stairs to get a first-hand look at what Berlin was seeing. If the doros were going to counterattack and attempt to storm the opening, they would likely do so following this reprieve. For this fight was far from over; quitting wasn't the doros' style. They'd shown a willingness to suffer heavy losses it if meant punching the Republic in the nose. There was no reason to think they'd back down against a small band of marines in the middle of their turf.

"What's the word?" Berlin asked over his shoulder as Wash bounded down the steps toward him.

"They broke off contact for the time being. What have you seen from here?"

"Whole lot of nothing." Berlin sounded annoyed, as though being denied the opportunity to get more doro kills was eating away at him. He was a legionnaire in that way at least, even though he was looking for those kills mostly to shore up his political aspirations, while the average legionnaires looked for kills because... KTF.

By contrast, the marine accompanying Berlin seemed relieved at the relative peace and quiet his new position had afforded him. But that wasn't going to last long.

Wash patted his friend on the shoulder. "Don't worry, buddy. They haven't left for good. Probably just finding a less suicidal angle of attack."

"Which means this entryway. So we can expect a charge, right?"

Wash was impressed with Berlin's tactical observation. Or maybe it was simple common sense. Either way, it was the truth.

"Yeah," Wash confirmed. "They'll throw everything they've got at us in order to get inside."

"Sket," mumbled the marine.

Wash studied the young man. He looked afraid, but not cowardly. No more fearful than they all were. Except for perhaps people like Denturo—who either really were afraid of nothing or had just mastered acting like they weren't—and Berlin... who maybe didn't know any better. The major was full of surprises.

"Hey, Marine," Wash said, unable to read the man's rank or name in the darkness. "I need your help with something."

"Sir?"

"I'm not up to speed about everything your team brought with you. Legion recon teams always carry anti-personnel mines and occasionally a mobile auto-defense turret. How 'bout the marines?"

"We have mines, yeah. I've got two in my ruck. And we usually hump at least one auto-turret..." The marine looked to Berlin and back to Wash. "But this wasn't set up exactly as a textbook operation, sir."

Wash nodded. Was that ever the truth?

He hitched his thumb toward the steps leading up to the parapet. "I want you to find Sergeant Shotton up there and tell him I need those mines and the turret if you've got it. I'll take your place here, but make it quick. We need to get set up before the doros find this back door."

The marine was gone in an instant.

Wash shouldered his rifle and peered down its sights, joining Berlin in the jungle vigil.

"This as bad as it seems or...?" asked Berlin.

"Yeah. Pretty bad."

"Well, this mission has been more than I expected almost from the get-go. But now we absolutely *have* to survive long enough to get out of here."

Wash nodded grimly. The mission had been everything Berlin had hoped for... and then some. After what they'd done so far, all Berlin needed to do was make it out and his political future would be a done deal.

Berlin continued as if reading Wash's mind. "You probably think I'm saying that because I want to win that seat in the House. But I'm not, Wash. If you can believe it, the House of Reason has barely been on my mind since we saw those artillery. All I can think about is what this mission could mean to the Republic."

Wash smiled. "You're just saying that to get a good quote out of me once you're running for office." Wash spread out his hands as if revealing the headline of a holonews article. "Fellow Legionnaire Says: Republic Was Only Thing D'lay Berlin Thought About on Psydon."

While Wash chuckled, Berlin looked on stoically. "I'm serious, Wash. I didn't know what—I mean, I had an idea something was out here, but I didn't know what we'd actually run into. I figured maybe we jump a doro patrol, wipe them out, and head home. I never actually thought we'd find that artillery."

Wash sniffed in the thick, humid air. He knew that, and part of him wanted to ask his friend what he was thinking to take the lives of these marines and throw them onto fate's game board. But what was done was done.

"Wash..." Berlin said. "I know I'm not the legionnaire you are. Hell, I'm not a *real* legionnaire at all. I'm self-aware enough to know that."

"No one thinks I'm a real legionnaire, either, buddy."

Berlin shook his head. "No. They do. The points all do. They know what you did at Academy and they hate your guts for it. Why do you think you're only a second lieutenant stuck doing jack-diddly in a broken-down office hab? That wasn't the Legion, that was the other points. The ones who got major like me."

"Well, I'll take it as a compliment to be hated by people like that. Badge of honor, really."

"My point is... you're a leej. You *know* how important finding those platforms is to the Republic. If we can get word of their location before they get away... if the Republic can take them out... Wash, this war will be over in a matter of weeks."

Wash sighed. Unfortunately, the biggest obstacle to getting the word out was being trapped in the ruin that Wash had led them into. "You're right. The problem is, we're trapped here, and help isn't coming—for us, anyway. The doros'll get reinforced, and although we'll kill heaps of them until our charge packs and supplies run out, eventually they'll wipe us."

A pause. The jungle hissed and thrived, providing no hint that the doros were on the move.

"Berlin, I've got us defending a death trap. We've got to take the opportunity to get out of it now that the dog-men broke contact."

Berlin rocked forward on his haunches. "So... we make a run for it down the steps?"

"No. I'm not saying that at all. I think that would get us killed. But I do have a plan."

"Spill it."

"It's going to require something of you, specifically. I know you didn't pay close attention, but you're going to need to behave like an honest-to-goodness Legion officer. And I know you're capable of that."

Berlin straightened. "Just tell me what to do."

"The doros think we're bottled up in here: only one way in or out. But I found a loose block that we can push out and exit from. I'm guessing when the doros return, they'll bring all their forces to bear here on the stairs. They won't be guarding the other sides of this place, not with any sort of strength, because they believe we have no means of escape that way."

"This sounds good."

"There's a snag, though. I need to make sure they continue to believe we're all still inside here even as we're escaping. If they think they're fighting all of us, and if the mines and turret—and I—can keep them back long enough, you'll hopefully get a large enough head start to make for the peak and send the all-hail."

"So... you stay here and shoot them while I play Legion hero and lead them all out?"

Wash nodded. "It'll be an amazing campaign story."

"The hell with my campaign, Wash." Berlin sounded hot. "Let's be realistic about this. Once we get out, we still have to make it across the valley to the peak. That's a short march, I know, but a hard one. These marines need you and Sergeant Shotton leading the way, not me."

Wash held out his hand helplessly. "I don't know any other option. I'm not going to order a marine to stay back and sacrifice his life. I got us into this..."

"No. I can't allow it. You know from the POW camp that I can light up any doros who come my way. I'll hold them back."

"Berlin, I can't let you—"

"You can't let me anything, I know. But I can *order* you. I'm still a major in the Legion, Lieutenant. And I'm ordering you to make it happen the way I said."

Sergeant Shotton came down the stairs behind them. "Make what happen, sir?"

Wash was too shocked by what his friend had said to answer the marine, but Berlin jumped right in.

"Sergeant, we're taking advantage of the doros breaking contact to get out of here. Our primary mission objective—at all costs—is getting the location of those artillery platforms to Legion command."

Shotton gave Berlin a look of newfound respect. And Wash could understand why. This was a side of Berlin that he'd seen before, although in other areas of life—social gatherings, athletics, academia. He *could* take charge. It was what would ultimately make him a powerful House of Reason delegate. And now he was using that innate talent to rise to something more than an appointed officer in the Legion.

"Sir," Shotton began, "I agree with everything you just said. But I don't know how we'll achieve that. It's not like we can all run down those steps and expect the doros not to chase us down. Or is that what you wanted the mine and auto-turret—we do have one—for?"

"That's exactly why I want them, yes. Have your men deploy them outside for maximum effectiveness. I want the auto-turret set up to pick off any doros who make it to the bottom steps. Something to keep them honest. Let them know that if they rush, they'll feel the heat."

Shotton signaled for three waiting marines to get to work. "And after that, sir?"

"After that, I'm ordering you and Lieutenant Washam to get out of here. The lieutenant says he's found another way out."

"Uh-huh," grunted Shotton. "And... what about you, Major?"

"I'll add a few more doro KIAs to my résumé while you're getting out. I'll attempt to follow if it looks like the worst is about to happen. And if I don't catch up... it was nice serving with you and your marines, Sergeant."

Shotton pushed his helmet to the back of his head and wiped his brow. A smile was on his face. "I don't believe it."

Wash didn't believe it either. Yet he found himself going along with it, at least for now. He still hoped to convince his friend to switch roles. But for right now... something was showing itself in Berlin that these marines—and he—needed to see. Something that gave him a new hope and compelled him to obey the major's orders. The magnetic will of someone who was determined to see that what needed doing would be done. It was that spark inside Berlin's family that had driven them to the heights of wealth, launched them into the social stratosphere of the Republic's core. A sheer force of will that made anything possible.

18

Corpsman Hellix stood just outside the triangle of parlaying leaders, seeming to wait for an opportune moment to impose on Wash, Berlin, and Sergeant Shotton's conversation.

"What is it, Corpsman?" Wash asked.

"Sir, I'm hoping to know if I can perform some more thorough treatments on the men. Are the doros gone for good?"

"I'll give you one guess," Shotton grumbled.

Hellix nodded. "Understood. They've been in sustained combat for hours and need a rest—for their mental health as much as physical. Some of them are also going to need more treatment than I can provide. Biggest problem could be that I'm out of disinfecting ointment. The jungle isn't going to be kind to all their cuts and scrapes."

"Do what you can," Shotton ordered, "but make sure everyone is prepared to move out at a moment's notice."

The marine sergeant faced Wash as his corpsman ran off. "So where's this other way out you mentioned?"

Wash pointed to the opposite end of the temple. "I saw a loose block when I was taking a tour earlier. I tested its strength. I think we can push it out and slip through the opening."

"Unless the wall comes tumbling down on us all."

"That won't happen. This ruin is still structurally sound."

Berlin interjected himself in the conversation. "You know, I was thinking... are we sure this is what we want to do?"

Wash had expected this. Eventually. His friend had been acting heroic—brave, even—but that was in the heat of the moment. Marching to your death is a much harder thing when you've had time to think about it. He didn't blame the man, and was ready to step back into the role he'd initially intended for himself.

"It's all I've got," Wash said. "And I don't exactly like it, but I'm willing to stay and hold the doros back."

Berlin rubbed where his chin would be through his helmet. "No, it's not that. I'm thinking... Sergeant Shotton, you still have the ordnance you brought, right?"

"Yeah... but not enough to take care of that artillery. Not by a long shot."

"No." Berlin shook his head. "Not that. I was thinking... Maybe instead of trying to keep the doro out of the temple as long as possible, we want them to get *in* the temple. As many as possible, and then..." Berlin made a show of exploding out his fingers. "Boom."

Wash nodded. Slow at first, but then picking up steam. This was actually a really good idea. One he should've thought of. "Yeah. If we can figure out a way to funnel enough of the doros in here and then initiate a remote detonation… that could cause a *lot* of damage."

Shotton let out a considering grunt. "Hmm. But how we gonna get them in here without taking casualties?"

Berlin shrugged. "Don't ask me. I'm saying that sounds a lot better than final suicide stand. What you say, Wash? If someone is gonna figure it out, it's gonna be you."

Wash looked around at the temple. The doros could regroup at any time. If this was going to be the plan, it needed to be done quickly. "I think we can do it. Sergeant Shotton, have some of your men plant the mines and get back inside the temple. And then… we need to set up some charges."

* * *

Every marine was stationed on the parapets, evenly dispersed and watching for the doros. And they were definitely still out there. Their odd yipping, growling language carried through the night like haunts in the jungle.

"Everybody be ready," Shotton urged his men. "No telling what direction these dog-men will come from."

No telling for certain, but Wash had a pretty good idea. The doros weren't fools—as far as Wash knew, there were no points in the doro insurgency—and they were unlikely to keep trying something over and over again with the hopes that, this time, it would work. If Wash's guess was right, they'd stage another attack on the temple's protected walls, much like the one before—but it would be a feint.

By now they should have spied the temple stairs, and they would try to exploit it. That would be their real focus.

In fact, Wash's plan depended on it. He wanted them to throw everything they had toward the open steps of the temple, taking heavy casualties in the process. And he would make them believe that they were dishing it out as badly as they were taking it.

A shot rang out from Parker's sniper rifle. A split second later another of the doros' odd buzzing projectiles sailed over the marines' heads.

"Here they come!" shouted Denturo.

The doros began to fire at the three protected sides of the temple, but the incoming fire seemed halfhearted—much less than what had been sent in earlier.

It was a feint. Just as Wash had anticipated.

"Make those doros pay!" Wash called out, his voice echoing across the stone parapet. "But be ready for the main assault at the steps."

The ground outside the steps exploded upward, causing Berlin to temporarily duck back inside.

"Here they come!" Berlin shouted, swinging his blaster back around and shooting hot, undisciplined fire into the jungle. "Pile up to defend the entrance!"

Wash was about to remind his friend to make his shots count, when the jungle erupted right where Berlin was shooting. Doro soldiers emerged from the verdant leaves firing their blasters from their hips. Several fell as Berlin's shots hit home. Soon the other marines stationed with Berlin joined the legionnaire major in cutting them down.

But the doros kept coming. It seemed that two more emerged from the jungle for each one who fell with a smoking blaster hole somewhere in its body.

"Light them up!" shouted Sergeant Shotton, and soon virtually all of the marines were concentrating their firepower on the advancing doros.

There were so many of the dog-men that Wash was afraid they would overrun the marines' position before the escape plan even had a chance to begin. The massive wave of doros advanced as far as the bottommost steps of the temple before the marines' fire became all too much for them. They broke and retreated back into the jungle, leaving the field littered with the corpses of their dead.

The marines gave a cheer at this bloody repulse.

Wash turned to the small marine contingent. "Did everyone remember to die who was supposed to?"

"Yeah," called a few marines.

The plan was for a few preselected marines to go down in the fight, feigning that they'd been hit. But the doros had come on so thick that Wash had feared they might not have to pretend.

"Did anyone die who *wasn't* supposed to? Speak up now if you did."

This was met with a morbid chuckle from a few of the men.

"Good. How are the other three sides?"

Denturo called down from atop the parapet. "They disappeared as soon as the main assault began. Haven't seen a sign of them since. Bunch of cowards."

Wash knew that behavior was driven more by doro psychology than by cowardice. The doros attacked in packs to overwhelm the opposition. But that tendency, that pack mentality, could at times be a tactical weakness. It meant the doros didn't perform as effectively in isolated groups, such as the ones required for coordinated assaults with lots of moving parts. So no, they weren't cowards; it was just that those doros who found themselves scattered or split up in the chaos of battle would instinctively scamper away in an attempt to find a larger force to join.

"Okay. I don't think were going to get another chance at this. That last wave almost overtook us. Everybody get in position and be ready to move out as soon as you hear us reopen fire."

The marines hurriedly followed orders. Wash, Sergeant Shotton, Denturo, and Parker moved to a rear parapet with a clear line of sight through the front opening and down the steps. From there, they would attempt to keep the doro charge at bay long enough for the others to retreat. Everyone else moved to the great, loose stone, lining up to begin their escape.

"Here they come again!" Denturo shouted.

"That didn't take long." Parker lined up the lead doro runner and dropped it with a single shot. The dog-man's head burst apart as if someone had stuck a det-brick in its mouth.

Wash could hear Berlin calling for the marines to "Go! Go! Go!" out of the hole in the back of the temple. A quick glance over his shoulder showed him that the doros had indeed abandoned all the other sides of the temple.

Tactically that was a colossal mistake—and worse, it had been predictable. The Legion's victories over the enemies of the Republic—regardless of what species they were—were driven in part by species research: getting to know the enemy and exploiting its weaknesses.

That was Legion 101.

The doro assault was more cautious this time. They were mindful of the full brunt of firepower that had broken their last charge. Yet Wash hoped enough marines had feigned injury to give the dog-men hope that this might be the time they would break through.

And so they would. The result just wasn't going to be quite what they'd hoped.

"Last man out!" shouted Berlin from below.

Wash was proud of his friend. He'd made sure that everyone else got safely outside before escaping himself.

Emboldened by the lower volume of fire coming from the temple, the doro charge intensified. More doros emerged from the jungle and ran toward the steps. But between the four who stayed behind and the auto-turret, they were still taking severe casualties.

One fleet-footed dog-man sprinted through the hail of blaster bolts, made it to the top step, and crossed the threshold into the temple courtyard. The stones shook from the explosion of the antipersonnel mine that blew him to pieces, painting the stone floor red with his blood.

"Time to go!" shouted Wash.

The four remaining soldiers ran swiftly down their defensive steps to the hole in the temple wall. Parker and Denturo went first, followed by Shotton and then Wash.

But as they raced down the temple stairs in the darkness, the sergeant missed a step, or maybe caught his foot on an uneven bit of broken stone. Either way, he flew face first down the stairs, taking a swan dive to the bottom.

"Sarge!" Wash shouted, holding out his hand impotently as the marine crashed hard onto the stone floor below.

With a groan, the sergeant rolled from his stomach onto his back.

"You all right, Sarge?" Parker asked. He was bouncing up and down on his feet, eager to get out of the ruin before what was coming next... came next. The auto-turret continued to fire, but the doros would swarm past it in seconds.

"No." Shotton was holding his knee. "These damn knees. I think I tore something."

Denturo said nothing beyond spitting onto the floor, yet it was clear he was as concerned as anyone for his sergeant.

"Let's pick him up," Wash said.

"Don't be stupid. You all can't take me along—I'll only slow you down. Just prop me up against that wall. I'll make sure the dog-men don't follow you out."

Wash moved to the hole and readied to put himself through it.

"You just gonna leave him like that?" protested Denturo. "Not even say goodbye?"

Wash slid through and called from the other side, "I'm not saying goodbye because we're not leaving him. Pick him up and slide him through."

Shotton began protesting even as Parker and Denturo lifted him up. "Don't get yourself killed on my account! My knee is worthless. I'm telling you I can't keep up."

The marines passed their sergeant through the opening, and Wash hoisted him over his shoulders in a fireman's carry.

Shotton chuckled. "You really think you can carry me all that way, Leej?"

Wash started running. "Legion's been carrying the marines for years. What's one more night?"

Shotton laughed. "You SOB, I'm going to remember you said that."

Wash and the marines ran to the predetermined rallying point. The path was free of any doros. They really had devoted every last dog-man to the one angle of attack. Explosions boomed behind Wash—the remaining mines. The turret could no longer be heard. The temple had been breached.

Wash looked back over his shoulder as he ran. The second he saw doros on the parapet, he shouted, "Now!"

The temple was engulfed in a thunderous fireball. The great walls toppled, with some of the stones flying nearly out as far as where the marines had taken shelter. The ziggurat at the center of the ruin swayed, but held. Not that it would do the doros any good.

"That got 'em!" Berlin shouted.

But as the dust began to settle, angry, vengeful barks could be heard rising above the whining howls of the wounded.

"It got 'em, but not enough of 'em. Everybody, let's move toward that valley!"

It was their only chance at salvation.

And they couldn't stop until they got there.

19

Subs cautiously emerged from the trees; the medical bot and Alistair remained hidden. They'd heard a thunderous boom while traversing the jungle earlier in the night—loud enough that those observing the listening bugs back at Firebase Hitchcock had to have heard it too. It was quite clear that Subs was now standing at the epicenter of the blast.

Massive blocks of stone lay strewn in every direction. They'd apparently been hurled from what had once been a four-walled structure, but which was now no more than a partially crumbling ziggurat. The stones had carved out large swaths of jungle as they skidded and rolled to a stop.

Oh, and there were pieces of dead doro everywhere.

Recon marines packed notoriously heavy when it came to ordnance. That was in large part due to their modified role as sappers—at least when they were battling with the Legion through the cities. While the Legion cleared the streets in the pursuit of hostiles, the marines came along to destroy weapons caches or bring small structures to the ground.

But why would they be carrying that much boom out here in the jungle? Maybe it was just standard marine procedure. Subs didn't know; he'd never been a marine.

As he walked over the bodies of dead doros, one of them flinched, dragging its mangled head across the green where it lay, leaving a streak of blood. Most of its skin was burnt or torn away. It whimpered, whether seeking sympathy or out of fear, Subs couldn't guess.

He raised his boot and brought it crashing down on the dog-man's throat. It crunched beneath his heel.

Even a dog-man deserved that much mercy. And anyway, Subs wasn't about to leave behind someone who'd seen him and could report on his location.

Once Subs was satisfied that the site was secure, if not clean, he returned to the waiting bot and Republic Army comm tech.

"There appear to be mass casualties at this location, sir," the med bot intoned. "Should I search for survivors and begin triage according to Republic Samaritan directives?"

"Sorry, bot. We don't have time for anything like that. Anyway, I don't think there are any left alive."

"Yes, you are very likely correct. However, my programming states that if there is no immediate need of medical help for those serving the Republic, my directive is to provide what medical aid I can to those fighting on the other side."

Subs looked around as the bot spoke, not ignoring it, but not diverting his attention from the surroundings. The sun had peeked over the horizon, and the jungle was growing in brightness with every passing minute. "The thing about that directive is this: What you're seeing here was caused by some resourceful marines... and a couple of legionnaires, I guess. And from looking at the way the foliage is displaced, I can tell that our soldiers left here in a hurry, and whatever dog-men they didn't blow to kingdom come were hot on the trail after them."

Alastair had already thrown up whatever was in his stomach upon first seeing the grisly aftermath of the explosion. The subsequent minutes had done little to bring color back to his face. "So what does that mean?" he asked.

"Odds are it means the doros caught up with them, and when we follow their trail, we'll find the marines slaughtered. But we also might find the doros... and if we do, we can pay them back."

Alistair frowned. "There's no chance that the marines are still alive?"

"There's always a chance."

Subs tracked the obvious path left by the marines and the doros. It was clear that both groups had been in a hurry; neither had made any effort to hide its presence. Leaves were bent, plants had broken stocks, and prints were everywhere.

There were far more doro tracks than marine. And that was *after* a considerable number of the dog-men had been shredded in the explosion at the temple.

Alistair held his rifle at the ready. His eyes were wide and unblinking. "Should we be ready to fight?"

"We were supposed to be ready to fight as soon as we stepped into the jungle. Psydon's a war zone, remember?" answered Subs.

The basic rolled his eyes. "Right, I get that, Dark Ops. But—i what I mean is: Is this it? Are we about to catch up to them and mix it up?"

As if in answer to this question, a distant snapping and shuffling of dry underbrush sounded in the distance, followed by the barking growls of doro conversation.

Subs motioned for Alistair and the bot to hide. The three of them slipped into a thorny, black-leaved swath of undergrowth, disappearing completely from view.

A band of doros emerged from the direction in which the tracks led. They moved casually, with rifles slung over their shoulders.

Subs's first thought was that this group had just returned from destroying the marines. But missing were any signs of battlefield plunder. The dog-men commonly took weapons, flak jackets, and accessories from the Republic's battlefield dead. But these were dressed up like vanilla doro insurgents, in a mishmash of khaki military fatigues and green pajama-like jumpers, and their weapons were old, Independent Arms–model blaster rifles popular with non-Republic militias.

So Subs adjusted his thinking. These doros likely had no idea what had occurred here, nor that they were traversing a trail used by Republic marines scant hours earlier.

Still... that didn't mean he could let them go.

He waited for the doros—they were seven of them—to pass him by, then noiselessly emerged from the undergrowth behind them, a grenade in hand. He stalked the pack's trailing member, creeping closer and closer until he could literally reach out and touch the dog-man.

He hung the live fragger onto the doro's belt loop.

Before the doro had the chance to bark out a warning or turn to see what had caught its pants, Subs shoved him forward. The doro stumbled, crashing into the rest of the group, while Subs dove for cover behind a tree.

The grenade exploded right in the midst of the pack.

Subs rolled back into view, a mist of smoke and blood still hanging in the air. All the insurgents were down.

Alistair came out from hiding with a look of awe on his face. "That was the most frightening and incredible thing I've ever seen."

Subs was already moving among the doros, using his knife to end the lives of those who—though not moving—were just barely hanging on. Wet mercy killings, but not worth the depletion of a charge pack. "Any leej can do that. It's the first thing they teach you at the Academy."

Alistair shook his head. "I've watched plenty of legionnaire combat holos. That's Dark Ops voodoo and you know it."

Subs cleaned his blade on the khaki uniform of the last doro. "Maybe. How's your stomach?"

Alistair looked to the side. "It's fine. Earlier... It was just the smell more than anything else."

Subs nodded, knowing the truth of that statement. He'd had his helmet on when they'd arrived at the temple, but he'd seen enough battlefields to know what the basic was talking about. "Jungle has a way of really making things stink, doesn't it?"

Alistair nodded grimly. The glamor of it all—experiencing the ruthlessness of combat with a legionnaire—it was starting to lose its sheen.

The medical bot strode into the midst of the dead doros. "I see that, once again, there are no beings for me to treat."

"Sorry about that," said Subs. "But I can almost guarantee we'll make use of you before we get back to the base."

The bot nodded. "I am not sure that what you guarantee is a thing I should hope comes to pass."

Subs sheathed his knife. "You and me both. You and me *both*."

20

Wash felt the effects of the hard marching keenly as they stepped past the jungle tree line into a vast, rock-strewn open stretch of land—Cuchin Valley. Poro-Poro Peak stood tall on the opposite side.

The marines filed along, weariness weighing heavily on them. You could see it in the hanging heads, the slumped shoulders, the listless eyes as they moved into the open field, each man panting, trapped in his own personal trial. Carry on... or die.

They'd lost the doros somewhere back in the jungle, but not before driving them back with a firefight that claimed the life of a marine whose name Wash couldn't remember. He felt shame at that. Felt like he *should* know the man's name, even if it had only been a day. Because it felt like they'd all been together much longer. A bond had been forged.

Sergeant Shotton was being carried by Denturo and Corpsman Hellix in a makeshift stretcher they'd lashed together after losing the dog-men. Wash had carried him the whole way prior to that, and his body was punishing him for it now.

The two marines halted next to Wash, allowing their sergeant to get a view of the open terrain, the ridges, and the valley.

"It's gonna be a hard climb down and then back up to the other side after all this," Shotton said, shoveling a slab of processed meat in gravy from a ration pouch into his mouth.

Though Wash hadn't called for it, the marines had dropped gear and were hydrating and refueling with water and rations. Perhaps their action was triggered by the crisp breeze sweeping down from the ridges; it felt like magic after so much time in the steaming jungle. A bit more marching would have let the patrol rest behind the cover of the boulder-studded ridge that rose up before falling away down into the valley, but Wash didn't have the heart to tell everyone to get up and head that way. They were exhausted. Running on fumes. And the rations these marines were downing—the last of what they had—wouldn't even make up for the calories they'd depleted just reaching this point.

Still, they *had* made it.

"It'll be tough," Wash agreed. "But we can't just stay here in the open. Ten minutes, then we need to get dug into that ridge. You and anyone else Corpsman Hellix says needs to stay behind will remain there, and I'll make the run with Berlin to the other side to see about getting the comm transmission out."

Shotton leaned back on his stretcher, closing his eyes against the cloudy skies overhead. "I hate being a liability like this. Shoulda had my knees fixed and let someone else take my place."

"I don't think we could have done any of this without you, Sergeant," Wash said, placing a hand on the man's shoulder.

"Bunch of queers," spat Denturo. But Wash could see that the big man agreed with the sentiment.

"Who's minding the store?" Shotton asked.

"Parker's still back there, watching for any doros who picked up the trail again."

"Let's hope we lost 'em for good," said Hellix. "The men are about at their limit."

"Speak for yourself," Denturo growled. "I could do this all kelhorned day. Hey! Which one of you's got my ruck?"

"I do," said a marine. "And you can have it back. Thing weighs a ton."

He dropped a massive pack at Denturo's feet.

Denturo glared at the man. "Careful with that. My girl's inside there."

The big marine's "girl" was a massive, rapid-fire portable blaster cannon capable of bringing down a shuttle if he got one in its sights. Wash had seen Denturo clean it obsessively when they weren't patrolling... or running away from doros. He carried it along with his service rifle, but so far hadn't used it in battle. The unwieldy thing required a heavy, non-standard charge pack, and Denturo hadn't yet deemed its use necessary.

But now he was apparently changing his mind. The big marine began to assemble the weapon as his compatriots rested and ate. He strapped the whole rig to his body, hoisting the heavy barrel onto his thigh.

"Way I see it," he said, "we're either gettin' rescued or the dog-men are gonna kill us. And I ain't dyin' today."

"Glad to hear it," Wash said. He looked around at the rest of the marines. "Everybody, I know it sucks, but we need to make for the ridge ahead. Once we're behind those rocks, we'll take a good, long break. But out here... we're sitting in the open."

A couple of marines moaned, but Sergeant Shotton was on them in an instant. "You heard the man and you know he's right. Get your asses off the ground unless you wanna take a *permanent* rest when the doros come and put a blaster bolt through those thick skulls of yours!"

Reluctantly, the patrol picked up their weapons and began to trudge across the clearing toward the ridge.

"You all look like a basic just stole your girlfriend!" chided Sergeant Shotton. "Pick it up, Marines!"

The men moved faster, but by no means fast.

The exception was Parker, who came sprinting from the jungle, holding his helmet to his head, his chin straps flapping in the wind. "Doro! Comin' this way! Right behind me!"

As if to verify the truth of the sniper's cry, an errant blaster shot sizzled overhead, and the marines dropped for cover.

Wash pointed at Berlin and Hellix. "You two! Carry Sergeant to the ridge. Now!"

The two men hoisted Shotton up and ran as fast as they could to the rocky haven that was the ridge.

Wash ordered the rest of the marines to stay down. There was no cover to speak of. He kicked himself for not making the team move to the ridge sooner.

The marines, lying prone, charged their rifles and kept them fixed on the tree line some fifty yards away. Parker swiftly joined their ranks, but Wash motioned for him to continue onward.

"Get up on those rocks and set up. We'll need some covering fire in order to reach you." Wash kicked the boots of the two marines nearest him. "Go with Parker and be ready to support us while we draw back."

The doros erupted from the jungle, blasters blazing. Energy bolts danced around Wash where he stood shouting instructions. It didn't dawn on him the courage he was showing under fire. He just... made sure things got done.

But the marines noticed. And it motivated them to fight through their fatigue. They hammered back, dropping the doros as they advanced.

An incoming shot sizzled so close to Wash's head that he felt the heat against his ear and heard the bolt cracking past him. He turned as if to watch the bolt fly by and saw one of the two marines running after Parker drop hard to the ground, shot in the back.

Corpsman Hellix reached the ridge and set Shotton down behind cover. As Berlin, Parker, and the other marine set up to return fire, Hellix turned and sprinted through a hail of blaster bolts to get back to the downed marine.

He reached the kid's side, knelt down, and rolled the man onto his side.

Wash returned his attention to the battle and added his own rifle to the mix. The doros were slowed, but they definitely weren't stopped.

Wash's hands were trembling from adrenaline. He dropped to a knee to stabilize. The intense flash of all the incoming fire dazzled his eyes.

There were too many doros and not enough cover for the marines. The dog-men could afford to expose themselves and take casualties; Wash didn't have the same luxury.

"Denturo! Is that gun set up? I need you to pour it onto them while the men pull back."

Denturo spat out a spent wad of stim. A strand of saliva thin as spider-silk drifted from his lip. "You can count on that."

The big marine jumped to his feet and added his blaster cannon to the mix. It sent furious sprays of fire into the advancing doro line, and for the moment, it completely halted the doros' progress. The dog-men either dropped for cover or retreated back into the trees. If Denturo could do this all day, the marines could simply hang out in the open until help arrived.

But the weapon's charge pack wouldn't last that long.

At Wash's shouted orders, the marines sprang to their feet and ran toward the safety of the ridge. Wash joined them, keenly listening to Denturo's merciless fusillade for any hints of it letting up.

It didn't. But the charge pack had to be close to depletion after so much KTF.

The marines were nearly to the ridge; in fact the fastest runners among them had already reached the safety of the protective boulders and rocky outcroppings.

"Let's get Denturo some covering fire!" shouted Wash.

The marines put everything they had over the head of the hulking marine, attempting to replicate the withering fire he'd been laying down long enough for Denturo to join them.

The big man's heavy blaster cannon ran dry just as the incoming barrage came in. Denturo shrugged off the heavy weapon's rig, let it hit the ground, and turned and ran as fast as he was capable, bending down on his way to pick up the discarded rifle of the marine Hellix had been unable to save on the way to the ridge.

With the suppressing fire reduced, the doros began to gather themselves, and sent shots chasing after Denturo. He ducked instinctively as blaster bolts streaked by him in both directions.

Wash took a quick count. They'd taken casualties, but eight marines were left alive, plus Shotton, who was immobile but still in the fight. The survivors covered for each other as they leapfrogged toward the ridgeline. Wash stood out in the open, some twenty meters away from the rest of the team, taking a count of the enemy.

The doros had been hit hard as well, but more than twenty of the dog-men were still in the field. The rest littered the open ground with their bodies.

Denturo finally streaked by Wash and reached the other marines. He was gasping for air, and even in the confusion, Wash thought it was a good thing the marine had spit out his wad of stim before he'd started firing. There was no way he could have made the run without swallowing it, and the last thing they needed was for one of their rifles to be out of the fight, puking his insides up.

"Get on up and find some cover!" Wash shouted.

The doros were advancing, and Wash, being out in the open, was a magnet for their blaster fire. Shots arced all around him, impacting at his feet and sending up plumes of scorched rock and debris.

"Get your ass up here behind some cover, you dumb leej!" screamed Denturo.

Wash turned about-face and dashed up the ridge, hopping over a flat stone slab and landing firmly between Berlin and Sergeant Shotton. Both men were blasting away at the doro with their rifles.

Looking farther up the ridge, Wash could see the surviving marines doing the same. Parker was relentlessly dropping a dog-man with each disciplined squeeze of his trigger. Denturo, still sucking wind, was practically frothing at the mouth as he sent charge pack after charge pack into the advancing aliens.

Shouldering his rifle to join in the fight, Wash saw that the doros had been reinforced from the jungle. Even though more of them had fallen, there were still perhaps twenty fighters.

Berlin suddenly dropped, his palm pressed against his helmet, his back against the cover of the boulder.

"Check him out!" demanded Sergeant Shotton.

Wash ducked down. "You all right, buddy?"

Berlin looked okay. There were no blaster scorches on his armor, nor any telltale blood seepage indicating that some shrapnel or other projectile had gotten through the armor's seams.

"Somebody's talking to me through my helmet," Berlin said. "He says he's with Dark Ops and that we need to stop shooting toward the tree line."

21

Subs first began to hear the L-comm chatter when he was within a kilometer of Cuchin Valley. It wasn't standard legionnaire transmissions; it sounded more like someone was panting and speaking without knowing his comm was on.

And that told Subs that the person wearing the helmet was someone who, technically, wasn't supposed to possess one.

It was a point.

Since it sounded like the point was in the middle of a firefight, and since Subs wasn't close enough to do anything about it, he waited to make contact until he could better assess the situation.

Now he, the med bot, and Alistair were on their stomachs trying to avoid the incoming marine blaster fire that ripped through the jungle. About eight doro were likewise hugging the dirt about ten yards ahead of them. Beyond the trees, another dozen or more were attempting to take a ridge where the marines were holed up.

Those marines had good position, but it wouldn't last long. Subs needed to link up with them—for his sake as much as their own. The sounds of the jungle had told him for some time now that he was traveling just ahead of another dog-man force—perhaps even a company-sized element—that had materialized out of nowhere. Like the jungle was hiding a big doro base in this sector that had escaped the Republic's notice. And when those doros arrived, Subs didn't want to still be lying here in the jungle.

"You heard me right," Subs answered the point over the L-comm. The doros ahead of him were oblivious to his presence, utterly blind to the fact that he was orchestrating their deaths. "I need you to stop firing so I can destroy a pack of doros you have pinned down. You and your marines can then focus on the doros making their way toward your position."

Subs listened as the point relayed the message to someone else. Maybe the marine sergeant. Or maybe to the guy Subs thought was in Nether Ops. Either way, it was clear that the point Subs was speaking to wasn't the one calling the shots.

"So, I'm supposed to ask for the authenticator challenge," said the point.

Subs ran his tongue along the inside of his bottom lip, trying to keep calm. Soldiers were trained a certain way, and you had to know how to deal with that training. Just like bots were programmed in certain ways and you just had to know how to deal with that programming. And points... they were essentially civilians who were unqualified to be in a war zone. Subs would have to deal with *that* reality.

It would do no good pointing out in frustration that he was communicating over L-comm, and that therefore his authentication signal would be popping up on the point's HUD.

"Six rendered truces waddle shellacked ruby nine."

Subs heard the point relay the passkey.

The point came back and said, "He says that was last week's passkey."

"It is, and I don't have this week's, and it's a long story why. I'm DO-13-RD, and if you want Dark Ops help, you need to do what I'm asking and quit the suppressing fire in the jungle. Otherwise, I'm gonna have no choice but to bug out."

Of course, Subs had no intention of leaving those marines. But he thought the threat might spur the point into doing what he needed to do.

"Okay," said the point. "Going to cease fire and focus on the doros trying to get at the ridge. They've taken cover behind the rocks below us and we can't get a clear shot at them anymore, but we'll make sure they don't get any closer."

Likely the doros were only waiting for their reinforcements to arrive and end the whole thing, Subs thought. He considered suggesting they toss down grenades, but the marines would have done so on their own initiative if they had any.

"Understood. I'll do what I can to clear them out once I take care of the dog-men behind the tree line."

Subs stood up even though the marine suppressing fire continued on, trusting it would cease as promised. He needed to leverage those critical extra moments to advance on the doros still hugging the dirt in front of him.

The incoming marine blaster fire abruptly stopped as Subs sprinted toward the doros. He reached them just as they were starting to push themselves up off the ground, evidently thinking that their pack brothers had finished the job out by the ridge.

Subs switched his blaster's selector to full auto and, without a word, opened up on the dog-men.

They dropped back to the ground they had been clutching moments before, mixing their blood and dying breaths with the jungle soil. The engagement lasted all of five seconds.

Subs motioned for Alistair and the bot to come forward. He preemptively told the machine, "No survivors. We need to move quickly now."

As the trio crept toward the tree line, Subs let the marines know they were coming. "The doros in the jungle are dead, and now three of us are about to come out into the open. Do not open fire on us. Copy?"

"Okay. Thank you. We won't shoot you." Then the point, still not knowing how to mute his L-comm, relayed the request to those around him. "Nobody shoot at the Dark Ops guys when they come out of the jungle!"

* * *

Wash peeked around the boulder he used as shared cover. The doros had managed to advance to a point where they were no longer in the open, though they'd paid a hefty price to get there. The dog-men and marines were now playing a game of cat-and-mouse, each side popping out long enough to try to find a target of opportunity and then slink back behind cover to avoid becoming a target themselves.

In short, what had been a hot and heavy blaster fight petered out into the sporadic report of a few errant bolts flying in either direction. It would be a great time to toss a grenade down on the doros, but Wash was totally out after the action at the temple, and evidently so were the marines.

Thankfully the doros seemed to be equally ill-equipped.

Berlin was communicating with someone over L-comm who professed to be a member of Dark Ops. Wash wondered how the ultra-elite and obscenely dangerous operators had managed to find them out here. Maybe someone had noticed that he wasn't answering resupply audits after all.

The speaker's passkey was stale, but Wash imagined that if this was a doro trick, the doros wouldn't have been throwing themselves into the meat grinder until *after* their deception had had a chance to succeed or fail. So he'd ordered the marines to halt what had been a steady stream of suppressive fire into the jungle. If this was in fact a doro trick, it would give them the opportunity to strengthen their numbers at the foot of the ridge. And if their numbers were sufficient to swarm up the ridge, Wash didn't think he or anyone else would survive.

And they *had* to survive. They were *so* close to where they needed to get. A swift descent down into the picturesque valley studded with immense gray rock formations brushed with leafy greens growing from ancient, weathered crags like bonsai plants. A run across the creek running down the middle of the valley—more of a canyon bottom in spite of what the maps said. And then on up the other side, which had a much more gradual incline. Then the climb up Poro-Poro itself.

Easy.

Even if it was a death trap should the doro artillery descend between the canyon walls.

Wash looked into the trees, watching for some evidence that he'd made the right call in telling the marines to cease their suppressive fire. He saw a sudden flashing in the darkness, deeper within the jungle, like localized lightning that temporarily revealed the rainforest's features in sudden contrast among the deep dark shadows.

"Well, something just happened," commented Sergeant Shotton.

Wash nodded, then forced himself to look down at the boulders where the doros were now holed up. They hadn't moved.

"Okay," Berlin said over his external comm. "He says he just wiped out all the doros we had pinned down in the jungle."

That was a good thing, if true. But the proof would be in what happened next.

"Now he says he's coming out and that we shouldn't shoot him."

Wash nodded. "Pass the word on," he said, meaning for Sergeant Shotton to do it, but Berlin shouted to the marines instead.

"Nobody shoot at the Dark Ops guys when they come out of the jungle!"

Wash strained his eyes to see who, if anyone, would emerge from the jungle. For a long while no one appeared, as though they were taking extra care not to bound out and draw friendly fire. And then, like ghosts rising from the grave, a lone, black-armored Dark Ops legionnaire appeared.

So it was true.

Dark Ops had come to save the day. They would take control of the situation, and finally all of this would be over.

Wash watched in rapt attention as a medical bot followed the legionnaire from out of the jungle. And following the machine was... a basic?

Wash shook his head. This was shaping up to be an unorthodox quick reaction force, to be sure. But then, two points and a recon marine team wasn't exactly textbook either. And in any case, the med bot made sense; it could certainly be put to good use—although Wash had always thought the Dark Ops kill teams relied on each other for emergency medical help. As for the basic... maybe he was a liaison for the Republic Army.

A small burst of blaster fire zinged down from one of the marines above. Keeping a peeking doro honest.

The Dark Ops legionnaire moved swiftly to within for-ty yards of the doros hiding at the base of the ridge. He dropped to one knee and held up his hand to let Wash know that he was about to take action. Then he casually took aim and sent a blaster bolt sailing into the back of the rearmost rock, presumably killing the doro that hid behind it. The next shot was just as smooth and effortless. So was the next, and the next.

Four times the Dark Ops leej squeezed his trigger, and if the rumored prowess of the operators were to believed—and Wash knew they were—that meant four dead doros. At least half the number of those pressing up against the ridge—though in the chaos, getting a sure count hadn't been possible.

It took that same number of shots for the doros to re-alize what was happening. Wash could hear them barking and growling frantically. One of them stuck its head out from behind a rock for a second too long—and had it re-moved, courtesy of Parker.

Then blaster fire began to fly from the bottom of the ridge toward the Dark Ops legionnaire.

The operator held his ground and carefully aimed his rifle even as doro shots sizzled past him. He sent back three return bolts coolly—almost casual in his unflinch-ing performance—and the blaster fire coming from the ridge ceased.

The legionnaire lowered his rifle to the ready posi-tion before motioning for the bot and basic to move with him forward.

"Holy sket," Berlin said. "He's saying over the comm that they're all dead now."

Wash looked out at the legionnaire, who gave him a casual salute, just a flick of his wrist, before jogging toward the ridge as the bot and basic scrambled to catch up to him. It dawned on Wash at that moment that all of this was the action of a single, lethal operator.

The Dark Ops leej, the bot, and the basic would be all the help that was coming.

22

"Hey! Where's Hellix?" called a marine to Wash's right. "I think my ear got shot off."

One side of the marine's face was streaked with sweat and blood. His ear was mangled, dark, and grisly, so much so that Wash couldn't tell whether the ear was gone or not. But it was certain that at least *part* of it was no longer there.

"Corpsman up!" shouted Sergeant Shotton.

There was no reply from among the ridge.

"Hellix!" shouted Denturo, looking odd without a wad of stim in his lip. "Hustle your ass down here!"

Still no answer.

"Parker!" Shotton yelled, his voice echoing across the rocks where the marines were wedged. "You see where Hellix was?"

"Yes, sir," a standing Parker replied. He shouldered his rifle and began skipping across rocks, hopping from overhang to overhang and making a beeline to where Hellix had taken cover. The speed of his movement was a testament to his agility—he was like some kind of suicidal mountain goat. And with each landing, the amplified sound of his boots and gear could be heard over the grim silence.

Finally, he called out. "Oh, sket! Hellix is hit bad."

It was with that announcement that the Dark Ops legionnaire and his team—if that's what it could be called—arrived.

Wash wasted no time with formalities. "We've got a man wounded up there. Can your bot get to him or do we need to bring him down?"

"I am capable of climbing," said the bot. "I will attend to the wounded now."

The bot took to the rocks easily. It was nowhere as agile as Parker, but it impressed Wash with the way it was able to keep its otherwise lithe frame stable as it moved ever upward.

"Gotta do me a favor, Lieutenant," Shotton said, grimacing down at his knee. "Go up there and be with Hellix. I can't with my leg, but he deserves that much."

Wash nodded and started upward. As he climbed the rocks, he heard the Dark Ops legionnaire speaking behind him. "I need to know who's in charge of this operation."

That was Berlin, and Wash would have to leave his friend to go over things—and take the heat—with the operator. There was a reckoning coming, and it was time both points faced it.

Wash scrambled up the ridge, arriving by Parker's side—and Hellix's—at just about the same time as the bot. Hellix was conscious and in pain. His hand was clamped down on what was clearly a gut shot. The powerful punch of the blaster bolt had ripped through his flak vest at its zippered seam.

Parker was squeezing Hellix's other hand, and from the somewhat uncomfortable expression on the sniper's face, Wash could tell that Hellix was squeezing back with all his strength.

Good, thought Wash. *That's good. His strength hasn't left him. He still has some fight.*

The medical bot crouched and made itself compact, seeming to fold in on itself in order to squeeze between the rocks to get close to Hellix. "Regretfully," the bot said, "I do not have your medical records and am unable to download them. However, I shall endeavor to do my best with my knowledge of human anatomy and physiology."

The bot tilted its head toward the gut shot. "I will need to have an unobstructed look at your wound, Corpsman Hellix. Kindly move your hand."

When Hellix didn't—either because he wasn't present enough to hear the request or because he was simply unwilling to take it away—Parker nodded at Wash, prodding him to do it.

Wash gently took the corpsman's hand in his own and moved it away. Hellix didn't fight him.

The wound was ghastly: a fist-sized hole right in Hellix's stomach, blistered around the edges from the heat of the blaster bolt. The impact had punched pieces of the flak jacket inside the corpsman. Everything looked raw and ugly.

Wash knew enough about combat injuries to know that what he was seeing was not good.

The medical bot's head tilted from one side to the other. Its optics focused and zoomed, making miniscule servo clicks and whines. It looked like a curious child examining a butterfly for the first time.

After studying the wound intensely and scanning Hellix from head to foot, the bot held out its thin, mechanical arm. A syringe popped out of a compartment on its wrist. The bot rolled up Hellix's sleeve, exposing the man's shoulder. "I have something for you, and then I will have to go and assess any others. A marine below has lost eighty percent of an ear."

The bot placed its hand on Hellix's arm and caressed it in a soothing motion. But Wash could see the needle lunge forward and inject its contents into the corpsman's body like venom from an insect's stinger.

The bot stood. "You are a brave marine, Corpsman Hellix. The Republic and any who know you should be proud."

And then it turned and headed down the rocks.

"Hey!" Parker shouted after the machine. "Don't walk away! He's hurt. He needs help. You gotta stay with him, man."

The medical bot turned its head as if it wanted to reply, but something in its programming was prohibiting it.

Hellix was still holding Parker's hand. "It's all right, Park." The corpsman's voice sounded melodic and dream-like. The bot must have injected him with some kind of pain-suppressing narcotic. "The bot just means that it's done what it can. I'm not making it off Psydon alive."

"What?" Parker sounded like he couldn't believe it. Not when Dark Ops had just arrived. Not when a Republic medical bot was here just when they needed it.

"It's okay," Hellix said, somewhat more feebly, but no less strong in his conviction. "I've made my peace. And I don't feel bad about it. Had to happen someday, right? I don't feel bad... I don't feel... *anything* right now except... *good.* I feel good."

Parker leaned down, not letting go of his friend's hand. "Don't get all defeatist on me, buddy. Hang in there."

Wash could see that some of the other marines were craning their necks, watching the bot as it descended, wondering what was going on.

"I..." began Wash. Then stopped. The simple utterance of words seemed somehow... sacrilegious. As if he had no right to be speaking out loud in such a pivotal moment in a man's life. His mind supplied him with an abundance of phrases to say. They were all memorable, worthy things... in isolation. Things he'd read others saying at times like this. In the history texts. In the holofilms.

You did all that could ever be asked.

Your sacrifice will never be forgotten.

You did good, kid. You did good.

Each of these sounded, phony, hollow, forced. Unworthy of the final moments of the corpsman's life. But Shotton had sent Wash up to be here, to see through the hard reality of men wounded because they followed orders.

Because they followed two points into the Psydon wilds.

Wash looked down at the dying man. "I'm sorry," he said.

The other marines began to climb up the ridge, aware of the fate that had befallen their friend. He was not the first of their number to be lost, but he was the man who had most devoted his time and energy to helping them. Patching their wounds. Caring for them. Trying to save them.

As the marines gathered, Wash felt out of place and began to make his way back down.

On the descent, he passed Denturo, who clapped him on the shoulder. "Sucks, man."

Wash nodded. It did suck. And yet somehow the marine pausing to take the time to commiserate with him made him feel a little better.

23

Subs couldn't believe what he was hearing from the point major. He'd expected some cock and bull story. Some kind of excuse for why the point had had to bend, if not break, the chain of Legion command and put not only his own life, but the lives of these marines in danger.

He didn't go into the conversation angry. He knew the point would pay the price for his decision. If anything, this might in the end be a good thing for the Legion, if not for the lives lost. The brass in Legion command would be well-supplied with the ammunition necessary to sink the House of Reason's appointment program once and for all.

But instead of scrambling to cover his rear, Major Berlin was open and candid. He talked about how he felt as though he had been missing the war, and how a future career in politics would be greatly benefited by him seeing action. And how that was something that the Legion—quite rightly, in Subs's opinion—would never allow to happen. So he used his rank to get a team of recon marines and a SLIC crew to move out dangerously deep into the jungle.

If nothing else, Subs admired the point's brutal honesty. Most of what he'd heard about this special class of officers was that they were feckless, conniving liars who would do anything to help themselves. Men who would throw you under the repulsor bus as soon as you look at you. But Berlin was making it clear that all the responsibility rested on his shoulders.

And then Berlin shared some news that utterly floored Subs. The team had somehow stumbled across an enemy outpost holding Republic prisoners of war.

They neutralized it—and while Subs *could* rebuke the point for his inability to save the POWs, given the circumstances described—details that were backed up by the marine sergeant—Subs wasn't sure even a legionnaire assault could have spared the POWs' lives. That was the sort of thing you sent in Dark Ops for.

The presence of Republic prisoners in that sector of jungle—one relatively close to Firebase Hitchcock but deemed by Republic strategists to be unoccupied—said something about the doros' ability to disappear into the terrain. The cunning dog-men were setting up where their enemy was not, a critical factor in waging a successful war. And yet they were also sending their forces each night in fierce attacks against Legion positions. Launching attacks from exactly where Republic intelligence said they were all concentrated.

The doros were cleverer than Subs had thought.

That fact made the major's next bombshell more believable. So despite how decidedly *un*believable it was on its surface, Subs had no doubt about its veracity.

"Mobile artillery platforms," said Berlin. "The prisoner we rescued—Tierney—she'd been taken back and forth between the camp and the mobile base for interrogations. So we followed the direction where she'd told us she'd last seen them. The things are massive. The guns themselves move on a base that sort of... well, I don't know what you'd call it. Not terraforming in the strictest sense, but they literally pick up the jungle, carry it over their frame, and set it back down behind them. It's like they have this sort of perfect..." Berlin snapped his fingers, searching for the right word.

"A constant camouflage," Sergeant Shotton supplied.

"Yeah. Like the platforms are always moling their way just below Psydon's surface, with only the guns sticking out right in the midst of the rest of the jungle. It's no wonder no one has seen them."

"Did you actually witness them firing?" asked Subs. That was the other thing that had been baffling the Republic. Even when operating, these artillery cannons left no visible trace, no telltale flash of hellfire.

"No. Never saw them fire in person. But we heard them after we'd marked the spot and left."

The man who'd gone up with the medical bot, the potential Nether Ops guy, came back down and interjected himself into the conversation. "I got a pretty good look at the guns."

"This is Lieutenant Washam," said Berlin. "But everybody calls him Wash."

Subs shook the man's hand, and suddenly remembered that Alistair was standing nearby, looking unsure what he should be doing. "I'm Sergeant Major Boyd, but call me Subs. It's less of a mouthful. My friend here is Specialist Alistair Loewns. He came with me from Firebase Hitchcock—the only one willing—just on the outside chance you didn't all get yourselves killed. So even though he's a basic, he's one who deserves your respect."

Alistair brightened at this introduction. He gave a fractional nod.

Wash nodded in return. "I'm grateful for you both. The bot came at the right time, too."

As the man shook Alistair's hand, Subs studied him. He had the bearings of a legionnaire. Rigid posture, standing tall. But there was also a sadness in his eyes that Subs didn't quite know what to make of. And if he was a legionnaire, he was ridiculously out of uniform.

"I'm going to cut right to the skinny here, Lieutenant Washam, because I need to know every card I'm dealing with. Are you in the Nether?"

Wash stared at him blankly. "I don't know what you mean."

"Nether Ops. If you're in, let's not play dumb. I'm a short hop to retirement and I don't need any more medals. I won't take credit for finding the artillery, Nether Ops can take all the credit. I don't care. But I do need to know."

"No," Wash said, shaking his head. "I don't know what you're talking about. What's Nether Ops?"

Subs examined the man for a beat. "So what are you, then? Because legionnaires have *armor*. That's sort of part of our shtick."

"He's Legion," insisted Berlin. "Appointed by Delegate Roman Horkoshino, same as me. But he's different. He actually passed the Academy on his own merits—just like all you other legionnaires do. He's a point... but he's a sharp one."

"Is that so?" said Subs, not believing it for an instant. He'd heard enough about points flaunting outright disorderly disobedience in the Academy and thereafter to know better.

"It's the truth, Sergeant Major," said Shotton. "I've served alongside enough legionnaires in my time—I'm not far from retirement myself—to know a leej when I see one. He thinks Legion, he walks Legion... hell, he was able to haul my butt all the way from the ruins to here on his back. And he fights like a caged devil, same as the rest of you bunch."

During all that praise, Wash looked down. Perhaps embarrassed, though humble was the word that came to Subs's mind. Humility wasn't always how a leej carried himself, but some of them did. And Subs always felt that the ones who went through their service showing humility... those were the best the Legion had.

Whether Wash was the real deal as his friends insisted, or if he had pulled the wool over their eyes the same way Major Berlin had the SLIC crew and recon marines, ultimately didn't matter. Subs was with them now, and if they had the approximate location of the doro artillery in their possession, it was crucial that word reached Legion command as quickly as possible.

"In the jungle, behind me," Subs said, "was a large force. They were slow-moving because of numbers, but I'm thinking now that they're a detachment from that mobile artillery platform you all saw."

Berlin looked over his shoulder, watching the tree line for their arrival.

"Which most likely means that the artillery division knows there's a Republic presence in the jungle who may have a bead on their location. And so they're gonna do two things: One, move that artillery as far from here as they can as quickly as they can. And two, send those doros to kill us to keep us from ever letting anyone else know about it."

Wash nodded. "Our plan was to cross the valley and do an all-hail from Poro-Poro Peak."

Subs looked at the round rock formation on the other side of the shallow valley. That was a good bet. Much as he'd tried, he'd been unable to reach anyone over L-comm except Berlin. There wasn't another legionnaire in range for a good distance. So unless they were able to maximize their comm range… they were stuck.

But that didn't mean the plan was an easy one.

"You go down in that valley, and you're gonna be visible to just about every doro around. A major topographical spot like that, you can bet the doro already have it zeroed in with their guns."

"Well, is there any alternative?" asked Wash. His tone wasn't challenging; he spoke as if genuinely seeking input on the best course of action.

"Potentially. Once Firebase Hitchcock gets its long-range comms back online, Captain Garcia there is supposed to scramble SLICs to come looking for us in this general direction. The comms may well be up by now, given the time. If we see the SLICs nearby, we can pop some flares and get them to pick us up."

"How long might that be?" Sergeant Shotton asked.

"No telling," said Alistair, speaking up for the first time. "The necessary parts were supposed to be in already, and I know the tech will get working on it right away. The rest of the base is probably geared up to rock and roll—but you know how supply schedules go."

"Do I ever," Wash said, a hint of a smile behind his lips.

"Whenever they arrive," Subs said, "hopefully the mobile platforms will still be close enough that a targeted carpet bombing of the jungle can catch up to them and take the artillery out."

Alistair looked doubtful. "I dunno if we want to pin our hopes on Hitchcock, Dark Ops. We traveled a pretty long way from the listening bugs to reach this place. If that's the first place they show up, they won't have much time to do a sweeping search before they have to refuel..."

His meaning was clear. There was no guarantee the SLICs would be coming to the rescue. Flares or no flares, Subs and the others were nowhere near where the SLICs would expect them to be.

Subs ground his teeth together. The kid was right. "Well, it's a tight spot, make no mistake. We can wait it out and hope the doros take a wrong turn and the SLICs find us here... or we can try to force the issue by crossing that valley."

Berlin, in a voice that caught Subs off guard due to its intensity and steadfastness, said, "Then we've got to move across the valley. I mean, even if we knew for sure the SLICs were coming, we still need to get ahold of the Republic as quickly as possible because those artillery platforms *have* to be destroyed. We're thinking about *our* lives, but taking those things out will easily save lives a thousand times more than our own."

What the point was saying was true. There was simply no argument against it, and Subs knew it. They would have to cross the valley. "Okay. Yeah. Let's do it."

Wash looked from Sergeant Shotton to Subs. "Do you think your bot can do anything for his knee? He can't run, and we aren't going to leave him here alone."

Shotton rolled his eyes and clenched his teeth. "Oba. Just leave me here, dammit."

Subs was about to explain that the bot could carry Shotton with ease, so long as no one else needed the stretcher, when a blaster bolt sizzled wide of the group, crashing into the rocks in a shower of sparks and stone.

"Doros!" shouted one of the marines above.

Everyone scattered for cover, hurling themselves behind rocks as the incoming fire intensified.

Subs swung around to see a horde of doros moving out from the tree line. They'd caught up.

It was too late.

24

The doros wasted no time pressing their assault on the ridge. The Republic soldiers were pinned behind rocks. The basic was practically curled up into a ball. Blaster fire zinked around them, impacting against the stone protection. Subs knew that if they didn't act quickly, this fight would be over before it started.

"Everybody get your rifles up and return fire! Return fire right now!"

The reality was that there were far too many doros for him and the marines to keep at bay indefinitely. The best they could do was to make them suffer for crossing the distance between the jungle and the ridge. And they could only do that much if they got up from behind their cover and actually started dusting them. Because every second that went by where they didn't contest the doros' advance shaved away minutes of continued survival.

"I said get those rifles up! Fire your weapons!"

To their credit, the two appointed legionnaires listened to Subs without hesitation. No sooner had he shouted the command than they both popped up, hugging the stones to keep as small a profile as possible, and sent effective blaster fire toward the advancing enemy.

The unarmored one, Wash, was much more accurate with his shooting, taking careful aim and generally scoring hits at center mass. The other was less disciplined, but he made up for that by carrying a high-cycle rifle that required him to do little more than squeeze the trigger and let the weapon put in the hard work. Subs had used one of those when he was in the regular Legion; it wasn't as lethal as a standard rifle, or as accurate, but it had very little recoil. The major was using this to his advantage, adjusting in real time when he missed the mark and walking his fire back, sweeping the blaster back and forth on the advancing dog-men until the barrel overheated and it flushed out a mandatory cooldown as it recycled its charge pack.

The few marines that remained were more of a mixed bag. Some of them were up and firing at Subs's command, but about half picked up the fight only when their crippled sergeant screamed for them to do so.

"Get your guns into this fight or else we're as good as dead! And don't let up! Don't stop! Quittin' is the same as dyin'!"

The sergeant's injury had done nothing to keep him out of the fight. The old hullbuster was lying down, scratching and fighting like a cornered wobanki, peering between two large stones and sending well-aimed fire into the doros.

The firing continued. Beyond the initial first moments, Subs was too busy dropping doros and changing charge packs to get a sense of what was happening around him.

There was so much noise, so much blaster fire in both directions, that for all he knew he might be the last man alive. And if that was the case... well, there wasn't much else he could do beyond what he was already doing.

"Changing packs!" shouted someone—Wash, Subs thought. The point knew to do that much. He was actually helping out in this fight, something Subs hadn't expected.

Wash then sprinted over to Subs as blaster bolts zoomed nearby. The point crashed hard against the rock Subs used for cover. The kid wasn't wearing any armor, and throwing his body into something so unforgiving surely didn't feel nice.

"Is there a problem, legionnaire?" Subs asked, not taking his eyes off the doros.

"Yeah, I count about a hundred of them," shot back the point.

Subs smiled at the comment. "Pretty sure there's still more comin'. They know that we know about the guns, and they're gonna do everything they can to dust us."

"I know," said Wash. "That's why we gotta switch things up."

"You got a SLIC on a string that can make a gun run that I don't know about?"

"No, but if we can get across the valley we can still do an all-hail on the comm and try to get help to our location."

Subs didn't see much of an alternative. He'd been trying to find someone—anyone—over L-comm, but he'd gotten absolutely nothing. No more legionnaires from Victory Company who just happened to be close enough for him to find while groping through the dark.

Three doros sprinted on all fours to the head of the charging force. Subs tracked each one and dropped them with a single blaster bolt each. He then seamlessly changed his charge pack and slammed home a new one using only one hand. "Okay. Who's the runner?"

"I think it needs to be me," Wash said. "I'm conditioned as good as any legionnaire, and I know how to use the L-comm."

"Yeah, but you don't have a bucket," Subs said, taking down two more doros.

"Major Berlin does, and I can take his."

Subs thought this over. He trusted himself to get to the peak of Poro-Poro more than he did anyone else. But taking his gun out of this fight could have serious consequences for the marines. "Okay. That sounds good. I'll keep in contact over L-comm. And if you don't make it, I'll be next up."

"Wish me luck." Wash gave a fractional nod and left Subs to continue holding off the doros.

"KTF!" Subs called after him.

He looked down at Alistair. The kid was still cowering behind the rock. Subs didn't blame him. But the game now was to stay alive long enough for help to arrive. And that really did mean having every rifle in the fight.

"Alistair, buddy, listen to me. I know you're scared right now." Subs shot out a doro throat. "But you need to use your weapon. They might kill you if you come out, but they'll for damn sure kill you if they take this rock. And trust me when I say that the way they'll do it will hurt a lot more."

This seemed to get through to the kid. He shook his head, took a deep breath, and sprang up firing his weapon.

"All right!" crowed Subs. "You're halfway to Dark Ops now, buddy!"

* * *

Wash moved from rock to rock, never slowing, but trying to make things as difficult as possible for the doros taking shots at him. At the same time, he had to be careful. A sprained ankle or wrenched knee would kill his plan before it had a chance to even get off the ground.

Kill his plan, and kill these marines. He had to get across that valley if they were going to survive.

He crashed behind the boulder from which Berlin was spraying blaster bolts.

"Where'd you go?" Berlin asked.

"To see the Dark Ops leej. We can't stay here, Berlin."

"Changing packs!" Berlin dropped down, removed his charge pack, and replaced it with a fresh one from his chest rig. He'd picked up the habit of calling out ammunition changes during the fight at the temple. It was something he should have learned in the Academy, but it was good to see he'd learned it now. "Well," he said, "I don't know what to say. I don't see anywhere else we can go except up, and they'll pick us off for sure if we start climbing."

"We need to get across that valley and up on the other side. We gotta call in the Republic for help."

Berlin looked at his friend, his face unreadable behind his bucket. "Well, if we're gonna do it with all these doros coming, we better do it now. If they get any closer, they'll for sure shoot anyone who tries to cross that valley."

He popped up above the rocks and began firing again.

Wash almost wondered what *he* was doing for the fight, seeing how dedicated his friend was. He felt like a spectator in comparison. "I'm going right now, Berlin. And I need your bucket. The L-comm has a much better chance of reaching the Repub than anything else we've got."

"Why can't Dark Ops go?" Berlin asked, looking back at Wash for a split second as he continued to fire into the doros.

"You haven't seen how much damage he's doing. Every single shot kills at least one doro. We need him defending the ridge… not everyone can make this trip."

Berlin dropped back down. "Okay. Then we both go."

Wash shook his head. "Berlin, this isn't gonna be easy. I gotta get down, run across, climb back up, and then scale Poro-Poro just to have a shot at making the call."

"I didn't ask if it was easy, and I'm not gonna let you go it alone. I got us all into this, so I'm taking the trip. Besides, if anything happens to you, it'll be better for you to have someone else there."

"You think you can carry me if I get hit?"

"Not carry you, Wash. I mean keep going. If one of us gets hit, the other has to take the L-comm and keep going."

Wash considered whether to argue the point further. He could see that Berlin had that same stubbornly determined quality in his voice that he'd known since forever. And there wasn't time for this. While the doros weren't right on top of them yet, they were advancing, splitting up into smaller packs supported by heavy fire from the jungle tree line. How much longer would the joint Republic force on this ridge be able to hold them back?

"Okay. Dark Ops knows I'm going, so you better tell him over L-comm that you're coming along."

"He already knows. He's been listening in. He says it's a better idea if we go together." Berlin gave Wash his politician's smile.

Wash shook his head. The man was incorrigible. "On three, and then we run for the edge over there and start the climb down."

Berlin nodded.

Wash counted down to their departure. "One... two... three!"

He leapt from the rock and began running for the drop-off into the canyon. Berlin's footsteps crunched behind him.

The doros caught sight of them and sent blaster fire their way. Several bolts sizzled just a few feet in front of Wash, the dog-man shooters leading the target too much. But they soon adjusted, and the bolts were closer to his feet, kicking up rocks and dirt, causing him to squint, his eyes watering from the dust clouds.

When Wash reached the edge, he was greeted with a momentary bout of vertigo. The valley seemed to spin down below. But the climb would be short. After a sheer, vertical descent, the canyon wall let out to a still-steep, but manageable grade. This first part would be a stand-up climb, but after that they could descend using a crab-walk. They'd tumble head over heels if they tried running down.

"You with me?" Wash shouted.

The major practically ran right off the edge, using his momentum to take his legs over the side as he turned and fell onto his stomach. He scrambled for a panicked hand-hold, and finding one at the last second, began to climb down as if descending a ladder, picking out the ample toe and handholds studded in the canyon wall. "To the end, Wash!"

25

The two men moved from rocky handholds to sturdy hanging vines and rock-cliff trees growing from cracks in the canyon's façade.

Wash looked up into his left and saw a dog-man close to the jungle tree line pointing them out. Another was communicating with an old handheld comm device, while two more aimed blaster rifles in their direction.

All Wash could do was hope that they were lousy shots.

The doros opened up, and blaster bolts sizzled around them, some zipping past and striking the valley below, others crashing into the cliffside as they climbed down.

Wash and Berlin picked up their pace. Hopefully the increase in speed wouldn't lead to one of them missing a handhold and tumbling into the valley.

"I asked Dark Ops," Berlin grunted, "to shoot those guys!"

"Good!" shouted back Wash as a bolt struck the rock just meters from him.

They climbed another few feet down, and Berlin gave an update. "Never mind. He says he can't see them from the ridge."

"Not good!"

More blaster fire chewed up the sheer cliffside around the two legionnaires. But they were closer to the change in gradient now. It was perhaps another five meters of sheer climbing and then they could begin moving more quickly down the slope.

The blaster fire intensified. Shards of rock and dirt fell down on them like a hailstorm. Wash felt fragments of stone dust his neck and slide down his shirt. He chanced a quick glance up, only to see that more doro shooters had gathered, crowding around each other to take aim at him and Berlin. If they had the leisure to do that… there must be quite a press against the marines.

Wash was about to ask Berlin to check on Subs when he felt something sharp nick the top of his ear. A trickle of warmth began to roll down his face.

"You're bleeding, buddy," Berlin said. He was protected from such injuries by his helmet and armor.

Wash had figured as much, but it didn't much matter. He couldn't exactly stop and dress the wound at this precarious moment.

A blaster bolt struck one of the trees jutting from a crevasse in the wall, sending a shower of needle-like splinters at them. Again, Berlin's armor shrugged it off, but Wash felt the tiny pricks all over his head.

Berlin shouted at the doros, "Can't you just stop shooting for one second?"

Wash almost smiled. Shouting at the dog-men was about all they could do right now.

But the blaster fire picked up even more. These doros were intent on taking them down.

In a dusty part of Wash's consciousness, he wondered why they were so set and determined to kill him and Berlin, just two soldiers out of the many still defending the ridge. A dark part of his mind told him it was because they'd already killed everyone up top. But a more rational part of his mind reminded him it was because they knew what Wash and Berlin might be able to do if they reached the other side of the valley.

It hadn't been an overstatement when Berlin said the war would be over with the destruction of those artillery. And the doros knew it.

The blaster fire only grew hotter. Wash didn't take the time to look, but he had no doubt more dog-men had added their guns to the fight. He felt there was no choice left but to drop the remaining three meters or so and hope that he didn't break a leg. "Gotta get down the fast way!"

Berlin said nothing in return. He simply swung himself around so as to face away from the wall... and jumped. His arms flailed as he dropped, like a bird without feathers trying to slow his fall.

Wash followed him in almost exactly the same manner.

He saw Berlin hit the ground ahead of him and bounce forward into a somersault, then Wash hit the ground himself. Hard.

All the air seemed to leave his body, and then he was rolling and bouncing down the loose shale grade.

The jarring tumble barely allowed him to take a breath. Everything was happening faster than he could process. He couldn't breathe, he could barely string a thought together, and the only one that came to mind was a favorite Legion curse. His ears were filled with the punishing crash of the rock coming up to meet his body again and again, and his own grunts and groans in response. The horizon spun at a dizzying, terrifying speed. He finally had to squeeze his eyes shut.

The path he was slide-tumbling down was not without stray trees, logs, and spires. His eyes still closed, Wash hoped that none of them got in the way of his roll. If he found the sharp end of a broken branch, that would be the end of him. Even Berlin in his armor was at risk of not making it to the bottom alive.

It seemed to Wash that he bounced and fell for an eternity. His mind escaped the broken loop of repeated swears to wonder if the doros were still shooting at them. He vaguely thought they might be, and knew that when he finally stopped—*if* he ever stopped—he would need to scramble to his feet and start running immediately so as not to be an easy, stationary target.

His hip crashed hard against a rock. The impact made his knees slam together and left his groin feeling as though it were pulled. He bounced high in the air from the impact, almost as though he'd gone off a ramp. He did a half rotation in the air and landed flat on his stomach. He continued to slide, like a deer on ice, with his belly to the ground... but at least there was no more tumbling.

He could feel the rocks biting at his flak jacket and cutting up his arms. His gloved fingers felt numb from trying to grab enough ground to slow himself.

When he finally came to a stop, it took him several nauseating moments to realize it. His head still spun from all the cartwheeling and somersaulting. It was the sudden relative silence that told him he was stationary.

When he opened his eyes, the world still reeled, but he knew he was at the bottom.

Wash spat and saw blood. His mouth felt caked with dirt and grime. He had more little nicks and cuts on his arms than he could count, and his gloves were frayed and torn from where he'd tried in vain to grab the earth and slow his fall.

Berlin came toward him through blurry eyes.

Blaster bolts danced at the bottom of the valley. The doros were indeed shooting at them from the cliff above. But all were very wide of the mark.

Wash ached all over, but nothing felt broken. Or perhaps everything felt broken. But nothing felt *more* broken than anything else.

"Come on!" shouted Berlin, evidently no worse for wear. Say this much for Legion armor: it makes tumbling down a hillside more tolerable than it ought to be. Wash *really* should have brought his armor. "The doros are climbing down after us. We gotta get out of here!"

Wash understood, vaguely, that Berlin wanted him to get moving. He nodded, feeling unable to muster enough breath to give a verbal reply. He wasn't sure his tongue would even form speech. He felt so… wrecked.

Berlin pulled him up at the armpit, getting him to a knee, then to a woozy stand. Berlin was supposed to just keep going if something like this happened. Instead he stayed, helping Wash take a first, tenuous step.

So far, so good.

Everything felt intact.

Another step.

He could walk. It hurt like the nine hells, but he could walk.

The walk turned into a jog, and then as much of a run as he was capable of coaxing out of his battered and bruised body. Berlin kept prompting him along. Berlin was in the lead—the first time the appointed major had out-paced Wash in the entire operation.

The two men ran across the valley, approaching the creek that snaked through its center. Wash didn't know how deep the thing was, and with the doros still firing at them, it didn't matter. They splashed through, the water rising to waist-level at its highest point.

As they scrambled to the other side, Wash looked back at the cliff face. The doros were following, but they weren't throwing themselves down the slope; they were climbing down slowly. That crazy tumble had been less than ideal, but it had given them a huge head start.

Wash allowed himself to feel a moment of hope. They were going to make it up and out of the valley.

They were actually going to make it.

But then came the whistling sound. At first Wash thought it was simply the ringing in his ears hitting a different key. The deafening explosion that followed, no more than a hundred meters behind them, told him otherwise.

His hope had been premature. The doros were so intent on keeping their location a secret that they had instructed their artillery—artillery that had been focused for weeks on battering Legion firebases and hilltop defenses—to kill two lone legionnaires running through a once-serene valley.

Neither legionnaire needed to tell the other to pick up the pace, and soon Berlin was creating an ever-widening gap between himself and Wash. When he looked over his shoulder and began to slow, Wash shouted at him.

"Keep moving! Don't wait for me!"

Artillery continued to fall, and it was gradually getting closer. Some doro spotter on the ridge must have been providing real-time corrections.

"Hurry up, Wash!" Berlin had come to a stop some twenty meters ahead. "I'm not goin' up without you, so get going!"

And then the lights went full bright as Wash was thrown hard against the ground. The last thing he saw before things went dark was a great object streaking directly in front of him, landing between him and Berlin, completely engulfing his friend in its blast.

26

Wash rolled onto his back and sucked in lungfuls of air with a loud, raspy gasp. He sounded like Tierney had when she'd awoken from the dead in the POW camp.

Surely he wasn't still alive.

And if he was, he wouldn't be for long.

Slowly, his head groggy and ears ringing, his nose bleeding, he began to feel his own body as though he'd just discovered the sense of touch. His face was wet with blood. His arms and legs seemed unbroken. He couldn't hear anything distinctly. Not even his own breathing.

Wash propped himself up onto an elbow, coughing like a H8 addict, expecting his body to fail him at any moment. But it persevered. It went on as it always had, and Wash—gasping, coughing, feeling as though he'd died—rose to his feet.

He stumbled several steps to his right and fell down. But that was only because of how everything spun inside his head. His body was working, but an equilibrium couldn't be found.

On his hands and knees, his nose dripping blood, he closed his eyes and took several breaths. He waited until the spinning subsided. Then with an effort, he rose again and began to stagger toward where he'd last seen Berlin.

There was a small crater where the artillery hit. Wash staggered around its rim like a drunken man, peering down, searching for his friend. Looking for Berlin in a freshly dug grave.

But Berlin was nowhere to be seen. And Wash wondered if the man—his friend since youth—had simply been vaporized.

It was worse than that.

Another fifteen meters or so ahead, Wash found Berlin lying on his back, covered in dirt and debris. He was alive. Holding up a wavering arm as though he were waiting for someone to give him a boost off the ground.

The sight of this energized Wash, and he ran to Berlin, his knee threatening to give out with every few strides. The artillery had stopped—or at least Wash didn't hear or feel its concussive blasts. He looked back and saw that the doros were now making the transition from the sheer cliff to the steep decline into the valley.

Wash reached Berlin, who was waiting for him.

"Wash," coughed Berlin. His voice sounded dirty and mechanical through his helmet's speaker. "Help me, Wash. I can't stand up. Help me stand up."

Wash reached down, wanting to do nothing more than what his friend pleaded for. But as he pulled on the outstretched hand, he realized that Berlin wasn't partially buried in the upturned soil as he'd thought, but rather that Berlin had no legs on which *to* stand.

There below the pelvis, which Wash could now see plainly, shattered and sloppy, mixing with the dirt on the ground... was nothing.

"Help me up, Wash," an oblivious Berlin begged again.

Wash's eyes were wide with horror. "Buddy... Berlin... your legs... I don't think you can stand up."

"Why?" There was a note of panic in Berlin's voice.

"I... I think they're broken."

Wash didn't exactly know why he lied to his friend. It wasn't to calm him, he knew that much. It was more like he didn't think telling the man what really happened was morally right. As though speaking the ugly reality was giving assent to something that wasn't supposed to happen. At least, not to Berlin.

This kind of... damage... it was for the doros. Or for the unnamed souls who required all those coffins and body bags Wash had continually audited the resupply of back in his sweltering, hellish office hab.

This wasn't supposed to be happening. *Couldn't* be happening.

But it was.

And the doros were still coming.

Like your life depends on it. The voice of Wash's drill instructor lit a fire in the back of his mind. His life *did* depend on what happened in the next few moments. His life, and the lives of all those marines still fighting to keep the doros at bay. And Berlin's life...

Wash couldn't leave his friend. Not like this. Not to be slain by a pack of ravaging dog-men.

"My legs are broken?" Berlin said. "Oh." He sounded as though that made all the sense in the galaxy. He couldn't stand up because his legs were broken. And that was okay. Because whoever died of a broken leg?

"Yeah, that's it," said Wash. "So I gotta get you out of here."

"You're too beat up to carry me, Wash," mumbled Berlin. He sounded like he was under heavy sedatives, or like his mind wasn't all there. Like the shock of what had happened had fractured his psyche.

Wash didn't argue. He grabbed his friend by the webbing on his armor and hoisted him onto his shoulders, hoping it wouldn't cause Berlin any additional pain.

Berlin didn't even seem to realize it was happening.

Staggering, Wash started to run toward the edge of the valley. Already he could feel the incline, but it was far less steep than the side they'd come down. Wash's legs burned as he made his own switchbacks, zigzagging his way up, taking both himself and Berlin closer to the top.

It actually wasn't as bad as he thought it might be, carrying Berlin on his back. The weight of the legionnaire was less than he expected.

That's because his legs are gone. And he's bleeding out. He'll be dead soon.

A lump formed in Wash's throat, and he felt as if he would cry at the terribleness of that reality.

He used the emotion to climb up with gusto, but he felt himself losing steam. The time in the jungle, the fall, seeing his friend maimed… it was all too much.

"Come on," he urged himself. "Come on, Wash."

"You can do it, buddy." Berlin's voice sounded thin and weak. "You can do anything you put yourself to. You always could, Wash."

Wash took another step. His legs felt no more energized for the encouragement. But he knew he couldn't stop. He talked himself along. "Come on, Wash. Come on."

Berlin continued in his dreamlike cheering. "You'll do it, Wash. You can do whatever you want to do. You always could. Not me. I could do the things that I was good at, but those were the only things. But you… you can always do everything."

Wash felt the sting of tears in his eyes as he carried Berlin up closer and closer to the top of the ridge. His friend was dying, and Wash had neither the energy nor the heart to say goodbye.

When at last he reached the top of the slope, Wash gently cradled Berlin's head as he laid him down. This was where they would have to part. Poro-Poro was still a long climb, and it wouldn't be possible for Wash to drag Berlin up to the peak. No matter what his friend had said, that was something Wash could *not* do.

There wasn't enough strength left in him.

"I can hear things," Berlin said. Wash could hear him breathing shallowly. "I hear voices."

Wash's nose was still bleeding and his eyes were watering. His face felt hot and red and flowing everywhere.

"It's okay, buddy," he said, unable to control the emotion in his voice.

"Republic voices. I hear them. I can't hear Subs, but I can hear... Legion things." Berlin coughed violently.

"Legion things?" asked Wash. "What do you mean?"

"I don't know... Legion people talking about... stuff."

Wash wiped his bleary eyes with his ripped and filthy gloves. Could it be that scaling the peak wasn't necessary? Could they reach the Republic from here, through the L-comm? He desperately wanted that to be so.

"Berlin, I need to take off your helmet."

Berlin shook his head slowly. "Wash, you said you didn't want one. Remember? I was going to get you one, but you didn't want one..."

"I remember. It was my mistake. I should've let you." Wash's voice bubbled with emotion. He began to pull the helmet up, not needing his delirious friend's permission, but trying to convince him all the same. "But I didn't, and now I need to use yours. Come on, buddy, just for a little bit."

"You... can... use it," Berlin managed, his breathing even more labored than before.

Gently, Wash pulled the helmet fully from his friend's head.

Berlin squinted and fluttered his eyes at the radiant daylight. He stared up into the sky. His face was pale to the point that there didn't seem to be any blood left behind his skin at all. His hair was matted down with a cold sweat.

Wash could hardly bear to look at his friend. He held the bucket above his own head and looked down at Berlin. "Just for a minute. Okay?"

Berlin gave a fractional nod that transformed into a cough.

Wash put the helmet over his head. This one wasn't fitted for him; it felt a bit tight. And the external visor was off, so that he lost some peripheral vision and wasn't able to see down as well as he should. Not without moving his whole head. It was amazing the number of idiots in the galaxy who assumed a fully enclosed helmet would be a one-size-fits-all ordeal. That wasn't even true of ball caps.

But even though the fit wasn't optimized for combat— and in fact keeping it on might get him killed—the comm was right where it was supposed to be. Wash activated it and began an all-channel transmission over the L-comm.

"This is LS-12-OC. I'm part of a detachment of legionnaires and marines organized by Major D'lay Berlin to locate the doro artillery platforms. We have found those platforms and require immediate fire support."

There was a pause.

And then…

"We hear you, LS-12-OC. We've been looking for you this morning."

Wash let out a sigh of relief.

A new comm channel opened up, picking up with it the background noise of a SLIC in flight. "This is Captain Uwler. SLIC attack force Gray Ghost. We're patrolling near Firebase Hitchcock and having zero luck getting visuals. Advise your location so we can find you."

Wash wanted to cry tears of joy. He had never imagined what would happen if the all-hail worked, but he couldn't have dreamed it would go so well. "We're near the Cuchin Valley across from Poro-Poro Peak. We're taking heavy fire from a considerable doro force detached from the dog-men's mobile artillery platforms."

"Copy. We were at the wrong end of the valley. We're now inbound. See you in a few minutes."

"Thank God," Wash said, not caring whether his comm was still live or not. He keyed the L-comm to Subs's direct channel. "Subs! Did you hear that?"

There was no reply.

"Please don't be dead," Wash mumbled into the ether, this time sure to mute his comm before uttering the words. "Subs? Do you copy?"

Still no reply.

Maybe his bucket had gone offline. Maybe it was some sort of transmission trick caused by the gap of the valley.

Wash tried not to think about the more likely explanation as he keyed the comm for Legion command, using the access code he'd been provided—to the chagrin of his superiors—as a point in case he ever needed to "bypass" traditional comm lines.

"This is Lieutenant Washam, LS—"

"We're already listening to you, Lieutenant," a gruff-sounding legionnaire responded. "I need hard confirmation. You are near the mobile artillery, is that correct?"

"Yes, that's correct. From Poro-Poro, it's approximately in a five- to ten-kilometer radius after crossing the Cuchin Valley."

"Intelligence has those guns placed nowhere in that vicinity. You're sure?"

"Yes, sir. I'm sure of it." Wash had no idea why he called the person on the other end of the comm "sir." Something about the tone of his voice, he supposed. "And sir, in addition, we need help, bad. We've got wounded marines and legionnaires, with Dark Ops and Republic army in support. I'm not sure how much longer we can hold on."

A new voice came on the comm. This one no less commanding than the one before. "You said you have a Dark Ops operative with you? What's his name?"

"I didn't catch his name and rank, but he told me to call him Subs."

There was a long pause, during which Wash's intuition told him that lots of people were listening in on this comm transmission. People in the Legion who mattered.

"You tell Subs... his kill team is coming for him."

Wash had no way to do so. Subs hadn't responded to his direct L-comm transmission. But he answered, "Yes, sir."

Because... what else could he say?

"Sir, I have to go offline. The doros are pursuing."

Wash moved to the edge of the cliff to look down at the valley. The doros were already climbing up this side.

He looked around for his rifle. It was nowhere to be found. Neither was Berlin's. He didn't even remember when he'd lost it. In the artillery blast? Or maybe in the fall down into the valley. It was all a blur.

He wondered if he had a concussion.

They needed to get out of here.

He ran back to Berlin. "Hey, buddy! We gotta keep moving, all right? Let me pick you back up."

There was no answer.

Wash still had the helmet on, and couldn't see his friend very well due to the misalignment, though he knew the man was right at his feet. He pulled the bucket off to get a real look.

Berlin wasn't moving.

27

Wash dropped the helmet at his side. He knelt down, picked up his friend's limp arm, and released it.

It dropped to the ground like a stone.

"Berlin?"

His friend was dead.

Wash closed his eyes. He felt numb. He didn't know what to do or what he could ever say to anyone about... anything. His mind was in turmoil, and he was losing his grip.

All the Legion training reminding him to stay aware, to stay cool and deal with this later... it was there, but all Wash could think about was what he would say to Berlin's parents. What his own parents would say. How would he handle it when people snidely talked about that legionnaire major, the point, who got himself and everyone killed?

A dog-man scrambled to the top of the cliff, the first to arrive. It was panting heavily from the exertion and seemed surprised to see Wash just kneeling there. The doro hurriedly raised its rifle and sent a shot above Wash's head.

If the doro was surprised, Wash was stunned. Stunned that he was being shot at here and now. This was a private time. A time of grief between him and his friend.

Get angry.

But instead he felt... morose. He had no blaster rifle. He was resigned to joining his friend in death. He'd done what they'd set out to do.

Handle these last few seconds like your life depends on it.

Something clicked, deep down inside of him. Wash's hand brushed his hip, and he felt his sidearm.

The doro was carefully lining up for a kill shot, sensing no threat from the broken human before it.

Wash drew the weapon in a flash and sent a blaster bolt straight into the dog-man's head, causing it to drop in a heap and roll back over the side of the ridge.

Feeling like a zombie, Wash trudged to the edge of the cliff and looked down. The other doros were still climbing up to him. His eyes unblinking, Wash shot the climbers one by one, driving smoking holes in their skulls and watching their bodies tumble back down to the valley.

Some of the doros leapt away, slip-sliding on the shale. But most kept climbing.

Wash kept firing until his charge pack was depleted. Then he threw the useless weapon at one of the doros, turned away, and took a seat next to his friend.

Now.

Now he had done all he could. He'd lived his last few moments fighting like his life depended on it.

Now he wanted to die next to a friend he'd had since youth.

His best friend.

Berlin was his best friend.

The roar of incoming SLICs raced in from behind Wash, and the wind they generated blew his hair and billowed his fatigues. A bird hovered above him like a protective mother, orienting its door gunner to face the approaching doros.

The guns rang like unholy chimes, ripping the climbing doros into ribbons while Wash could only sit there, stunned. Drained.

More SLICs roared overhead. They tore across the valley and launched rockets into the doros still charging the ridge where the marines had dug in. Pluming fireballs erupted amid the dog-men, sending them flying in all directions, in pieces and aflame.

The versatile craft were flying around the battlefield like a coordinated swarm of locusts. Guns buzzed and blazed, and rockets utterly demolished the jungle tree line where the doros tried in vain to damage the craft with small arms.

Three more SLICs shot over Wash's head, hovered protectively at the base of the ridge, and descended until the wheels kissed the ground. A platoon of Republic Army soldiers jumped out and immediately began to swarm over the rocks, strengthening whatever marines remained.

The SLIC that had arrived first—the one that had taken out the doros coming for Wash—had moved down into the valley to pick off any straggling and fleeing dog-men. But now it popped back up above the canyon wall, directly facing Wash. He could see both pilots plainly through the front canopy window.

Wash didn't move from his place, slumped on both knees at Berlin's side.

The dirt and wind kicked up as the craft came to rest several meters away. A med bot hopped out and helped to lift Wash to his feet. Then it removed its collapsible stretcher and laid it next to Berlin.

"No." Wash shook his head. He bent down and scooped Berlin up in his own arms.

No one else could touch him.

No one else would carry him off of Psydon.

* * *

Inside the SLIC, the med bot delicately placed Berlin inside a body bag. Wash watched the bot work with a sort of morbid fascination. Like he was entranced by what, for the bot, was a mundane aspect of its basic programming.

Through it all, Wash couldn't stop staring at Berlin's ghostly face. His friend's eyes were still looking, now fixed on the metallic roof of the SLIC instead of Psydon's skies.

Somebody should close his eyes. So he can rest.

But Wash didn't move. Or rather, he couldn't move. He felt frozen in place. His body had exerted itself to the limits of its ability and now would do no more.

So he merely watched as the bot closed the body bag over Berlin's face, his open-mouthed friend staring upward until he was sealed in darkness.

Wash wondered if Berlin would be interred in his armor. That was how it usually went with legionnaires. The armor was iconic. A part of them.

He remembered Berlin's helmet, still sitting discarded on the ground a short distance from the SLIC.

"Hey!" Wash called for the crew chief, surprised by the strength of his own voice. "I gotta go outside to get something. It's important."

"Can I get it? You look pretty beat up, pal."

Wash shook his head. The med bot had been trying to treat him since he and Berlin first came on board, but Wash had insisted that he wouldn't go for it until Berlin was taken care of. "I gotta get it myself."

The crew chief nodded. "Okay, but hurry up! We're about to hop over the valley and load up with any wounded before we make the trip back to Cinder Air Base."

Wash jumped out of the SLIC. He attempted to bound toward Berlin's bucket, but managed something more like a shambling hobble. He found the helmet lying where he dropped it. He picked it up and stared into the visor, feeling like Berlin was somehow looking back at him through it.

The SLIC waited for him, and in a few short moments they were in the air, making the short trip back to the ridge. Wash felt his soul would take more hits over there. A part of himself that he called cowardly wanted to just leave the battlefield and go straight for the hospital at Cinder.

The battle at the ridge was decidedly over. The arriving SLICs had routed the doro forces, scattering them deep into the jungle. Republic Army soldiers had formed a perimeter while more SLICs arrived to relieve those craft that were low on fuel. The whole area was buzzing with Republic military strength and might.

The SLIC touched down, and the med bot immediately departed. Wash remained in his jump seat, keeping Berlin company for a few moments. Then he, too, stood up and stepped outside. The crew chief didn't try to stop him.

As Wash crunched his way along the rocky ground toward the ridge he'd helped defend, he heard the low, overhead droning of Republic quarter-five bombers. It occurred to him that the artillery had been silent for some time. No doubt they were doing their best to disappear into the jungle.

The bombers were coming to throw darts in an attempt to find them.

The first payload dropped by the quarter-fives wasn't far from Wash. Close enough that he could feel the concussion in his chest and sinuses. The jungle was exfoliated in great plumes of fire, thick with black smoke, annihilating any doros lying in wait for the eventual Republic pursuit.

More bombers came, systematically carpeting the jungle with their ordnance. Entire trees were uprooted and sent flying as the jungle incinerated at the point of impact. Wash could *see* the concussive wave of the blasts reverberate through the very humidity of the jungle itself in a radius of boom that he could feel in his chest, in his molars, in his very soul. It was the most fantastic display of firepower he had ever seen.

Finally, one of the geysers of fire, perhaps twenty kilometers away, flared up even higher than the rest, with a massive secondary explosion. It blew so high into the sky that pursuing bombers had to peel away to avoid the skyward funnels of flame.

They had found the artillery.

Wash let out a heavy sigh. Someone—a Legion company, or a Dark Ops kill team—would travel into the jungle to verify that they'd gotten them all. Later, they'd send basics in to recover bodies. Probably a firebase would be set up right were Wash stood.

But he and the marines had done their part. Those other actions were all yet to come. Meant for people other than Wash. His fight—and more than likely his career—was over.

As he turned away from the raging inferno in the jungle, he saw a med bot approaching the SLIC. It was the same machine that Subs had brought with him, and it was carrying a stretcher with Sergeant Shotton lying atop it. Denturo and Parker were trailing behind.

Wash ran as fast as he could toward them. All the little bruises, cuts, nicks, and gashes were starting to be felt. Starting to take their toll.

Denturo held up a strong arm to stop Wash's progress. "Don't bother," he said. "You're looking at the only marines who made it. No sense goin' up any farther."

Wash looked up at the ridge, now studded with Republic Army basics. It had been hit with so many blaster bolts that the natural deep gray of the mineral now looked almost black.

"How's Sergeant Shotton?" he asked.

"Bot says he'll be all right," answered Parker. "Got clocked in the head by a piece of rock, but otherwise he's okay. Had his helmet on."

Wash nodded.

"How 'bout the major?" Parker asked, his voice subdued, barely audible.

Wash shook his head. He was already fighting back tears. He didn't want to look weak in front of these men who'd lost more friends today than he had. "Didn't... didn't make it. Guess it's only the four of us."

Denturo spat clear saliva. He was still out of the stim. "Like I said... wasn't plannin' on dyin' today. Neither was you. Ain't nothin' to feel bad about."

Wash looked around, unsure what else to say.

Was that all it came down to? Berlin simply planned on dying? Maybe he had. Why else would he have stopped and waited for Wash? He'd planned on dying rather than leave his friend behind.

More SLICs poured in as the Republic continued to show its strength. Now legionnaires were jumping out of newly arrived SLICs, hustling all out to set up perimeters of their own, relieving the basics. A few squads seemed to have orders to immediately enter the jungle, though it was still smoking and burning in parts.

The basics from the rocks began to make their way down from the ridge. They seemed to Wash to almost be marching down on parade. Their shoulders were back and their heads were held high. They looked victorious... though perhaps it was more accurate to say they appeared to be crowned with honor.

Wash spied, in the middle of the procession, a stretcher carrying Subs's lifeless body. The Dark Ops legionnaire's arms were folded across his chest, marking his eternal repose. The other legionnaires pulling security nearby, the SLIC crews... they all stopped what they were doing and watched as the Dark Ops legionnaire's body passed by.

Wash felt himself straighten up. He didn't know whether to salute or cry.

This was because of him. He had done this.

A new SLIC appeared over the horizon. It was unique in how quiet it was, and instead of the deep jungle green of the other craft, this one was painted a black that seemed to absorb light itself. Six Dark Ops legionnaires jumped from the craft as soon as it landed.

Or at least that's what Wash took them for. They were in a state of half-dress for combat, as if the SLIC they took was leaving before they were ready, like a repulsor bus arriving at a sleeping kid's building. Some were armored from the waist down. Others had only torso pieces and buckets on. A few didn't even have helmets, just shades and shaggy hair—a sure sign of Dark Ops.

The new arrivals made straight for Subs. They stopped next to one of the basics carrying the stretcher, who Wash only now realized was the basic Subs had brought with him through the jungle—Alistair. Tears flowed freely from the man's eyes.

One of the men without a bucket—wearing a thick blond beard—leaned down and whispered something in Alistair's ear. The Republic Army soldier said something in return, then stood aside as two Dark Ops legionnaires took up the stretcher containing their fallen comrade.

Subs's body was carried to the black SLIC and set gently on board. One of them picked up Subs's rifle from its place on the stretcher next to the Dark Ops legionnaire's dead body. Then they all gathered around Alistair and clapped the basic on the back and shoulder. He was crying uncontrollably now. At the order of the bearded man, who appeared to be the team leader, the legionnaires snapped a salute at Alistair.

Wash realized that Alistair wasn't the only basic weeping. All the soldiers who came down from the ridge seemed just as affected by Subs's death. He wondered if they knew the man—if these were the men from Firebase Hitchcock, where Subs had come from.

The legionnaire holding Subs's well-worn blaster rifle—the weapon Subs had used with such ruthless aggression to hold back the doros while Wash and Berlin traversed the valley to call for help—handed it to the team leader, who in turn held it out for Alistair to take. The basic did so, his face red and ugly from the ravages of sorrow. The kid made no attempt to hide his grief.

And then the Dark Ops legionnaires got back on their high-end SLIC. The vehicle's thrusters whined to life, kicking up as it picked up altitude. It banked over the valley, then flew behind Poro-Poro Peak, disappearing from sight, along with the body of their fallen brother.

Wash wished he were dead. Not out of a sense of suicidal depression. But out of a desire—perhaps a fantasy—

that he could be the one whose heart had stopped so that Berlin and Subs and every marine could go on living.

But that wasn't the way it happened. So Wash would have learn how to go on living.

It seemed a daunting task.

The Republic Army soldiers began to file back onto waiting transport SLICs, no longer needed now that the Legion proper was filling the area of operations. Parker and Denturo helped the bot load Shotton onto the SLIC that Wash had arrived on. Some of the dead had been loaded on that SLIC as well, and Wash wasn't sure there would still be room for him. But he would hang off the sides if he had to. He couldn't leave Berlin alone.

A trio of legionnaires approached. Their helmets were on, so Wash couldn't read their expressions, but they walked erect and with purpose. They stopped directly in front of Wash, and the lead man removed his bucket. The disgust on his face was palpable.

"So you're the point that got everybody killed 'cause you thought you could do what we do?"

Wash didn't reply.

One of the other legionnaires said, "House of Reason might call you a leej. But you ain't."

Denturo and Parker returned to Wash's side.

Wash was too tired to argue. And he didn't wouldn't have been able to defend himself anyway. He had left his post. He had gone along with a poorly conceived plan, and men and women had died because of it.

But to his surprise, Denturo picked the argument up on his behalf.

The big marine was half a head taller than the legionnaire who'd removed his helmet. Denturo walked forward until he stood toe to toe with the man, like a pair of fighters preparing for the pre-fight photo op. The legionnaire got an up-close look at the cleft in Denturo's stubbly chin.

Wash was sure that if the marine had any left, he'd spit a wad of stim juice on the leej's hair.

"Fact is," Denturo said, "the lieutenant saved my sergeant's life—not to mention the life of every other marine that don't have to worry about that artillery. Doros weren't just lightin' up the Legion."

The legionnaire scoffed and looked from side to side as if looking to his buddies for backup. "What? Your hero didn't save your life too, big man?"

"Nope. I don't need savin'. But your ass is about to."

"I'd step off if I was you," warned Parker. "Denturo's left leejes in traction before. Y'all ain't invincible."

Finally, the three legionnaires' CO realized what was going on, and he shouted for the men to return to their squad. "LS-18, get your butt back here! I'm trying to wade out into the jungle to kill some dog-men, and you're over there makin' kissy-face with a marine!"

The legionnaire took an easy step backward, his eye on Denturo. "See you around another time, huh, hullbuster?"

"You'd better hope not, you queer sonofabitch."

The legionnaire snarled and looked at Wash, not slacking his slow retreat, stepping backward along with his two buddies, refusing to turn his back. "Watch your back, point. Don't think you're safe just because you go back to your little cushy base in the rear. This is Psydon. And that means you can still pay for what you did."

And with that, the legionnaire turned and rejoined his unit.

"Forget that guy," Parker said. "He doesn't know anything. What we did today won this war for the Republic. Every leej out here knows it. We saved a lot of lives, Lieutenant."

Wash felt utterly spent. It seemed to take everything in him just to muster a few words. "Thanks. To both of you. At the Academy, they'd say that a hullbuster is just a wannabe leej without the armor. But you guys are a breed of your own. The Republic is lucky to have you."

"Damn right," said Denturo.

That was the last Wash spoke to the marines. The crew chief called out that they'd made room for him on the SLIC carrying Sergeant Shotton and Berlin, and Wash got aboard.

Parker and Denturo waited around for the next one.

There was nothing else to do.

38

EPILOGUE

The Planet Spilursa
Galactic Core

It was raining on Wash's home planet. Washam, now a captain thanks to a relentless press by the House of Reason, sat in a covered grandstand. He felt like a fraud in his Legion dress uniform, occupying a place of honor, up front with Berlin's parents, among the elites of the planet.

Spilursa's planetary governor was finishing his remarks as the keynote speaker at Berlin's memorial. It was a deliberate rebuke to House of Reason Delegate Roman Horkoshino, who by all rights should have been the one giving the address, having been the one to appoint Berlin and Wash in the first place. But his endless anti-Legion rants now looked to much of the galaxy as petulant and out-of-touch. Instead he sat at the edge of the grandstand, openly sulking with arms crossed. Berlin had been right: Horkoshino's time in the House of Reason was drawing to an end.

"Critics of the House of Reason's appointment program," the governor said, "were quick to point out that most of the officers appointed to the Legion came from core worlds like Spilursa. They called it a social club for the elite. Painted the brave officers as spoiled children eager to play war for their own personal advancement.

"But now, as we gather in memory of Major Berlin," the governor gestured to a gleaming white coffin engulfed with colossal floral sprays gathered from every planet in the system, "we know... *better*."

Wash stared numbly at the coffin, his friend moldering inside.

"Major Berlin has shown the galaxy that the desire to fight for our shared liberties and freedoms, the integrity required to lay down one's life for the good of others, is something that transcends all social, economic, racial, and species distinctions!"

The crowd gave respectful, but not boisterous, applause. It was a memorial service, after all.

"His sacrifice is a reflection of the character embedded in the heart of the citizen. And faithful citizens of the Republic can be found from galaxy's edge to the mid-core to the very core itself!"

The governor paused, lowering his head in a practiced show of sorrow. When he spoke again, his voice was quiet, so that you had to practically lean forward to hear the man. "I spoke today about a hero of the Republic. A man worthy of the respect afforded to the finest in our history. And now I leave you with this: the galaxy is worse off today for having lost Major D'lay Berlin..."

The words sat there, soaking into the audience in a way that the rain could never hope to do.

"... unless those of you hearing me today, wherever you are, follow Major Berlin's example of sacrifice and harrowing courage. Think now, fellow citizens of the Republic, of yourself—yes—but only inasmuch as you can contribute to the greater good for all those who share in this one unified Galactic Republic."

The gallery huddling under umbrellas and personal weather shields applauded loudly. Wash noted the moment his friend's memorial service crossed the line from reverential tribute to political rally.

A marine honor guard took the stage, and the cheering died down. The marines were in their dress uniforms, swords gleaming, flags held proudly aloft. Wash looked to see if any of the marines he'd known were among them, but he didn't recognize any of the men.

Following the marines was a Legion general. The man looked as tough outside of his armor as he likely did in it. And though he gave no outward indication of it, Wash was sure that the general was less than pleased to be here. Berlin had been a point, and to some, that was a stink that could never be rinsed off, no matter what he had done.

The general crisply saluted the governor and assumed control of the podium. "The Order of the Centurion is the highest award that can be bestowed upon an individual serving in, or with, the Legion. When such an individual displays exceptional valor in action against an enemy force, and uncommon loyalty and devotion to the Legion and its legionnaires, refusing to abandon post, mission, or brothers, even unto death, the Legion dutifully recognizes such courage with this award. Today, on behalf of the Legion and a thankful Republic, I award this honor to Major D'lay Berlin."

The audience applauded loudly.

The general walked to Berlin's parents.

Berlin's mother wept uncontrollably and buried her head in her husband's shoulder. Berlin's father did his best to hold back his tears as the general bent down to present the Order of the Centurion to him.

Wash saw compassion in the general's eyes.

"Mr. and Mrs. Berlin," the general said, his voice subdued and low, speaking for just the two of them to hear, "on behalf of a thankful galaxy, I award to you, in the place of your son, the highest honor the Legion can bestow: the Order of the Centurion."

And that was it.

There was no mugging for the holocams while the people shouted and cheered. Just a somber silence as Mrs. Berlin continued in her sorrow, tears streaming into her husband's chest. Wash could hear the rest of Berlin's family—siblings and grandparents—weeping in the seats behind him.

The Spilursan National Defense Force began to play an ancient piece of music known as "Taps"—its slow and haunting tune had supposedly played at the funerals of soldiers since the days of the ancients.

Marines fired their blaster rifles in unison seven times.

And then the crowd dispersed, leaving nothing but the echoing memory of the day's pageantry to comfort Berlin's grieving family.

Later was the wake, which always struck Wash as an odd custom—he never felt like attending a party after burying a loved one. Berlin's parents had accepted an offer to hold it at the capital's extravagant council ball room. There were holocams present, and though none were live-casting, the footage would surely be expertly produced and used by the House of Reason in what was already a public relations campaign to make a hero of the first appointed Legion officer to die in service.

No, Wash corrected himself. *Not* make *a hero.*

Berlin, despite his faults, *was* a hero. No one would ever convince Wash otherwise.

But he wasn't the only hero from that day on Psydon. Other men had fought just as hard—harder—had suffered just as much, and were just as dead. There would be no medals for them, no grand ceremonies for their grieving families. Just heartfelt condolences, a Purple Heart, and—Wash hoped—financial support for the fatherless children left behind.

Wash wondered if Berlin would have gotten the Order if he hadn't been a point. If he had been just another legionnaire doing his job. He certainly wasn't the first legionnaire to receive the honor for actions on Psydon.

Regardless, Wash was certain the Legion brass wasn't particularly happy about having to hang one under the name of a point. In fact, if Wash had to bet, he would guess the bestowing of this honor was merely a component of some backroom give-and-take between the House, Senate, and Legion in the halls of government.

Just the way business was done.

It didn't matter, though. Berlin deserved it.

In spite of Wash's best efforts to stay out of the lime-light—standing away from the high-traffic areas like the bar and refreshments table, while trying not to stand out in a secluded corner—a steady stream of visitors and well-wishers approached him. It was as if his Legion uniform were a magnet.

It was no secret that Wash had been with Berlin when he died. No secret that Wash had been part of the mission that, while not ending the war directly, had opened the way for Legion General Umstead's final push. The doro resistance was utterly destroyed, allowing Psydon to return to its rightful place in the Republic. A sizeable Legion garrison would likely remain on planet to make sure things never got so out of hand again.

"What really happened out there?" was a question Wash heard often that night.

Those who asked it meant well enough, but a truthful answer was one they would never be able to fully comprehend. Because it involved something deeper than a series of orderly facts. To know what really happened on Psydon required not a state of knowledge so much as a state of being. Either you were there, and you got it, or you didn't.

And that was that.

But Wash could hardly say as much to a mourner dressed in their best clothing inquiring—sometimes earnestly, and sometimes out of a morbid sense of curiosity—about the final minutes of their friend's, or acquaintance's, life.

In the end, Wash gave a stock answer: "He died a hero. He died trying to save the rest of us."

Usually that was the point where the small talk would end, because what else can you say?

Wash felt like he'd been holding the same snifter of brandy in his palm for hours. He made an effort to actually finish the thing and then see about getting out of there. But as he tilted it back, he saw through the orb-like distortion of the glass that the planetary governor was coming his way with a small entourage.

"*Captain* Washam, I believe it now is? Congratulations on a well-deserved promotion." The governor gave a warm smile and extended his hand.

"Yes, sir," Wash answered, feeling a new bout of depression coming on. Berlin was in the grave, and Wash was moving up. The Legion probably weren't crazy about the new rank, either.

The politician gave a knowing nod. "Well, let me express my gratitude for what you did on Psydon. I know that your friend paid the ultimate sacrifice, but that shouldn't diminish your own contribution. What I said about Major Berlin is just as true of you. I daresay more so, if the rumors about you actually completing Legion Academy training on your own merits are to be believed."

Wash nodded. They were true and would never be believed. "Thank you, sir. I don't think I did anything that anyone else dedicated to the Republic wouldn't have done. Certainly the marines served with great sacrifice of their own."

"Indeed." The governor moved to stand at Wash's side, looking down pensively, like they were two friends traveling down a road together, lost in conversation. "However, you say what you've done is what anyone dedicated to the Republic would do. Sad to say, such is not the truth. Or at least, not as true as it ought to be."

"Sir?"

The governor seemed lost in consideration of his own words. Then he waved forward a young man from his entourage. A handsome fellow, perhaps three years younger than Wash. "I'd like you to meet this sector's junior delegate, Orrin Kaar."

"A pleasure to meet you, Captain," said Kaar in a manner that made Wash instantly feel he was with a friend. Someone who understood... everything. "I'm terribly sorry about the loss of your friend. I daresay, if I may be so bold, that had he survived, he would be able to stand against foolish men such as Horkoshino—and win—this very cycle."

"I believe so," said Wash. "D'lay wanted very much to run once his time in the Legion came to a close. He felt Delegate Horkoshino's rather... *pronounced* disavowals of the military, and the Legion in general, were a denial of the will of the people."

The governor laughed into his glass of wine. "Major Berlin was a discerning man. In time, I think Horkoshino's undoing will be exactly as you say. And the sooner the better to make way for people who understand how the galaxy works. People who understand that it requires sacrifice to maintain unity in a Republic. Such is the very fabric of the freedoms and liberty we enjoy. It's truths like these that men like Major Berlin—may he rest in eternal slumber—fought and died for."

Wash felt like he was a test subject for the governor's next State of the Planet address. He nodded politely.

Kaar raised a glass of champagne. "To the major."

The entourage and the governor repeated the toast. Wash sipped his brandy.

The planetary governor beamed at Kaar like a proud father, then turned his attention back to Wash. "That brings us to some other business, and I do hope you'll forgive me for it, given the nature of this gathering. However, who can say when all of us will be gathered together again?"

Wash nodded, inviting the governor to continue, though he couldn't imagine what more there was to talk about.

"We want *you* to stand for the House of Reason in Major Berlin's place."

Wash nearly spit out his drink.

"We believe your service record and your close relationship with the major will bring you to an easy victory over Horkoshino. The time is right, and we need men like you in the house, Captain Washam. We've been at war with the Savages for over a millennium. The Republic needs men such as yourself to lead us into a new age."

Wash was stunned. He hadn't expected this, not by a long shot. And the House of Reason had never been something he aspired to. That was Berlin's dream, not his.

"I know this is sudden, Captain. But... there it is. Out in the open. I only ask that you consider it." The governor smiled, as did Kaar. They both seemed genuinely interested in Wash's potential future as a politician.

"For what it's worth," Kaar said demurely, "I think you would make a fine member of the House of Reason. That is… *if* you should decide that the House is where you can best serve the Republic, of course."

Wash smiled meekly and resisted the urge to shake his head in disbelief. "Thank you both. I'll consider the matter with the utmost care."

"That's all I can ask." The governor looked over his shoulder and saw Berlin's parents hovering outside of the conversation at a respectful distance. "Ah! I see Mr. and Mrs. Berlin are also eager for some of your time. I'll not keep you from them any longer. It was a pleasure to formally meet you, Captain Washam."

With farewell handshakes, the governor, the junior delegate, and the rest of the entourage departed.

Wash smiled forlornly as Berlin's parents approached.

"Did you ever think that you'd be rubbing shoulders with the planetary governor?" Berlin's father asked.

"No, sir."

Wash shook Mr. Berlin's hand. The hand of the man who'd let Wash and Berlin run amok in his house as children during those long Spilursa summers. The man who had often taken time from his busy workday to take them to the park to play seamball or goof around with them after school. He'd always been a strong man. But now, his handshake felt weak and almost limp.

"And if I'd have known what it would take to make it happen," Wash continued, "never in a million years…"

Mr. Berlin nodded and gave a sorrowful smile.

Berlin's mother wrapped her arms around Wash, hugging him closely and resting her head on his uniformed chest. "Oh, Wash," she said. That was the name the family had always called him, because it was what Berlin called him. "Thank you."

Wash felt a lump grow in his throat. His voice was scratchy with raw emotion. "For what?"

Mrs. Berlin looked up at Wash, tears welling in her eyes. "For being there. With him... at the end. There's not much comfort that I can find, but knowing that he wasn't alone is something I'm grateful for."

Wash felt as though he couldn't say another word for fear of bursting into tears and making a scene.

But somehow he managed. "My parents... hoped to be here. But matters outside of their control prevented them. They asked me to pass on their condolences." He felt a gnawing sense of anger over their absence, but it was his duty to cover for them all the same.

"Give them our best when you see them," Mr. Berlin said.

And then Mrs. Berlin brought out a black velvet box and opened it up so Wash could see inside. It was Berlin's Order of the Centurion medal. A golden pentagon-shaped medallion with a stylized, ancient-looking legionnaire helmet. It was attached to a blue ribbon with black borders.

Wash thought she was showing it to him so that he could see it up close. He was about to open his mouth to compliment its handsomeness when she said, "We want you to have this."

"What?"

"He didn't die on that planet by himself. We know you were with him every step of the way. You always have been, Wash."

Mr. Berlin squeezed his wife's shoulder. "We both feel that you deserve this as much as he did. And we want you to take it as a symbol of our gratitude for the friendship you always showed to our son."

This was a gift Wash couldn't possibly accept. And yet it was also an offer he couldn't refuse. He reached out and gently took the box from Mrs. Berlin, closing the lid. "We talked about the two of you while we were in the jungles," he said. "After we'd rescued the woman from the doros. And I... I asked Berlin if he thought the two of you would be proud of us." Wash gave Mr. and Mrs. Berlin a tight smile that just barely held back his emotion.

"And what did he say?" Mrs. Berlin asked, tears streaming down her cheeks, her voice quavering.

"He said you would be," Wash managed to choke out.

Mrs. Berlin hugged him again, and then Wash felt Mr. Berlin come to his side and wrap his arm around his shoulders.

"He was right," Mrs. Berlin said.

The three of them stood there together, relying on one another to help heal the pain of the love they'd lost.

* * *

Wash sat in a busy terminal lounge at Dorn VI's primary spaceport. He had flown in on a luxury liner—Berlin's parents had connections that gave him a free flight. He had things to do: rent a speeder, buy some flowers, pick up an acquaintance. But he didn't want to leave the port. At least, not yet.

He was having doubts about whether this was the right thing to do, whether he was even really welcome in spite of assurances otherwise. But he was on the planet now. And short of buying a return ticket and disappearing, this was all he could do. And it was the thing that needed to be done.

But... just not yet.

Wash looked down at a steaming bowl of scarri—a local soup made with diced crustaceans and spiced enough to make you feel warm long after the contents in your stomach cooled. That would be a welcome thing—the warmth. Hyperspace travel always left Wash feeling chilly. And after all that time on Psydon, the whole galaxy seemed a cold place.

Though the spaceport thoroughfares were busy with the bustle of travelers moving from docking gate to docking gate, the adjoining lounge Wash had found was relatively empty. And he had been the only patron at the restaurant. It wasn't the local meal time, and Wash's ship had had a farewell dinner an hour before arrival. He wasn't actually hungry. Just... cold.

The point was that there were lots of seats available. So it seemed odd when a man came up to Wash's table to ask, "Can I sit down?"

As though the place were so packed that strangers had to dine together if there was to be room for all.

"Be my guest," Wash said distractedly, reading the news headlines on his datapad. He casually held out a hand inviting the stranger to sit.

"What's new in the galaxy?" asked the stranger.

That was a loaded question. No sooner had Psydon wound to its close, with an official end to hostilities, than the House of Reason had begun talking about some new system threatening to walk away from the alliance forced during the Savage Wars.

"Not much," Wash answered.

As the man sat down, Wash pulled his eyes away from his screen to study him. He was dark-skinned, with short hair, mostly gray but still with a bit of his youthful color. An older man. He was dressed in casual clothing, slacks and a pull-down, but there was an edge to him. A certain awareness of his surroundings, like he was on guarded alert. Not panicked, but not taking everything at face value either.

Wash realized that he'd allowed himself to completely retreat into his mind. He needed to do a better job of observing life. Like the Legion had taught him.

Like your life depends on it.

"So, what did you want to talk to me about?" Wash asked the stranger.

The man didn't smile. "What makes you think I want to talk at all?"

"Because this place is full of empty seats where you can not talk to your heart's content, but you chose this one. And... you asked me what was new in the galaxy."

"Maybe this is my favorite table."

"Sorry to intrude." Wash stood, grabbing his bowl of soup and datapad.

The man thrust out his hand and chuckled. He looked around as if laughing with someone else unseen. "Okay. All right. Yeah. We want to talk to you, Captain Washam."

Wash settled back into his seat. "Who's we?"

The man gave a half grin, showing the creases of age around his mouth. "I could play coy and ask you who you *think* 'we' is, but I won't. 'We' is Dark Ops."

Wash nodded.

"And we've been watching you for a while now. Because... we weren't exactly sure about you. At least not until you booked this jump."

"And what does that mean?"

"It means that we've heard things about you, Captain. But since we aren't the type that trades in unsubstantiated rumors, we started looking to see whether what we heard was true."

Wash was interested. He stirred his soup, watching the steam rise from the bowl to fog the metal spoon handle. "And?"

"And as it turns out, you did graduate from the Legion Academy as the top point in your class."

"The only one to show up is more like it."

"But you did show up."

"I did."

"I know you did. But I had to work to find that out. Your drill instructors weren't keen on talking about you. Didn't want to admit it. But they came clean. Eventually."

The Dark Ops stranger leaned forward. "They said you took every little bit they threw at you and then some."

Wash let his spoon clink to the side of his bowl and leaned back in his chair. "That's the truth. So why wouldn't they just tell you the truth?"

"Don't think less of them—they're good men. But there's a fear that every inch the Legion gives to this new program will spell the eventual ruin of the Legion. And admitting that some point is capable of meeting Legion standards... well, that feels like much more than an inch."

Wash went back to his soup, blowing on a spoonful before quietly slurping in the spicy broth. "So you know my commission is legitimate. But you said you were watching until I booked this trip."

"Right. The Academy was step one. Then we started going over Psydon, tracking down SLIC crews, bots, soldiers—anyone who spent time with you while stationed there." The stranger laughed. "There was a basic supply clerk who gave us an earful about your response to improperly submitted requisitions."

Wash smiled at the memory and took in more soup, content to let Dark Ops do the talking. The way he saw it, they were either going to burst in with a kill team and arrest him for what happened at Psydon, or they were going to ask for a favor.

"Those three marines who made it out of the jungle with you, they spoke *real* highly of you. But... it wasn't until now that we finally decided to have this little chat."

Wash dabbed his mouth with a napkin. "Is this about my being asked to run for the House against Horkoshino?

Is that some sort of violation to my remaining terms in the Legion?"

Wash was on prolonged administrative leave pending a full review of Psydon. He figured it would drag out long after his commission ended, and then he'd be quietly discharged.

"Hell, I don't care about your politics, Captain. You're free to do what you want as far as we're concerned. But we *hope* that what you want is what we think will be best for the Legion. Still, I couldn't ask you about all that until we were sure about you. And now... I'm betting that it's okay to ask."

"Ask what?"

"Whether you still care more about the Legion than yourself."

Wash felt more kinship with the marines than the Legion, truth be told. But that didn't mean he harbored the Legion any ill will; he had simply reconciled himself to the fact that they would never let him in. Still, that didn't diminish what they stood for, or the men like Subs who exemplified everything good in a broken galaxy.

"I'd like to think I do. I didn't join the Legion because I needed the money."

The Dark Ops stranger smiled. "Over here, in my little neck of the woods, what we do goes without much recognition. What will earn a basic a Senatorial Valor Award is considered part of the job for Dark Ops."

Wash nodded. He knew that much to be true.

"So here's my offer to you, Captain. And it'll only be on the table for you to decide until that bowl of soup of yours goes cold: Don't stand for election to the House of Reason. Remain in the Legion—the inquiry is already decided, and nothing's happening to you. The House of Reason knows what a good story they have with Major Berlin. They might let your name slip from view so his can shine brighter—the Order was part of that—but they aren't going to let you go to trial for doing the same thing he did. No matter what the Legion proper might want."

Wash cleaned his teeth with his tongue to remove a willowy strand of some leafy vegetable. "I'm not sure how giving up the chance for a seat on the House of Reason is much of an opportunity. Especially when staying in the Legion probably means spending the next however many years until retirement or discharge auditing supply requisitions."

The stranger laughed. "No, man. You're too big a fish for that now. Your future in the Legion as we see it involves serving as a House of Reason attaché. A career in the finest offices in the capital. You advocate to the Legion on the House and Senate's behalf. And trust me, they'll love trotting out an appointed officer who proves that the Legion was wrong about the benefits of the program. Basically the same thing they'd have done if you were a delegate. But with one important difference."

"And what's that?"

"You work for Dark Ops. Not the House. Not the Legion commander. Not the Senate. But us."

Wash gave the stranger a quizzical look. "I'm not sure I follow."

"No one is going to buy you being a true leej, Captain. That's just a fact. But those of us in Dark Ops who took the time... we know. And if this whole thing, this whole Galactic Republic, ever goes sideways—and if you ask me, one day it will—you'll be in a position to do something about it. If, say, Article Nineteen ever needs to be invoked, you're the man up front who can help it go the right way. And we want you there, because we've been watching you. You care more about the Legion than you do about yourself. Is that right?"

It was. Wash cared about the legacy the Legion had crafted for itself throughout the Savage Wars. For the sacrifices the Legion had made on behalf of the galaxy. Sacrifices personified in men like Berlin. Men like Subs.

The man from Dark Ops looked down at the bowl of soup. "That looks like it'll take a little bit of time to cool off. But if you know your answer now, I'd just as soon take it and get on the next transport back to where I need to go."

Wash looked straight ahead, almost past the man. "I'll do it."

The stranger rose from his chair. "All right. We'll be in touch."

Wash finished his soup.

* * *

It was strange to pick up Alistair from his hotel. It wasn't exactly like the two men were friends. In fact, other than a very short time on Psydon, they were complete strangers. But it was that common experience—Psydon—

that opened a conversation. And it turned out neither of them could shake the ghosts of that battle, and neither had a road map for how to repair their soul-scarring wounds.

How do you make better something that's so horribly wrong?

Wash had called Alistair with a plan to try to do that. To try to heal and make things right. The basic had been enthusiastic about the idea. But now, sitting together in a rented speeder winding along dark, country roads, the comm tech seemed nervous.

"You think this is a mistake? I'm worried this is a mistake."

"I've been worrying the same thing, and I have no idea what will happen," Wash said. "But… she didn't have to say yes. And, anyway, the only true mistake would be for us to do nothing."

"Yeah."

The pair didn't talk after that. No reminiscing about Psydon or swapping perspectives of that thin sliver of time where they'd both experienced the same doro assault. One that had cost them both their best friends.

Maybe that would come another day. When the pain wasn't still so raw and fresh.

The speeder's internal navigator chimed to tell them that the modest cabin they'd reached was their destination. The surrounding trees—the cabin was nestled at the bottom of mountain foothills—were lit by the cheerful glow of the cabin's windows, which sent a warm yellow into the darkness.

Wash killed the speeder's forward lights, and the stretch of forest the vehicle faced was instantly draped in darkness. That was something one rarely saw, as it was only visible out here, far removed from the city: pure night.

"Here we go," Wash said. He stepped out, stretched off the long drive, then retrieved the flowers from the back seat.

Alistair repeated the phrase. "Here we go. Here we go." As if hyping himself up for the meeting.

The two walked up to the cabin, the soft pine needle carpet reminding Wash of the cushy jungle floor. He wondered if everything for the rest of his life would remind him of Psydon. Wondered whether that planet had become the measuring stick for all of his life's experiences.

The front door was heavy and wooden, with no chime or automated greeting program. Just a slab and metal knocker. Rustic and charming. An entryway to the sort of place you'd visit and then spend your entire vacation contemplating never returning to civilized life.

Wash used his fist to pound on the door, then stepped back.

The door swung open, and they were greeted by a slender woman not a day over forty. Too young to be a widow, but she was.

She smiled somewhat awkwardly at the strangers. "Captain Washam and Specialist—"

"Alistair," the basic interrupted her, sticking out a trembling hand. "Just Alistair. Thanks for agreeing to see us, Mrs. Boyd."

"Gloria," Subs's widow said. She invited the men inside.

The cabin was modestly decorated, something of a hunting lodge. An old slug-throwing rifle hung on one wall. An antique. All the furniture was crafted out of logs. Other than the lights, the place seemed to purposely eschew all modern trappings.

"Did you have trouble finding the cabin?" Gloria looked down at the flowers.

"Uh… no," answered Wash. He held up the bouquet he'd forgotten in his hand. "These are for you."

"Thank you. I'll just go find a vase. Make yourselves comfortable."

Wash and Alistair didn't wander far from the door. They inspected the books and the paintings on the wall. Kicked their toes dumbly against a well-worn area rug.

"I feel like I'm going to be sick," Alistair said.

Wash looked at a photo of Subs's wife and two young boys. They were smiling with a man who had to be Subs himself. It occurred to Wash that he didn't actually know what the Dark Ops legionnaire looked like under the armor. "Is this him?" he asked Alistair.

Alistair's eyes grew wet. "Yeah."

"Thanks again for coming," Gloria said, returning with a glass jar containing the flowers. She set it on the mantel. "I'm sorry about how long of a drive it is from the spaceport. Ellis liked to come out here whenever we could. He didn't really like the city."

"Oh, it was no bother," Wash said, standing awkwardly with his hands in his pockets, feeling the velvet box he'd brought for the occasion.

Gloria smiled, then bit her lip as a fresh sting of sorrow rolled over her face. "So. You two, you said you were with him... when..."

"We were," Wash said, stepping forward, cutting off the need for Gloria to say out loud words she no doubt dreaded. He retrieved the box containing the Order of the Centurion and held it out to her. "My friend, D'lay Berlin, he also... he was there too. His parents gave me this, and... we all feel it rightfully belongs with you."

Alistair opened the box for Gloria to see. The medal caught the light of the fireplace and reflected the gleam onto Gloria's face.

"That's... thank you." Gloria took the box and closed it. "The boys would probably like to see this. They're actually excited that you're coming, since you knew their father."

That sentence struck Wash like a punch to the stomach. He tried not to wince. Tried to smile. "Of course. We'd love to meet them."

"Boys!" Gloria called. "Come down, please."

There was a scuffling of feet, and then two boys, maybe ten or eleven, Wash wasn't good at guessing children's ages, stood next to their mother. They were on the verge of becoming men, just starting the transformation.

"Hello, sir." They politely greeted each man.

Alistair and Wash shook their hands, and Wash felt a sense of pride at the composure they both showed. As though he were in a place of privilege and honor for being able to meet them.

"Captain Washam and... Alistair both knew your father. I thought you might like to talk with them about Daddy."

"Can we go out by the campfire?" one of the boys asked.

"That sounds like fun," Alistair said, sounding like it was the best thing he'd ever heard.

"Why don't you two go set up some extra chairs and we'll be right out?" Gloria said.

The boys hastened to follow their mother's wishes.

She turned back to face Wash and Alistair. "I didn't... couldn't ask this with them in the room. But... what really happened out there. At the end?"

Alistair looked down.

"He died a hero," Wash said. "He died trying to save the rest of us."

HONOR ROLL

We would like to give our most sincere thanks and recognition to those who supported the creation of Order of the Centurion by subscribing as a Galaxy's Edge Insider at GalacticOutlaws.com

Elias Aguilar
Tony Alvarez
Robert Anspach
Sean Averill
Russell Barker
Steven Beaulieu
John Bell
WJ Blood
Aaron Brooks
Brent Brown
Marion Buehring
Van Cammack
David Chor
Kyle Cobb
Alex Collins-Gauweiler
James Conyer
Robert Cosler
Andrew Craig
Adam Craig
Peter Davies
Nathan Davis
Tod Delaricheliere
Christopher DiNote
Matthew Dippel
Karol Doliński

Andreas Doncic
Noah Doyle
Lucas Eastridge
Stephane Escrig
Dalton Ferrari
Skyla Forster
Mark Franceschini
Richard Gallo
Christopher Gallo
Kyle Gannon
Robert Garcia
Michael Gardner
John Giorgis
Gordon Green
Tim Green
Shawn Greene
Michael Greenhill
Jose Enrique Guzman
Ronald Haulman
Joshua Hayes
Jason Henderson
Tyson Hopkins
Curtis Horton
Jeff Howard
Mike Hull

Wendy Jacobson
Paul Jarman
James Jeffers
James Johnson
Noah Kelly
Jesse Klein
Mathijs Kooij
Evan Kowalski
Mark Krafft
Byl Kravetz
Clay Lambert
Grant Lambert
Dave Lawrence
Paul Lizer
Richard Long
Oliver Longchamps
Richard Maier
Brian Mansur
Cory Marko
Pawel Martin
Trevor Martin
Lucas Martin
Tao Mason
Simon Mayeski
Brent McCarty
Matthew McDaniel
Joshua McMaster
Christopher Menkhaus
Jim Mern
Alex Morstadt
Daniel Mullen
Greg Nugent
David Parker
Eric Pastorek

Daniel Caires Pereira
Jeremiah Popp
Chris Pourteau
Eric Ritenour
Walt Robillard
Joyce Roth
David Sanford
Andrew Schmidt
Brian Schmidt
Christopher Shaw
Ryan Shaw
Glenn Shotton
Daniel Smith
Dustin Sprick
Joel Stacey
Maggie Stewart-Grant
John Stockley
Kevin Summers
Ernest Sumner
Travis TadeWaldt
Tim Taylor
Steven Thompson
Beverly Tierney
Tom Tousignant
Scott Tucker
Eric Turnbull
John Tuttle
Allan Valdes
Christopher Valin
Paden VanBuskirk
Andrew Ward
Jason Wright
Nathan Zoss

Jason Anspach and Nick Cole are a pair of west coast authors teaming up to write their science fiction dream series, Galaxy's Edge.

Jason Anspach is a best selling author living in Tacoma, Washington with his wife and their own legionnaire squad of seven (not a typo) children. In addition to science fiction, Jason is the author of the hit comedy-paranormal-historical-detective series, *'til Death*. Jason loves his family as well as hiking and camping throughout the beautiful Pacific Northwest. And Star Wars. He named as many of his kids after Obi Wan as possible, and knows that Han shot first.

Nick Cole is a dragon award winning author best known for *The Old Man and the Wasteland, CTRL ALT Revolt!,* and the Wyrd Saga. After serving in the United States Army, Nick moved to Hollywood to pursue a career in acting and writing. (Mostly) retired from the stage and screen, he resides with his wife, a professional opera singer, in Los Angeles, California.

Made in the USA
Las Vegas, NV
03 February 2023

66519780R00175